# THE
# NEVER DAWN

R.E. PALMER

FrontRunner  Publications

ISBN: 978-0-9562593-6-3
www.FrontRunnerBooks.com

# DEDICATION

For my wife, Bernadette.

# ACKNOWLEDGMENTS

A huge thanks to Cary and Mara Morton for their support. I doubt this series would have been finished without their valuable feedback.

Also a special mention for Meenu Khela for taking the time to read my early drafts and provide much-needed encouragement.

And lastly, a big shout out to all the book bloggers who review the work of indie writers – thanks guys!

# 1

I had touched the sky. Not the real sky; that, of course, would be soft. The one under my fingertips had felt hard and scratched my skin. I know I shouldn't have done so, but after thirteen years in the confines of Education, the high dome of The Workers Level had been too much to resist. Together with Reuben, I had climbed onto the factory roof to take a closer look. My stomach had churned as I'd gazed down onto the jigsaw of grey rooftops below. But it was the sky I'd come to see. Standing on Reuben's shoulders, I barely had time to run my outstretched fingertips across its rough surface, before Mother's booming voice had sent Reuben toppling forward leaving me dangling over the edge, hanging by my fingers.

But it was worth it. I'd touched the sky! My skin tingles even now at the memory. But that was a long time ago, almost five years, and I learned my lesson. Mother banned me from the bedtime story for a month, and I still feel the shame of being excluded from those magical evening sessions. But she knew what was best for me as always. She knew back then, that with the right encouragement, I would become one of the most productive workers in The Ark. I won't let her down. I, Noah, will make her proud.

The patch of blue showing through the tiny skylight above my workstation, reminds me of Mother's promise— if we work hard she will let us go outside. It's been weeks since we last had a blue sky. Mother must be happy.

I look back to my desktop, annoyed at letting my concentration slip. I push the memories aside and pick up a number six fastener from the tray on my left. With a flick of my wrist, I attach it to the protruding bolt holding plates A and B together. Next, the middle finger on my right hand feels for the groove beneath the box and I fix the bracket my left hand has already taken from the top shelf, and snap it shut. Thirty-six! I reach thirty-six and I'm well on schedule to finish fifty-two before lunch—that's two ahead of the target Mother has set for me.

I reach for the next plate and look up to the giant poster on the far wall beyond the rows of workstations. The determined face of Moses, our hero-worker, watches over all five floors of the factory. His eyes shine as he stands in front of his shelf stacked high with the record number of units he produced in one shift. I take encouragement from the words, '*Remember Moses!*' Perhaps one day that will be my face on the wall.

'Mother will be pleased.' I jump as Abe reaches over to place the tray of parts I need for the next batch. 'You're way ahead of the rest, Noah.'

I nod. 'I'm going for my record today. I've worked out how to make each unit twelve seconds faster.'

Abe glances down the row. He lowers his voice and leans forward. 'Have you cleared this with Isaac? He hasn't said anything to me.'

I stutter, suddenly ashamed. 'No… no I haven't. I'm sorry. I'll go back to the old way until I get approval.'

Abe's shoulders drop. 'Yes, that would be best. You can put forward your idea at the next production meeting, then if Mother approves, you can show the rest.' He starts to walk away, but stops and turns. 'I know you mean well, but you must remember to ask before you change anything. If you want to break the record you must use the correct procedure.' His eyebrows rise and he manages to smile. 'Mother knows best, eh!'

I duly repeat his words. 'Yes, Mother knows best. I don't know what I was thinking. Sorry.' Abe turns his back and pushes his trolley along to Reuben's workstation. Once he's collected all the units from our row, he will leave them by the small door at the end of the workshop to be collected by Rachel's team. *We work together. We succeed together.*

I wait until he completes his collection from Reuben before I breathe out. *You fool, you should have checked first.* Was I showing off? My jaw tightens. I should not put my pride above the team's objective. I hope Mother won't be displeased.

## 2

'*We work together. We succeed together.*' The wrought-iron words, emblazoned across the entrance to The Square, remind us of our purpose as we pass beneath in orderly lines. Everything we do, we do as a team. From five in the morning when we wake, to ten at night when we go to bed, we work together. From cooking breakfast and the daily routines of the dormitory, to the important jobs at our designated workplaces and evening lectures, we succeed together. Mother says work is good for us because agents find work for idle hands and minds. *Mother knows best.*

I enter The Square. Before me lies the largest open space on the Workers Level situated at its center. I allow myself a moment to take it all in from the edge. Two rows of benches stretch across three sides. In a few minutes, six hundred workers will sit shoulder to shoulder anticipating our special audience with Mother.

I shuffle forward and sit at my allocated place with my team amongst the factory crews with our grubby faces. To my left; the farm workers in their dirt-encrusted overalls and grimy hands filter through, and to my right, the clean-faced laboratory teams. But we all share the worker's badge of honor—our hunched backs from hours of stooping over microscopes, seed beds and workstations.

The fourth group of workers never join us here. They're the slow learners, the clumsy and who Mother tells us 'live in a different world'. They prepare, cook and serve the food in the work's canteen or to our dormitories.

The remainder are never seen. Sanitation is made up of weak-minded shirkers who repeatedly fail to reach their targets. We rarely mention them—no one wants to think of the work that goes on beneath the lower levels in The Trench. Rumor and scare stories whispered in the classroom help to keep our minds focused on achieving our challenging daily goals.

I look up to check the clock: three minutes before twenty-hundred hours on Thursday, the twenty-ninth day of April. Above, the sky is now a dark blue above the lamps—it's a beautiful sight and a good sign. We call it the sky, but it's a large dome protecting us from the terrors above. To think of it as sky helps to keep our hopes alive. Mother has done her best to make The Ark look like the surface, but I wonder how it would feel to breathe the clean air under wide, open skies and not have to tolerate the stale odor of the Workers Level. But I mustn't hope for things that may never happen in my lifetime. I cannot let selfish thoughts distract me from the work.

I shake my head and look back to the benches. More workers stream through. I risk a glance. She's here! I follow her out of the edge of my vision, hoping no one notices my interest. It is wrong to focus my attention on this girl alone. *We work together. We succeed together.* But since the first time I saw her at the annual production review, I have committed this sin daily and can do nothing to stop myself.

She sits on the front row to my right with her colleagues from the laboratory. I long for her to look in my direction, but she turns to face the large screen. My heart sinks. Something stirred that day at the review. I had a strange urge that I hadn't felt before, the urge to be with this girl, to hold her and… I stifle a gasp as a strand of her hair tumbles from the headscarf onto her shoulder. I let the air from my lungs out slowly. Her hair is the color of the dying embers of our dormitory stove. My fingers tighten on the coarse material of my overalls—if only I could reach out and stroke her soft curls. If only I could—

'Did you hear me?' Reuben whispers in my ear. I turn to see his lips moving.

'What?'

'I said, 'that's odd'.' Reuben nudges me. 'Look, over there. There are empty spaces and… where's Isaac?' I tear my eyes from the girl and look quickly to where Reuben gestures. I count six empty spaces before I have to look back for another glimpse of the girl's red hair. But her colleague behind taps her on the shoulder and she tucks it quickly back inside her headscarf.

'What do you think it means?' I grit my teeth as Reuben interrupts again. But before I can think about the mystery, the prefects enter. We stand in silence.

All present follow the twelve upright bodies in their immaculate black uniforms as they take their positions in front of the benches. I'd always hoped to number amongst this noble order, but Mother gave me the grey overalls of a factory worker and I take pride in my duty. Perhaps if I expose an agent, or report a poor worker, she may one day reconsider. *We fight together. We win together.*

The lamps dim. She is here. My chest rises as the screen wall glows brighter. Mother enters The Square. We hold our breath—she has a new dress. The blue material glimmers as her tall, slender body glides effortlessly towards the center. She stops and smiles. Six hundred pairs of lungs release their precious air: Mother is happy.

Her head tilts as she scans the gathering. Her blue eyes fall upon me; I look down feeling I'm not worthy to hold her gaze, but I can still feel her love as she sees directly into my heart. My face grows hot, grateful for everything she has done; keeping us safe from the terrors above and working relentlessly towards the day we can return.

She holds up her hands. I watch as her long, white hair flows over her arms. Mother speaks. 'Please sit.' She waits until we're comfortable. 'My children! It is good to see all of you together again.'

We respond. 'And to see you, Mother.'

She nods in appreciation. 'Now. Before I come to tonight's… special purpose.' She pauses as a low murmur dares to fill the air. 'I want to give thanks for the sacrifices made by those who have gone before you. Especially one man.'

I turn to Reuben and whisper. 'She means Moses.'

'Yes, Noah.' Her eyes find mine. I freeze. 'I do mean Moses, our very own hero-worker.' My heart swells as she smiles *at me!* She continues, her voice rising. 'Did Moses ever turn from his duties?' We shake our heads. 'Did he ever doubt that one day we would leave this place?' A few mutter 'no'. 'Did he ever stop working for The New Dawn?'

Reuben stands and shouts, 'We thank you, Moses! We remember!' We eagerly follow his lead and jump to our feet to show our gratitude, gazing up to the large sculpture given to Mother by Moses. We call it The Metal Sun. It sits proudly next to the clock with its radiant beams depicting the first sunrise of The New Dawn. We all make gifts for Mother's Day, but only the work of Moses hangs on her wall. I hope one day my gift will be up there for all to see.

Mother's voice carries clearly over the top of our cheers. 'Moses knew he would never return to the surface. But did he stop? No! He worked selflessly every waking hour so that day would come for those who came after him.' She pauses. We stop and sit. Mother lowers her voice. 'You must all take courage from the example Moses set. Work hard and stay on your guard for the enemy.' Her eyes drop to the floor and The Square holds its breath as we strain to hear her shaking voice. 'I am afraid enemy agents will do whatever they can to prevent our return.' My jaw and fists clench. She looks across the front row. 'And if their main force gets out first, they... they will come here and,' she whispers their threat, 'bury us for good.'

I stand and call out. 'We won't let that happen!' Reuben and Abe join me, quickly followed by everyone present. We repeat our vow over and over. No one is going to take the chance of returning to the surface from us. I see the picture from my book of the tree on the hill. I've climbed it a thousand times in my mind, up through its branches until I can stroke the sky, the real sky, the soft, smooth sky.

'I am encouraged by your determination.' Mother calls over our protestations. My vision shatters and I'm back in The Square. We sit. Mother appears to grow taller as her voice rises. 'I made a promise to the first people of The Ark, and I will keep it for you. *We* will be the first to return so *we* can bury them!'

She lets us stand and cheer once more, before a slight nod and a raised eyebrow brings our shouts to an end. Mother waits for us to sit. 'Now, on to tonight's business in hand. Someone here has already noticed there are some empty spaces…' Reuben stiffens beside me. Should I tell her it was him? Heads turn and notice the gaps. Mother laughs. 'No need to look concerned. This is good news.' She gestures to one of the prefects. 'Jared, could you show them in now please.'

Jared stands at the end of our row. We were together in school, but at eight he was selected to be a prefect, while Reuben and I were left to build pretend houses with wooden blocks.

Jared nods to Mother and steps aside. I grasp the edge of the bench as a dozen oddly-dressed workers enter. They're not wearing overalls, but clothes that look thin and… clean, and soft shoes instead of worker's boots. They hesitate at the edge until, encouraged by Mother, they make their way to the center. No one dares speak. I see Isaac in the middle—he looks uneasy in his new, light blue uniform. I catch his eye, but he quickly turns his attention back to Mother. Reuben grasps my arm. 'Do you think they're going to—?'

Mother's glare rips the question from his lips. She looks away, then smiles and raises both arms with her palms face up. 'Before you, stand those who have followed the example of Moses. They have worked hard so others that follow will see the light of day.' I glance sideways at Reuben—his mouth drops open and I hear his short intakes of breath as if about to sneeze. Mother continues. 'They have been chosen, they have earned their place in...' she looks at our frozen faces, 'Paradise!'

Heads turn, a murmur rises from the benches. 'Yes!' Mother's eyes flash towards me. Now it's my turn to hold my breath, but then she smiles. 'Yes, the manual work has finished for The Chosen before you. A life of study *and* leisure awaits. They will learn new skills that will be passed on to the next generation, valuable skills that will help *when* The New Dawn is upon us.'

It still doesn't sink in. The Chosen look unsure of what to do next. I recognize Eli from the dormitory next to ours. He suddenly throws out his arms and hugs the girl next to him. I flinch, waiting for the prefect standing nearby to pull them apart. But he doesn't move.

We stand and begin to chant. 'We work together! We succeed together!' I'm shocked to see tears stream down Isaac's face, but also feel my eyes well up. I will miss him. He was my mentor when I arrived at the factory. It was Isaac who took our team to the top of the production tables after Enoch lost his mind and was taken away.

I see Rachel turn to Mother and run with her arms outstretched ready to embrace her. *No! She mustn't.* We are always to keep a respectful distance. Thankfully, a prefect steps into her path. She realizes too late her error of judgment in her impulsive act. The cheers stop. She sinks to her knees and clasps a hand to her mouth. I feel her pain. Will she lose her place in Paradise? Or be sent to Re-Education? Mother takes one step towards Rachel. She holds out an arm and turns to the prefect.

'Please. Help Rachel to her feet.' I cannot read Mother's expression, or tell from the tone of her voice what's on her mind. Silence. I'm sure I can hear Rachel's heartbeat. The prefect takes hold of her elbow and helps her to stand. Mother smiles. 'You do not want to miss the opportunity that awaits you.' Rachel breathes out for us all. 'But!' The smile leaves Mother's lips. She turns to us. 'Remember, you have to earn the right to become one of The Chosen and enter Paradise.' She looks at David, and then to others around the benches. 'There are other… less pleasant tasks that need to be done.' She claps her hands. 'Now! No one here will speak of this moment again.' The younger members of our team frown, but Reuben and I nod. Mother takes a step towards us and speaks slowly. 'We work for the greater good of us all, and not for personal reward. Banish such selfish thoughts from your minds, work hard and we will succeed.'

She turns to the brightly-clad Chosen. 'Come, all of you, follow me.' She walks towards the screen. It parts at the center. I peer into the gap trying not to look too interested, but I see nothing in the darkness beyond. The screen glows, and Mother and The Chosen leave the Workers Level to the sound of our appreciation. I watch as the back of Isaac disappears. I wish I could have said goodbye and thanked him for his help. I will miss him.

'I wonder what it's like not to go to the factory every day?' Reuben turns to me as we depart The Square. 'I mean, what would they do?' Ahead, the caps on workers' heads bob left and right as we move at the slow pace of the walkway. The walkways are the only place where it's possible to talk without the whole team listening in; but it's also where you can get into trouble. Speaking out of turn to someone you thought you could trust, might be an agent of the enemy only too keen to piece together every small piece of information that would lead to our undoing.

'I bet they eat cake every day!' David licks his lips and Reuben laughs at him.

'When have you ever eaten cake? You're too young.' Reuben yanks David's cap from his head and holds it up beyond David's reaching hand. He draws back his arm to throw it into the crowd in front.

I hiss, 'Prefect!'

Reuben places it back on the boy's head. He grins at David. 'I'll let you have a sniff of my cake when I'm eighteen, but that's all!' We check the prefect has passed out of earshot and laugh with him. Reuben gestures to me to join Abe and Barnabas at the front. He taps Abe on the shoulder. 'Did you know this would happen tonight?'

Abe sighs. 'Yes, but I wasn't allowed to say anything.' He glances at Reuben and then me. 'Look! Remember what Mother said—we do not speak of this again. We work for the good of all and not for personal gain.'

Reuben isn't satisfied. 'But—?'

'But nothing!' Abe holds up his finger and points to the sky. Reuben closes his mouth. No matter how much he wants to ask the question, he won't want Abe to mention his behavior to Mother. Abe raises his eyebrows. 'Am I clear?' We nod. I shake my head at Reuben. His antics keep our spirits high, but I worry he doesn't know when to keep his mouth shut and may let down the team. My thoughts return to the evening's event. Mother told us not to speak of it, but she didn't say we couldn't *think* about the ceremony. I wonder what those brightly-colored clothes would feel like against my skin; to not have the constant scratch of my overalls would alone make it worth getting into Paradise. But first I have to work hard for at least another three years before I can be considered for a place.

Abe slows in front. The factory looms ahead—its five stories tower over the surrounding grey buildings. We stop. The crowd leaving The Square part around us and stream both ways along the main route that runs adjacent to our workplace.

Reuben speaks barely above a whisper. 'But just imagine what it would be like to not come here every day.'

David straightens his cap and blurts out too loudly. 'No work! I can't wait.' We freeze. I look to Abe. He's heard David. He turns and nods to me. I step forward and speak quietly into David's ear.

'Careful what you say. Remember, no work, no getting out… for anyone. We work together, we leave together.'

David's head drops. 'Of course, I'm sorry. I spoke without thinking.'

But I haven't finished. 'Look at me, David.' He raises his chin but his eyes drop to the floor. 'Look at me! You're fifteen, it's time you grew up and acted your age. I don't hear this sort of talk coming from young Amos and Caleb. You're on the best crew in this place, but you could just as easily be transferred *elsewhere*.' He knows of what I speak. His face turns white. I wonder if I've overdone the threat. I put my hand on his shoulder, he stiffens but I continue. 'Do your duty, and one day you could be chosen, just like Isaac.'

His lip quivers. 'But I don't want to be chosen, I want to go outside.' I clench my fists but let them relax before I speak.

'We all do. But if it's not us, we have to do all we can for those who come after.' I straighten David's collar. 'Remember, Moses, eh.' He manages a smile as the color returns to his cheeks. We both repeat the words that give us strength.

'Remember, Moses.'

Female voices! I glance up. I hope the others can't see the look on my face as the girl with red hair approaches. My stomach flutters as it had on the factory roof all those years ago. Her team will walk right by us. I have never been this close. But she's in conversation with her colleagues and I fear she won't notice me. I can't move. My feet take root in the path beneath as she nears. My heart thunders in my chest. *Calm down!* She'll hear my excitement and think I'm a fresh-faced new arrival from below, wide-eyed and overawed by the world of the grown-ups.

She's so close now I can pick out her voice. Her skin looks so smooth and soft. My fingertips tingle. She glances over as she passes and our eyes meet. Time stops. It's just the two of us amongst the crowds. We share a precious moment as I lose myself in her blue eyes – the color of a happy sky.

'Rebekah?' She turns to her colleague and she's gone. Sounds and smells crash back into my world. The girls stop to talk nearby. *Rebekah.* So that's her name.

'Move along! You need to be getting back to your dormitories.' Jared strides in between us. 'You heard what Mother said. You'll need your sleep if you're to meet your targets.'

I dare to look towards Rebekah. Her back is to me, but I see Jared watching her. I groan inside. I see something in his face that I don't like. Jared is a prefect. He can go almost anywhere in The Ark without Mother's permission. He can talk to Rebekah anytime he wishes. My face feels suddenly hot.

# 3

'Are you tired?' I look up to see the faces of my team watching me from around our dormitory table. Reuben leans over. 'You look pale.'

'I'm... I'm fine, it's been a long day.' *Did I say something out aloud?* I can't get Rebekah's face out of my mind, or Jared and the way he looked at her. I turn back to Reuben and try to smile. 'But don't worry, I'll be fine for tomorrow's shift.' I must push out all thoughts of her before they notice.

Abe taps my bowl with his spoon. 'Best eat your dinner then, we'll need all our strength if we're to stay at the top of the production table.' He glances up to the large clock dominating our living quarters. 'And hurry up about it, it's nearly nine-thirty.' I scope a spoonful of the re-heated cabbage and potato into my mouth. But I'm not hungry. I'm usually the first to finish supper, but tonight is different. I see the flash of red of her gleaming hair; I hear the sound of her voice.

A chair scrapes across the floor, wrenching her fair face from my thoughts. Abe stands and walks to the head of table behind Isaac's empty chair. He clears his throat and looks at each one of us. 'Mother has informed me that I will take Isaac's place and lead the team, Barnabas will be my deputy.' We turn to look at Barnabas. He nods in appreciation to Abe. He continues. 'From now on, you are to address me by my full name.' He runs his hands along the back of the chair. 'Tomorrow we'll get a new worker. His name is Seth. He came up yesterday and has completed his induction course.' He looks to me. 'Noah, you will be his mentor.' I catch Reuben's eye. I can see he is trying to hide his disappointment. *Mentor!*

I nod. 'It will be an honor, Abe... raham.' I try to keep the excitement from my voice. *Mother must be pleased with me.*

Abraham completes the formality. 'You have worked hard to earn that honor.' He steps back from the table. 'Now, let us all stand.' The first notes burst from the speaker as we remove our caps. I clear my throat ready to sing The Workers' Anthem, but it's my mind that needs to be focused as I raise my voice.

We sing of the daily grind and monotony of our tasks; we sing of our commitment to the cause and for the greater good of all workers; we sing of our gratitude to Mother and, finally, we sing of the sun rising on the glorious day of The New Dawn.

I watch the faces of the others as we renew our vows. It's our duty to look out for signs of weakness. If even the smallest cog in the machine fails, it could jeopardize our chance of being the first to resurface. If we fail, we'll be buried for good by our enemy – The Ark, a place of safety for all these years, would become our tomb. I know Abraham will be a good leader, he is clever, considerate and fair. Barnabas is strong, tireless and vigilant; Reuben is dependable, if a little impetuous, but he keeps our spirits high; Amos and Caleb may be the youngest, yet they are good workers. Caleb is tall and broad if a little slow at times; Amos is respectful and knows his place on the team. But I have concerns for David. I see worrying signs. He speaks without thinking and I wonder if he is really committed to the cause. *But what do they think when they look at me?*

We finish the song and sit. The loudspeaker crackles and Mother's harsh voice bursts forth. '*It has come to my attention there is an unauthorized book on this level.*' I glance around to the others; they're all looking back at me. Do they think it's mine? I turn back to the speaker. Mother continues. *'This book is spreading lies that seek to dampen your spirits and sabotage The Work. Must I have to remind you that it is your duty to report anything suspicious?'* I risk another look around the table and thankfully they're watching the speaker. Mother softens her tone. *'It hurts me to say this, but there will be no story tonight. I am disappointed with you all. Lights out in fifteen minutes.'*

It's a bitter end to what has been an eventful day. I climb the ladder to my bunk and collapse onto the bed. I look at the ceiling a few inches from my nose. She said fifteen minutes, that leaves at least five minutes before lights out. I reach under my pillow for my book. I open the tattered blue cover. I rarely read the words these days; I can almost recite the whole book by heart. I turn to the third page, the page with the only picture. Some of the others have books with many pictures that show the story, but I have to be satisfied with just one, one that I know every detail of the fine-line drawing of the tree upon a hill.

Two years ago, I'd found a pencil under a bench at the factory and had copied the picture onto a blank page at the back. The bird in its branches didn't look like the one in the original, but it was my creation, something that no one else had done. But it was wrong to waste time on work that didn't contribute to our objective. The next day I had carefully torn it out and tucked it inside a rip in my bed roll. But within a week it had gone. Someone must have taken it for themselves and not told Mother. Otherwise, she would have punished me for damaging the gift she'd given me on the day I left school.

The light above flickers and dies. I close my book and place it back under my pillow. A faint glow from the lamp outside seeps through the slit in the wall of our sleeping quarters. It too will go out soon, but for a few minutes I can look upon the space of the empty walkway. If only it was just the two of us. I could hold Rebekah's hand and go wherever we liked. We could leave The Ark and go up to the surface. Together we would be safe. I would protect her from the dangers and let her stand on my shoulders so she could touch the sky. Then I would stroke the smooth, clean skin of her cheek, and run my fingers down her slender neck...

The lamp outside clicks off. I lie in darkness—it will never happen. Instead, my fingers search for the headset on the hook and I attach it before the buzzer can alert Abraham—the last thing I need is a warning. Mother is angry; she didn't wish us goodnight. Tomorrow the sky will be the grey of our overalls.

# 4

*Large metal monsters hurl rocks at the outer shell high above. The Ark quakes in fear, knocking us to the floor. I look up to the small window—the sky turns black. We flinch as another huge boulder smashes against the last of our defenses. We'll be buried! I push the palms of my hands into my ears and screw my eyes shut. The inner shell won't take much more. The dome will shatter. Mother's voice screams in the dark. 'Do you see what you fools have done?'*

*The shell cracks. The sky crashes down onto the factory roof. The lights go out. The floor shudders, then collapses under the weight of the landslide. We'll be swallowed by the Earth as it takes revenge on those who dared to ruin its beauty. We tumble, tossed like pebbles, battered by rubble, dragged deeper into its dark depths, forever beyond the reach of the surface where we can wreak no more harm.*

*Then silence. Only the sounds of our sobs fill the small spaces between the debris. I hear Mother's voice. 'See what happens when you do not do as you are told!'*

I wake with a start and bang my head on the light above—it's still out. I look through the slit and am not surprised to see the gloom of a grey sky. Today I will work harder to make Mother happy again. I will be on full alert for any news of the unauthorized book. I must show Mother she can trust me.

The light above my bed comes to life. I turn to see Reuben sitting on the edge of his bunk rubbing and shaking his head. He looks up. 'We have to find that book. We can't let them find us or we're dead.' He swings his legs out of bed and shivers in the cold morning. We stand and stretch out our stiff limbs—I can't remember the last time my body didn't ache. I pull my overalls over my damp underclothes. Abraham is already up and urges us to action on his first day in charge of the team.

'Five o'clock! Everyone up. It's Friday, the last day of April. I want to see breakfast ready when I return.' Abraham shakes David's bunk. 'Get up, lazy bones, get that stove lit! Barnabas has already emptied the ash pan and cleaned the flume.'

I fasten the last button on my overalls and nod to Abraham. 'I'll get him.' He turns and strides off to deliver his morning report to Mother. I grasp the blanket and pull it back. David is curled into a ball with both hands covering his face. I hear him moan. He's crying! I quickly check the others. Thankfully they're busy with their morning duties and don't see him in this state. I kneel by his bed. 'Shush! The others will hear. Come on, pull yourself together.' I strain to hear his weak voice.

He snivels. 'I can't stand it. They're coming for us, you saw it. We'll never get out.'

I grab his shoulders, pull him up and hiss in his ear. 'You've got to stop this! Come on, get a move on and light the stove.' David looks up. Tears stream from his red eyes. I take his overalls from the shelf and thrust it at him, but stop short of pushing it into his face. I soften my tone. 'You have to try, you'll feel better once you start work.'

'I know. I'm sorry, but you saw... you saw what would happen if—'

'Stop! That's exactly why we have to keep going.' I lean closer and speak through my tight jaw. 'Look, if you can't handle it on this shift I'll have to speak to Abraham.' David's eyes widen, but I know my duty. 'I'm sorry but you have to think of everyone, we can't have you holding us back. You know what happens if just one of us falls behind and we don't meet our targets? It will upset Mother and we could all suffer.'

'David! Why isn't the stove ready?' Barnabas yells from

the living quarter. 'Caleb has collected the fuel.'

I reply for him. 'He's coming.' David wipes his cheeks with the back of his hand and climbs out of bed. I give him a stern look and leave him to get ready. I pass Barnabas as I make my way to the entrance. I speak so no one else can hear. 'The night story scared him, he'll be okay once he gets to work.' But I'm not so sure. I could report him to a prefect—Mother would be pleased.

Outside, I find the crate with the bread and milk. I grasp the handles and lift. As I rise, I keep my eyes fixed on the crate—I don't want to see the sky today. I hurry back inside to find David has yet to prepare the stove. The others won't forgive him if we have to eat the bread untoasted and go without coffee—to be late for the factory is a punishable offence.

I grab the flint from his shaking hands and shove him aside. 'Here, let me remind you how to do it.' The stove used to be my duty before David arrived, and my hands easily recall the technique. I strike the flint hard against the slate. The spark jumps onto the wood shavings and the satisfying crackle announces my success. I glare at David. 'Don't just stand there, pick up the bread and place it over the fire.'

I nod to Amos. He brings the pot of water and rests it on the rack, careful not to spill the water onto the kindling fire. We've lost three minutes. The toast will be ready, but we'll have to drink lukewarm coffee. David has failed the team. He must put in a good day at the factory, or it won't be long before one of us reports him.

Rebekah. I say her name in my head. I say it slowly and let the *arr* linger until it turns into a sigh. I place the assembled unit next to the others ready for newly-promoted Barnabas to collect. My eyes wander along the shelf. Two empty spaces! *Only forty-eight? What have I been doing?* I glance up to the clock and see the hand build up momentum, jump and come to rest on the last minute before break. I stretch out the tightness in my lower back and reach for a Plate A—at least I could fix it to Plate B and attach the bracket before the bell rings, but I will still be below fifty. I will have to work harder after lunch to make up my quota.

My fingers slip. I miss the bolt and the fastener scrapes the side of Plate B. I freeze. I dare to look down to the parts in my hand. *Dear Moses!* A small scratch, no bigger than my thumbnail, stands out on the gleaming surface. I peer closer. The squiggle looks like a bird from the picture in my book, the one flying from the tree towards the hills in the distance. The bell clangs. I don't have time to finish it. I place the plate face down to hide the damage—at least the terminal box will hide the mark once complete.

I join the line behind Barnabas. Reuben steps in behind me. He whispers, 'Two short? Anything wrong?'

I shake my head and shoot him a look. I whisper, 'I'm fine. I'll catch up after lunch.' Barnabas looks back. I speak louder. 'I've… I've been thinking about that illegal book.'

Reuben shakes his head for Barnabas to see. 'Yes, nasty business. Let's hope it's found soon and anyone who's read it is punished.'

We walk to the end of the row and head for the canteen. I should go straight to Abraham and report the damage to the plate, but it would look bad for us all. It's only a small scratch. Surely it won't be a problem.

The queue in the canteen seems to move slower each day. I glance to the clock above the food counter—in twenty-five minutes lunch will be over and I still don't have my soup. 'What are they doing in there?'

Barnabas turns. 'Careful.' I realize I've spoken out loud. He cautions me. 'Mind the servers don't hear you, you'll end up with the slops.'

I stutter. 'I… I didn't mean to criticize. I just—'

He shakes his head. 'Don't panic. I wasn't going to say anything. We need you on top form with the new targets coming up.'

The queue moves and we shuffle forward a few paces. I clench my jaw. Everyone needs to be fed, my needs do not override theirs. It's because I'm behind schedule, and that scratch. I'm on edge and want to get back to my workstation. Perhaps I could use my new procedure—just for this afternoon to catch up.

The queue edges forward. I take another step and reach the counter. Behind stand four servers in white coats. Three are covered with green flecks from the soup. The first pushes a tray towards me and places a bowl in the middle. I slide it along the counter to the next. He ladles the soup from a large pot and pours it from a height too great to be accurate. The third takes a slab of bread from a basket and drops it next to the bowl. I stop opposite the fourth. She smiles and nods. 'Eat, stay strong, and work hard.'

I respond, 'With your help, I will.'

I follow Barnabas and sit at our table. Forty-eight. I'm behind schedule. I have to get back and make up the gap.

'Hey!' Reuben sits and lowers his voice. 'Where's David?' I glance up from my soup to see the space next to Reuben.

I look back to the queue. 'He was at his workstation. Did he not join the queue?' As I scan the line, I see Abraham approach with a prefect. *Someone has reported David before me!* I dig my nails into my palm, annoyed that I'd delayed and let another please Mother. But who? I scan the faces at our table, but I see nothing that might give away the informer.

The prefect and Abraham stop at the head of the table.

Abraham shoots a sideways look at the prefect, then turns to us. He straightens his back and speaks. 'David has been excused his duties. Our targets will be temporarily adjusted.' The prefect nods at Abraham. His eyes wander across our faces. The prefect tilts his head forward and raises his eyebrows. Abraham continues. 'David has been sent for Re-Education to… to help him become a better worker.' He glances to the prefect. The prefect turns and motions Abraham to follow.

We watch as Abraham almost breaks into a run to keep up with the prefect. I look back to Barnabas and Reuben. Caleb blurts out, 'Do you think it has something to do with that book?'

Barnabas corrects him. 'No, not David.' I agree. I have my doubts about David, but only as a worker, not as a potential agent. I speak up for him.

'No, we would have known. He just needs some help, that's all.' They nod, and we say no more and I am none the wiser as to who informed Mother.

The Re-Education building is behind The Square in the prefects' quarter. It has no windows and a small door that is constantly guarded. Before David, Enoch was the only worker I'd known to attend. He'd had what Isaac called a *breakdown* shortly after I joined the team. I remember him being dragged away by the prefects as he shouted words that made little sense. He didn't return—we were told Enoch had been reassigned to a duty better suited to his abilities and condition. I hope the same fate doesn't await David. But if he can't pull his weight on the team, he doesn't deserve his place. *Mother knows best.*

Amos is only six units behind me and will meet his target. If I miss my quota it will not go unnoticed. Not since my third day at the factory have I failed to achieve my daily target. I clench my jaw. I don't intend to fall short today.

We take our positions at our workstations and wait for the bell to signal the beginning of the afternoon shift. My fingers twitch, itching to make amends. It chimes. I pick up the unfinished unit from the morning—the bird-like scratch flies off the surface and surely anyone within ten paces will see it. I check, but they're too busy with their own work to notice. I flip the plate over and complete the fixing and reach for the terminal box that will conceal my error from the outside world. I attach the box and relax a little as the evidence of my carelessness is hidden. A quick look to my left and right confirms no one saw it—I'm safe. I can put my new process into action. Instead of picking up each metal pin one at a time, I take all three and keep them in my hand as I complete the connections. Done. I place it on my shelf twelve seconds ahead of time. I do a quick calculation. Yes. I will make up for the lost time this morning and reach my daily target of one-hundred with almost nine minutes to spare. I decide to pick up only two pins at a time in order not to exceed the quota with my unauthorized procedure and raise suspicion.

Rebekah. I see her face once more but try to shake it out and replace her with David's. I will have to wait until I climb into my bed before I can think about her soft, clear skin and red hair.

# 5

I walk tall. My face feels strange and I probably look like a *third-timer*. I'd completed the last unit with just over a minute to spare, and reached my target. And I achieved it easily, even by slowing down towards the end. I will speak to Abraham to get my new process onto the agenda for the next meeting. Just think how much quicker we could be ready to return if we used my process. Mother would be pleased. I look up to the sky between the roofs of the dormitories—it's still grey.

The light from our dormitory window paints the walkway with an elongated, pale yellow triangle—our new arrival must already be here. We enter and see Seth. He's sitting in silence with Jared at the table. His straight back, fresh face and clean overalls make me feel old. But in a few days he will start to look like the rest of us. And within a month, he'll be proud of his worker's stooped posture as proof of his commitment and contribution to the cause. Seth stands at the prompt of the prefect. He looks so young. *Did I look like that at thirteen?*

It's difficult coming up from the Education Level. At first I wanted to go back down to the familiar surroundings of my early life, but as Mother says, there has to be a time to put aside childish things and work for the good of the people. I remember being overwhelmed by the induction tour of the Workers Level. It took exactly twenty-six minutes to walk around the inside of the perimeter wall—a trip I've never repeated, nor wanted to. In the nursery, Mother told us stories of the strange creatures with big, black eyes that prowl on the other side. We call them Outsiders and are grateful to Mother for building the wall. She says they're descendants of our race, banished from the surface centuries before and remain jealous of those who've seen the light of day.

Jared hands a clipboard and pencil to Abraham. I hear the pencil scratch across the paper as Abraham signs for the new worker. Jared nods as he countersigns and checks the paperwork. He looks to me. 'Noah, as his mentor, you'll be held responsible for...' he glances back to the document, 'Seth, for his one year probation period. Ensure he knows what is expected of him.' He places the clipboard under his arm with not a hint that we shared our early years together. He steps towards me and lowers his voice. 'And remember, you will be accountable for any misdemeanors.' Jared turns and marches out. I remember the feeling of guilt when Mother punished Isaac for my foolish act on the factory roof. But Mother had been right to do so, and Isaac accepted it as his duty and helped me find my way in the big, wide Workers Level. I will do the same for Seth.

We relax except for our new arrival. He looks down to the bag he clutches with his clean hands. This is a good sign. He should be nervous. He must earn his place before he can be considered part of our team.

I step forward and complete the formal introductions to each member of the team. His eyes jump from each of our faces, and I can tell his head is filled with questions. But this isn't the time. I speak before he can say something that would set him off on the wrong foot. 'We're the number one team here, Seth. We intend to keep our position, so you'll have to work hard.' He nods. I recall how it feels to be the new boy, but I was lucky to have Reuben with me on my first day.

Reuben asks the question on all our minds. 'So what book did you get for your leaving present?' This breaks the barrier and we step closer as Seth reaches into his bag. He takes out his book with a picture of a large green machine on the front. I bite my lip—mine has a plain cover. Reuben takes it from Seth; in a few days Seth won't let anyone touch it. Reuben reads the words on the front. 'The Big Book of Tractors.' He opens the book. 'Is it good?' I take a closer look—it's full of color pictures!

Seth rubs his fingers on his palms. 'I don't know… I've not read it yet, but I'm sure it's amazing. Mother knows how much I like big… machines. She always said I have an enquiring mind.' Seth glances to me. 'Mother knows best, eh.'

I nod. I take the book from Reuben and hand it back to Seth. 'Make sure you look after it, you won't get another. We keep ours under our pillows. Mother will be upset if you lose or damage her present.' He places it carefully under his arm. 'Oh, and don't forget to write your thank-you letter. She does like to feel appreciated,' I look around to the others, 'and I think we're all guilty of taking her for granted at times.'

'Well said, Noah.' Abraham pats me on the back. 'And while we're talking of letters, there is a special workshop coming up for those who are struggling to write their Thanksgiving Story. He glances to me. 'Now I know Noah has already written and submitted his entry.' Reuben's mock groan is cut short by a glare from Abraham. 'Remember, this is important. Mother devotes all her time to our welfare, so we should make every effort to write of our gratitude. And,' he smiles, 'Mother tells me there will be a prize this year for the best story.'

'A prize!' Seth almost jumps off the floor. 'I wonder what—?'

The first notes of The Workers' Anthem burst from the speaker. We straighten, quickly form a circle and remove our caps. I motion to Seth to do the same. We all stare—his hair is almost white, the same as Mother's! I have seen black, brown and the red of Rebekah's, but never anything as light as Seth's. We falter and miss the first line. Abraham flashes us an angry look and hisses, 'Concentrate.' We join in with the second line, but I cannot take my eyes from Seth. His face reddens with the attention, making his hair look even lighter.

The anthem finishes and we replace our caps. But my heart was not in the song and I have no memory of singing the words. We sit around the table in readiness for the bedtime story. I hope tonight's won't be postponed. Nothing more has been said about the illegal book, so perhaps it has been found and Mother will be happier. Was it David's? I wonder how he's getting on in the Re-Education Building.

The speaker sparks into life. *'Good evening, my children. I wish to congratulation you on a good day's work. All targets have been achieved.'* I see the scratch on the side of the plate. I have got away with it, but I really should have reported the damage. I push the thought away and listen to Mother. *'We have taken another step on the long staircase back to the surface.'* I smile at Reuben. *Could we be the first to return?*

Mother continues. *'As you all know, tomorrow is the first day of May. Which means it's… Moses Day!'* I'd forgotten! How could I have forgotten? Mother sounds excited. *'Tomorrow we celebrate the day Moses first broke the record by achieving one-hundred and fifteen percent of his quota. A special supper with readings from his diary will be held in The Square at the end of the shift.'* My heart quickens, but not for the ceremony, it is for Rebekah. I will see her tomorrow evening. Mother continues. *'Please shower and clean your overalls for this special occasion.'* I shudder at the thought of the cold water. No one likes the shower, but it will be worth it if I can see Rebekah. I sit straighter and look back to the speaker. I don't want Seth to notice my attention has slipped.

*'Now onto tonight's story.'* Good! She is pleased with us.

'*Make yourselves comfortable.*' My shoulders relax and I lean back an inch or two in my chair. '*Once upon a time, Mother climbed to the top of the tallest mountain to look down upon the Earth.*' I love this story. I see the mountain from the pictures on the classroom wall. Her voice rises. '*The gathering storm clouds in the West troubled me. But thankfully, I foresaw the coming danger and took steps to protect my good people. Many years before at the dawn of human history, our race was saved by building an ark. But a ship couldn't save us in the dark days to come this time, No, our redemption lay deep beneath the Earth, an ark large enough for...*' I let my eyes close to see Mother's story. I sigh and give thanks for her love and devotion to our cause. I think back to a day in school when Mother showed us a picture of a brilliant, fiery ball in a deep blue sky. She told us about The Sun and how it brought warmth to Earth and made everything grow. But it hasn't been seen for generations and nothing can survive until the clear skies return. Mother assures us that one day it will shine once more; so we work hard to be ready for that historic day.

'No, it goes on the other way around.' I show Seth how to attach the headset next to his bunk. He moves to press the button. I stay his hand. 'You don't need to press that yet. We have fifteen minutes to read before lights out.' His bright hair stands out against the pillow like the sun in a grey sky. I can see he is trying to look brave.

He whispers. 'It's different to the one in the nursery. What does it do?'

I glance to David's empty bed. 'We'll talk in the morning, you'll find out. We have to be up at five.'

'But my bed is hard.'

I try not to laugh, aware the others are listening. 'You'll get used to it.' I remember waking on my first morning in the dormitory – it took until lunch before my stiff muscles relaxed. I look back to Seth. 'Caleb will show you how to light the stove, and after breakfast, we'll go to the factory.'

He screws up his face. 'Is that what I can smell? Does it always—'

I sigh. 'No, that comes from the farm. You'll get used to that as well.' I smile and lie. 'I barely notice it now.'

'But—'

I raise my hand. 'We have a long day tomorrow.' I turn before he can speak again and climb into my bunk.

I let my heavy head sink into the pillow. Being a mentor is going to be hard work, but I have been given the honor and am happy to commit to Seth's training. I see the lock of red hair fall onto Rebekah's shoulder. My pulse quickens and I hear it echo back from my pillow. *Is she thinking of me right now?* She had looked at me. But why her? Why can I think of nothing else? Isaac has left; David has gone for Re-Education; I have Seth to train; and tomorrow is the second most important day of the year after Mother's Day. But still it's Rebekah who fills my mind. *Focus!* I think of the story Mother has just told and give thanks to her foresight to build The Ark as the war escalated to a global conflict. She took our people out of the reach of the enemy, and even now she protects us from their agents.

The lights go out and I reach for my headset. My book! I must be distracted by today's events. I haven't thought of looking at my book.

*The sirens wail in the dark. I run with hundreds of others but I know not where. Some scream; some shout; others cry, but I stay silent as I try to stay on my feet. To fall down will result in my death, trampled beneath a hundred feet in the frenzy and panic. Fork lightning splinters the black sky. It begins to rain, but not a cooling rain, it stings my head and burns through my clothes. I begin to scream.*

*But Mother is calling. She tells us to stay calm and walk. We slow our pace and stream down the narrowing path as it dips towards an entrance. A sea of bodies swell into the wide mouth, happy to gulp us down into its belly. Inside it is dark and quiet. Mother tells us we're safe now. She'll protect us from the horrors unfolding above.*

# 6

'It's five o'clock!' Abraham strides past my bunk. 'It's the first day of May so you know what that means.' It's Moses Day. But my first thought is of Rebekah; I will spend the day counting down the hours until we'll gather in The Square. I climb from my bunk and click my neck and feel the stiffness release a little. I shake Seth's bed. His white hair appears from beneath his blanket followed by his young face. He blinks in the harsh light above his bed—his mind is already in a whirl as he sits and stretches out his arms. 'Is that what it's like on the surface? What would have happened if Mother hadn't saved us?' He sits up. 'Are all the sleep stories like that?'

I shake my head. 'No,' I wriggle my fingers towards him and bare my teeth and growl, 'some are scary!'

He laughs. 'Do you—?' He jumps. 'Oh I forgot. It's Moses Day!'

I smile at his youthful enthusiasm. 'Not if you don't get out of bed and prepare the stove!'

Seth stops and glances around. 'Oh yes, sorry. Where's Caleb?'

'He's fetching the wood. He's big enough to bring it in all at once so you'd better be ready when he returns, Barnabas has already emptied the ash pan.' He climbs from the bed and pulls on his clean work clothes—they still have the creases. I remember my first morning and how the starched overalls had felt against my young skin.

He frowns. 'I thought Barnabas was second in command, why does he have to clean?'

I guide him to the living quarters. 'That's what he's like. He's a hard worker and says being a senior team members doesn't exclude him from humble duties.'

He shrugs. 'Oh, I see.'

I address his casual response. 'He sets a good example. Be sure to follow it.' I turn to the entrance and call over my shoulder. 'We're lucky to have him on the team, and don't you forget it.' My heart lifts to see the bright day beyond and I'm not surprised to be greeted by a blue sky. My body feels lighter as I collect the crate with the bread and milk. I return to see Seth has lit the stove first time. He learns fast. I have no doubt he will become a good worker. He frowns at his dirty hands and wipes them on his overalls before trying to rub the mark off with his sleeve. How long did it take me not to care about the grime?

He looks up and beams. I return his smile. 'Good work, Seth. We won't have to worry about the cold mornings if you're this quick every time.' I arrange the seven slabs of bread on the rack and place them over the fire. Next, I carefully lift the heavy pot Amos has filled with water and position it by the bread. It will be boiling, ready for coffee by the time we have eaten our toast.

Seth picks up more wood from the basket. He turns it over in his hand. 'Where does the wood come from? Do we have a tree?' I see the picture from my book. Strange, I'd never made the connection between the wood in our basket and that tree. The stove crackles, I wince; surely it would be a crime to burn a tree?

I turn to him, remembering his question. 'No, of course not. The farm makes the wood, the same place where they make the food, didn't they teach you anything at school?'

Seth places the wood onto the fire. 'Make? How?'

I sigh. 'We don't need to worry about that. It's in the basket every morning and that's all that matters. Our duty is at the factory.'

But he's not finished. 'Where does that smoke go?'

I turn the bread, worried it will burn with the distractions. I point. 'Up that pipe.'

'But where after that? Does it go up to the surface?'

'Err… I don't, yes I suppose it does. There must be a chimney.'

Seth wipes his hands again on his overall. 'But won't the smoke give our position away to the enemy?'

I turn. 'Amos! Show Seth how we set the table for breakfast.'

A buzz of excited voices fills the air beneath the blue sky. Faces, that would otherwise be fixed straight ahead, are turning side to side as we discuss what we might get for supper at the Moses Day celebration. I walk a little way ahead of Seth and scan the crowd for Rebekah. She will be making her way to the laboratory. Mother had the foresight to situate the dormitories for each sector on the opposite side to their places of work. She tells us a long walk is good for our health and motivation. I now thank her for another reason; if I'm lucky, I will see Rebekah before the evening. The clean faces of the dozen or so new arrivals stand out as they gawp up at the dome. But I don't see Rebekah—I will have to wait.

'This will be your workstation, be sure to keep everything in order as it is now.' I watch as his eyes flit across the component shelves. I continue. 'You have one week to get up to speed and achieve your first target of thirty-six units a shift. Mother will set new targets as you get more experience.'

Seth runs his fingers across the marked desk top. He picks up a metal plate from his shelf and holds it up for closer inspection. 'What do we make? What are these for?'

I try to laugh. 'Questions, questions!' *Did I ask this many?* I take the plate from him and replace it in the correct position on the rack. 'We make the parts that Rachel... no, it's now Lydia's shift, use to make the machines that will help us when we get back to the surface.'

'Like the ones in my book? Do you think these things are used to make tractors? We'll need those to grow food, won't we? Is that—?'

'We make machines, that's all we need to know.' I pick up a Plate A and hand it to him. 'You start with this in your right hand, and then...' I see the question is still on his lips. I put the plate down and speak slowly. 'We are small cogs in a big machine—' Seth opens his mouth. I lift my finger. 'And no, it's not a tractor. But we operate like one. Each one of us has a function to perform and that is our duty. We mustn't concern ourselves with things beyond this room and outside of our control. That is for Mother alone.'

Seth closes his mouth and nods. Is that a tear? I soften my tone. 'Come on. I bet you can soon reach your target.'

He turns. 'Is it true that yours is fifty?' I nod. His eyes widen. 'Wow, is that the highest since Moses? What was his? Fifty-eight, wasn't it?'

'It was.'

'Do you think you will reach that?'

My pride takes over. 'I have an idea that—' I stop myself.

Seth looks up. 'What? What idea?'

My jaw tightens. 'Nothing. I cannot say anything yet.' I reach for Plate B. 'Now take this and attach it to the other plate with this,' I reach across and pick up the next part, 'a number six fastener.'

Alone in the shower, I have time to contemplate the day. I made it through to the end of the shift without further mishap. Seth has proved me right and taken very quickly to his task, managing thirty-two units in the afternoon shift. I'm confident he will reach his target within two days. Lunch passed without further questions from Seth. I think he's learning to keep his thoughts to himself in the company of others. I managed to keep mine of Rebekah hidden by engaging with Abraham and Barnabas about the upcoming evening's event.

I grin. Seth's progress will help me look good in Mother's eyes. She will see I am capable of taking control and showing a worker what is required of him—that must help my case if she decides more prefects are needed in our fight. The first blast of icy water takes away my breath and I gasp out loud. I pick up the soap, still grey from Reuben's turn, and scrub my face. The soapy water stings as it gets into my eyes. I force them open into the shower stream and let the suds wash away.

I rub the last of the soap from my eyes. The white, tiled walls close in. I'm alone. Odd. Why have I never thought of this before? The only time I am truly by myself is when I'm in this cubicle. I can see no one else, and no one can see me.

I turn and gasp anew as the cold water splashes down my back. I check my arms; I'm as clean as I will get in my allocated time in the shower. I have two minutes to wash my overalls. I turn to take them from the hook on the back of the door. They hang limp, but straight without my body inside to disfigure their shape. I lift and hold them under the water. Grey fluid bleeds from the cloth and I watch it flow down the plug. *Where does it go?* I turn to answer Seth before realizing the question came from inside my head. *Stop!* It doesn't matter where it goes—that's nothing to do with me.

I turn off the shower and slap my overalls against the tiles, but my numb fingers fail to hold onto the stiff fabric. It slips from my hands and lands back in the murky pool of water yet to drain away. I crouch and look down into the plughole. The rhyme we used to whisper in the nursery comes into my head.

*Deep down below where the dirty waters flow,*
*Where the sun don't shine and the wind don't blow,*
*You can hear the screams as the Shovellers cry,*
*For a breath of clean air and an open sky,*
*Deep down below where the dirty waters flow.*

I peer closer into the dark hole. Do all the failing workers get sent down The Trench? Worse things than dirty water flow down the pipes. I wouldn't want to spend my day shoveling that!

'Noah! Time's up.'

I jump at the sound of Barnabas's voice. I call over my shoulder. 'Nearly done.' I do my best to dry my cold body and pull on my under-garments over damp skin; Mother is very strict about covering up in front of others. My face tingles and feels strange without the mask of grime that would conceal much of what's on my mind. I look down to my clean limbs covered in goose bumps and suddenly think of Rebekah. Has she just come out of the shower? What would her wet body look like? What would it feel like, pressed against mine, dressed only in her thin, white—? No! This is wrong.

'Noah!' This time Barnabas bangs on the door. 'It's getting late!'

'Sorry. Just coming.' I feel suddenly ashamed. I clutch my damp overalls to my stomach and open the door. Caleb and Barnabas are standing outside—Caleb grins but Barnabas's jaw muscles knot. They are right. I have spent too long in the shower with my private thoughts with no consideration for the needs of the team. I hold the door open and try to deflect the accusation. 'Don't look so worried, Caleb. It's hot water on Moses Day.'

It works. He straightens to his full height and beams. 'Is it? That would be—'

'Don't get his hopes up.' Barnabas scowls at me, then sighs and turns to Caleb. 'He's pulling your leg. Now get a move on.'

I try to laugh but Barnabas doesn't join in with the joke. His eyes stay fixed on mine. He opens his mouth…

'Hey look!' We both turn as Amos calls through. 'David's back.'.

# 7

David stands in the entrance looking like a new arrival in his stiff, clean overalls. His red-rimmed eyes stay fixed ahead and appear not to see us as we go to welcome him back. I am desperate to know what's happened, but Mother has dealt with him as she sees fit. It's not for me to ask. *Mother knows best.*

We gather around but no one speaks. Abraham returns from signing David's release form for the prefect. I'm grateful when he pats David on the back and breaks the silence. 'Just in time for the celebrations, eh!' The boy stumbles forward and looks down to the floor. He tries to smile but manages only a grimace. Abraham steps aside and looks back to us. 'Stop standing around like a bunch of new arrivals, get a move on. I want everyone dry, dressed and with their hair combed in fifteen minutes.' He glances back to David. 'Then we can all go to The Square.'

I turn away, guilty for watching him for so long. I hang my overalls over the stand placed next to the stove. It won't dry fully in the time we have left, but I don't care—I will see her shortly.

The excited murmur greets us long before we arrive. It spills from The Square, flowing down the walkways, wrapping itself around our bodies, drawing us in towards the celebration. Seth is almost skipping beside me. I think back to my first Moses Day Supper and can't blame him for getting carried away by the occasion. He opens his mouth but I cut him short, anticipating his question. 'Wait and see.' I grin as his brow furrows in the middle.

'But—'

'But nothing. Wait and see.' I cannot think of anything

but Rebekah and pretend to focus on the people ahead. We're almost at the entrance. I find a smile on my lips.

Reuben surges ahead. He glances back, his face beaming. He mistakes my private joy for anticipation. 'You can feel it, can't you?' He rubs his hands together. 'This is going to be a party to remember.'

I catch sight of Barnabas watching me and reply, 'Of course! It's something worth celebrating.' His eyes are still on me. I continue, 'Moses set an example for all of us to follow.'

Reuben frowns, then notices the attention of Barnabas and nods. 'Well, yes. Where would we all be without our Moses?'

Abraham stops us at the entrance to The Square and turns back to us. 'Where indeed.' He waits for David to catch up and join the group. 'Now remember why we're celebrating. Do enjoy the food, the readings and the songs, but don't forget the reason we're here.' He glances at me. 'If we work as hard as Moses, we'll be ready to return to the surface sooner.' I smile, but I'm impatient to enter and see Rebekah. Abraham raises his hands. 'Form two lines. Let's show everyone what the most productive team in this place looks like.' Reuben and I move behind Abraham and Barnabas. We glance up to the archway, now decorated with pale blue bunting woven around the metal-wrought words of our vow.

We pass beneath and I can't resist looking up at the dome as the space opens up before me—it's a beautiful deep blue. But I spend too much time taking in the sight and bump into the back of Barnabas, who's stopped. He spins around but before he can speak, the bulk of Caleb, then Seth bumps into me, and our combined weight knocks Barnabas to the floor. I should have immediately helped him to his feet, but my eyes are drawn to The Square beyond. The three of us gawp past Barnabas as he climbs to his feet unaided. He steps towards me, but his anger fades as he's disarmed by our wide eyes and open mouths. Barnabas turns to see what has struck us dumb.

Long tables covered with cloth, the same color as the bunting, stretch out towards the screen. This is new. I've attended four Moses Day celebrations, but I've never seen anything like this before—not even for Mother's Day. *What does this mean?*

A girl I recognize from the laboratory greets us. 'Please, come this way. You have seats at the head of the center table.' None of us speak as she leads our team along rows of equally bemused workers. She stops at the top of the table closest to the screen wall. 'Here, please be seated.'

Abraham finds his voice and thanks her. We sit in order and I find myself sitting opposite Barnabas. Seth blurts out. 'What are these? Where's the spoon? And what happened to the bowl?'

Reuben smiles. 'Put them down.' He points. 'That's a fork, that's a knife, and that flat bowl is called a plate.' Reuben's face lights up. 'Hey! A knife! We must be having meat.' We laugh, but I find Barnabas's eyes are still fixed on me. I look away and disguise my search for Rebekah as a child-like curiosity. But I can't see her. The places are now full, but she's not here. *Why isn't she here?* I mustn't let my disappointment show, but it's a struggle.

'Something wrong, Noah?' Barnabas is on to me. *Think!*

'Err… no, I was just,' *Come on! Think!* The others are looking, I have seconds to stop my secret being exposed. *Got it.* 'I was just thinking if we really deserve,' I take another quick look for Rebekah, 'all this. I mean, have we worked hard enough to earn such a party?'

Abraham slaps me on the back. 'Always the conscientious worker, eh. I think we have our very own Moses on the team.' But Barnabas doesn't look convinced.

I will have to be careful. My extra time in the shower has raised his suspicion. He suspects I'm having thoughts that may distract me from the cause.

I look away to the clock, just as the big hand clicks onto the top of the hour: eight o'clock, Saturday the first day of May. The lamps dim as the prefects arrive in line. We stand. I forget Barnabas—Mother is about to make her entrance. We turn to the screen and cheer as it begins to glow. I shield my eyes as it grows brighter. I've never been this close and notice rows and rows of tiny lights on its surface. They explode into a thousand brilliant suns bringing warmth, life, and Mother to The Square. The suns fade and transform briefly into stars as they go out. I blink, momentarily blind. When my eyes adjust, I see her, standing tall and magnificent, closer than I've seen her before. Her eyes shine in her pristine, white face, framed by her immaculate hair that flows onto her shoulders. I notice her dress—it's blue and glistens in the lamplight. I can't take my eyes from her as I shrink into my seat, suddenly feeling small, grubby and not worthy of her love. But I'm safe. Safe because of her knowledge; safe because she has everything under control; and safe because she knows how to get back to the surface only her eyes have seen.

We sit at her request. She scans our upturned faces, seeing and knowing each one of us, passing on her love. She breaks the silence. 'My children, this very day, exactly sixty years ago, Moses set a new record which still stands today.' We cheer as Mother reminds us of his achievement. 'His tireless work at the factory set us firmly on the path to meeting our goal. His unselfish attitude shows us how we can work for the benefit of all. His unquestioning faith sets an example of loyalty, diligence and belief in our just and noble society.' She turns to look up to The Metal Sun. Her voice falters. 'And I miss him.' I send my thoughts to her, to give her strength, to let her know I will do everything I can to fill the empty space in her heart for Moses.

Mother straightens. 'But let us not be downhearted. We are here to celebrate what Moses stood for, and what he has done for The Ark.' She takes a step back and looks to the right. 'The workers of the top laboratory teams have the honor tonight of serving you.' She claps her hands. 'Let us eat!'

The prefects step aside. A dozen or so workers enter carrying gleaming silver bowls—I see Rebekah and she's heading towards me! She stops at the head of our table with another girl. She looks down the line, but before she reaches me, her eyes drop to the contents of the bowl in her hands. Her face reddens. I hold my breath; my heart beating in my ears. *Don't stare!* If Barnabas sees me now, he will know. *Breathe!* I look down at my plate. *Stay calm.* My body is in turmoil. Rebekah stands only a few feet away, but I dare not look at her. I must control my heaving chest but I also need air. My face feels hot and beads of sweat trickle from my brow and down the sides of my face. I can't hold out much longer. Any moment, I'm going to pass out or explode.

I glance up. Barnabas is watching but thankfully the other girl reaches over his shoulder and places a slice of pink meat onto his plate. That must mean—Rebekah moves to my right. As she leans forward, I feel her breath on my neck. My head feels suddenly light. I barely contain a sigh as the soft skin of her forearm brushes mine. I look up—straight into her blue eyes just inches away. A flicker of a smile passes across her lips. She speaks. 'Enjoy your meal, Noah.' *Words meant just for me!*

I try to reply, but my dry tongue clicks as I open my mouth. I stammer. 'Th… thank you.' She holds my gaze for one more precious second then steps back. I release the air from my lungs that must blow like a blast from the stove into Barnabas's face. She moves to my left to serve Reuben. I look down and notice her arm doesn't touch his. She speaks. 'Enjoy your meal.' *She didn't say his name!* But she knows mine.

More servers place food on my plate, but I'm in another place. My arm feels the touch of Rebekah's soft skin; her breath still on my neck, and her words echoing in my head. *'Enjoy your meal, Noah'.* Behind my fixed face, I'm in a state of pure joy I have never felt before.

Movement. The others are eating. I pick up my knife and fork and start. I chew but taste nothing. Not even the flavors of the specially prepared meal can penetrate my new world. These are my thoughts, my sensations, and mine alone. No one needs to know. I don't have to share this moment with anyone. These are selfish thoughts—but I feel no guilt.

We finish the supper. We sing songs. Mother reads from the diary of Moses. We play games. I hope I am smiling and laughing at the right times. But I celebrate something else, and I know Rebekah is celebrating with me in her thoughts.

'Noah!' Reuben's knee nudges my leg.

I turn. 'What?'

He whispers. 'Is she talking about our team?'

'Who?'

Reuben gapes. 'Mother! Who else?'

*Focus.* My world shatters. I hear Mother's voice for the first time since her opening speech. I hope I haven't missed anything important and try to catch up. '...at the factory are achieving the new quotas, while the workers at the laboratory are continuing to improve the air quality.'

Barnabas leans over to Abraham. 'Yes, it does smell better.' Abraham agrees, but I can't say I'd noticed any difference.

Mother raises her voice. 'And,' she waits for silence, 'I

hope to have some good news for you soon, very soon.'
This gets my attention.

Reuben mutters loudly in my ear. 'Good news? What
do you think that could be?'

I shake my head. *Surely she can't mean...* but I reply. 'I
don't know. Perhaps she's found that illegal book, or we
might get another special day for our good work.'

'Or...' The table goes quiet. We turn to Barnabas—his
eyes are fixed on me. 'Perhaps she suspects an agent and is
about to make an arrest.' The others glance to David and I
follow their gaze. But David doesn't notice; his attention is
on the half-eaten food on his plate. Barnabas remains
silent, letting his words take root in our minds. No one
speaks and I'm grateful when Mother continues.

'So let us retire to our beds, and wake refreshed, ready
to accept the challenges that await us on the path towards
The New Dawn. Just as Moses did.' She turns towards the
screen as it begins to glow and leaves The Square.

A prefect claps his hands to summon the servers of the
evening. My heart lifts, but Rebekah is assigned to another
table. I turn to see her move to the next; Jared watches her
closely.

# 8

'Is every Moses Day as exciting as this?' I sigh. Seth resumes his skip as we make our way back to the dormitory block. 'What do you think the good news is?' I smile, but it's not for him. Barnabas is walking ahead, talking to Abraham, so it's safe to think back to the evening's events. But Seth has other ideas. 'Do we also get meat on Mother's Day, or any other time?' I must answer before the others notice I'm ignoring him. I wrench my attention to the moment.

'Yes, no idea, yes, and no.' Seth frowns. I try again. 'Yes, Moses Day is always that exciting. I have no idea what the good news is. Yes, we also have meat on Mother's Day, and no… we don't get it any other time.' He looks hurt. I must make an effort. I laugh, to let Seth think I'm joking.

The lines melt from his brow. 'Ha, ha. I'm asking too many questions again, aren't I.'

I feel a twinge of guilt for neglecting my duty as his mentor. I pull the cap from his head. 'Yes you are.' I look for somewhere to throw his cap without getting the attention of a prefect, but notice others are staring at Seth's light hair. I replace it and twist it so it's back to front. 'You ask as many as you like, but,' I lean closer and lower my voice, 'but just ask me.' Seth steps back. I try to make light of my poorly disguised warning and grin. 'You don't want to annoy every member of this team.' It works and I think he appreciates my help.

'Seth!' We both twist to see Barnabas glaring. He hisses. 'Put your cap on properly. It's still Moses Day! Show some respect.'

Seth adjusts his cap and mumbles, 'Sorry.' *He didn't*

*blame me.* Barnabas turns back to Abraham.

I mouth to Seth. 'Sorry, my fault.' He grins. I nod back and, for a moment, feel like I had on the factory roof with Reuben.

We arrive back at our dormitory in high spirits. Tomorrow we'll be back to the usual routine, but that's still several hours away—Mother lets us go to bed one hour later on special days.

'Hey! Look at this. We've got a surprise.' I follow Caleb into the living quarters to be greeted by a new and welcoming smell coming from a large, shiny pot on our stove.

'Stand aside please, let me through.' Abraham works his way between the throng gathering around the stove.

'What is it?' Both Caleb and Amos try to peer into the pot. Abraham holds up his hands.

'Move back, it's hot. Now settle down and I'll tell you.' We form a circle, making sure we're not too close to annoy Abraham. He smiles as he scans our faces. 'This,' he rests his hands lightly on the rim, 'is a special gift from Mother.'

'A gift?' Amos hops on the spot.

'For all of us.' Abraham laughs. 'It's in recognition of our contribution to the cause.' He leans forward and breathes in its sweet aroma. 'It's Mother's special recipe. Now get your mugs!' We rush to find them and form a queue in order of seniority. Abraham takes the ladle hanging from the side of the pot and fills Barnabas's mug, then mine and Reuben's. I lift it to my nose and let the steam warm my throat. 'Wait, Noah.' Abraham fixes his eyes on mine. 'We wait until everyone is served.'

'Yes, of course. I was just enjoying the smell.'

Reuben nudges my arm and leans over. 'It smells a bit like a birthday cake, do you think it has—' A glance from Barnabas ends his guess about the drink's ingredient.

Lastly, Abraham fills his cup and joins the circle. We hold our mugs, waiting for someone to drink. Abraham lifts his own cup. 'Congratulations, everyone, you deserve this. I believe the tradition is to say 'bottoms up'.'

Reuben almost spills his drink as he splutters, 'What?'

'He means the bottom of the cup.' But even Barnabas seems to find it amusing. 'To raise the cup to your lips, you have to tip the *bottom*, up.' Now we all laugh.

'Shush.' Abraham steps into the circle. 'Not too loud, we don't want to draw attention to ourselves.' He glances to the entrance. 'Let's try again, but quieter.' We follow his lead and take a sip. As the first gulp of warm liquid slides down our throats, our eyes widen and we lower the mugs.

Reuben speaks for us all. 'Dear Moses! That tastes good.'

My mouth waters, eager for more. I have to ask. 'Is this what a cake tastes like?' I see Abraham look to Barnabas. He smiles.

'Almost.' I take another sip and stop. I want to make it last, but before I can think, I tip back my mug and guzzle down the lot—the bottom coming into view all too soon. I look up to see the others have done the same. Reuben steps up to the pot.

'I don't suppose there's any more?' Abraham shakes his head.

'That's your lot, I'm afraid.' He wipes the back of his hand across his lips. 'But there'll be more next Moses Day if we can stay at the top of the table.' My whole body is filled with the warmth from the drink; my head feels suddenly light. I look around at the others, they look as if they're swaying, or is it the room?

We grin at each other. We're a team, the best team but they're also my friends. Mother talks about us all being friends, but I don't feel for the other team members what I'm now feeling for those around me. I look at their faces.

I want to tell them about Rebekah. How she makes me feel; that I want to hold her hand; stroke the soft skin on her cheek; and wrap my arms around her and pull her body close to mine. I open my mouth. I know I shouldn't, but I have to share this feeling. 'I... I want to—'

'Hey! Guess who?' Reuben steps into the middle. He bends down and pulls off one of his boots. He hops around the room, waving his arms and shouting gibberish. We laugh. We laugh hard. Tears roll down my face as I lose control—but I don't care.

Seth pulls at my sleeve. He giggles but shakes his head. 'What's so funny?'

'He's...' I choke before I can speak. 'He's pretending to be Enoch.' I wait for Barnabas to stop Reuben's antics, but he too joins in the fun. Seth is still none the wiser. I try to hold back my laughter long enough to explain. 'Enoch was head of this team before Isaac, but he went mad.' More rowdy bursts fill the room as the others pull off a boot and hop around with Reuben. I grab Seth, 'Come on, join in.' I bend forward and almost fall as I tug at his boot. My head spins so I sit on the floor to remove mine.

Seth beams, but still looks confused. 'I don't get it. Why the one boot?'

I try to stand but fall back. 'Help me up, Seth.' I take his hand, pull myself up and wrap my arm around his shoulder to steady my spinning head. 'The boot? That's how we found him. He came back from the morning report with a boot missing, and then started to flap his arms around and shout at us until the prefects came and took him away.'

'Like those.' Seth stops and points a wavering hand to the entrance. I turn to see two prefects watching us. But the odd thing is, I don't care. They look too serious, standing stiff as if made of metal. I prop myself against Seth and force my mouth to close, trying to shut off the giggles. But Reuben bumps into me and sprawls forward, landing at the feet of the prefects. I erupt, bending double as the delight erupts from my lungs. Reuben struggles to stand, but each time he gets halfway up, he slips on his sock and collapses back to the floor, and each time he fails, the more hilarious we all find his predicament.

The prefect opposite Reuben holds up a hand. He has the same face that Mother had when trying to calm us down in the nursery. 'Okay, that's enough.' They stoop to help Reuben to his feet. But Reuben fails to contain his amusement and squeals as they lift his floppy body. I glance to Seth—it's a mistake. Our lips are not strong enough to hold back the laughter; it explodes louder than ever. The rest follow, each ridiculous sound of mirth setting off another. My face, sides and stomach ache, racked with pain from uncontrollable spasms. I'm bent double, staring at the shiny boots of the prefects, who stand unmoved amidst our writhing bodies. I know I shouldn't be doing this but I cannot stop.

More prefects arrive. I'm aware they're standing in a circle around us and I try desperately to stand so as not to disrespect them. I look for Reuben and crawl to him. He sees me and smiles and clasps my hand. Reuben squints and speaks in a strange voice. 'Hey, Noah. Have I ever told you that if it wasn't for you, I think I'd have ended up just like Enoch?'

I help him to sit and hug him to me. 'No, it's you that's—' my tongue feels heavy and I slur my words. I speak slower. 'It's you that's the strong one, it's *you*,' I prod him with my finger, 'that keeps,' I point to my chest, '*me* going.'

Reuben claws his way up, using my body like a ladder. He bends and offers his hand. 'Well, let's agree that we couldn't carry on without each other.'

I take his hand. He pulls me up and embraces me once

more. Over his shoulder, I see the others. Abraham and Barnabas clasp hands. Seth, Caleb and Amos are in a huddle; only David stands alone. He chuckles to himself as he looks at his big toe peeping through a hole in his sock. Reuben pats me hard on my back. 'You're our hero, you're *our* Moses and an inspiration to us all, Noah.'

'No, you're the hero, Reuben.'

'No, it's you.' Reuben pulls back and looks me in the eye and blinks several times. 'When we were on the roof...' he sways back and has to grip my shoulders, 'I knew then that you'd be the one.'

'One what?'

He burps and I get a taste of the hot milk, only not as enticing as before. 'You know, the one that will get us back to the surface.' He grins. I have to look away to stop his expression setting off another bout of laughter. I see Barnabas. Tears streak his red face, but he's not laughing, he's crying. I feel his pain, and suddenly, our desperate situation, stuck far below the world we're so anxious to see, hits me hard. I blurt out. It surges from my stomach, gushing out in fits and starts, sounds that I'm ashamed to hear, coming from deep within. But I cannot stop, and soon we're all sobbing like infants.

'Okay, that's enough.' I look up to see Jared's stern face. *When did he arrive?* Eight prefects in total stand in the room, each with a clipboard and pencil. They tuck the boards under their arms and I realize Jared had spoken to them. He turns to Abraham, he sounds calm, almost sympathetic. 'Celebrations are over. Get your team into order and ready for bed.' The prefects turn as one and leave. I rub my tired face and wipe the tears with my sleeve. We stand in silence, glancing briefly at each other. In these exchanges, we agree to never speak of this again.

*Enjoy your meal, Noah.* I grin into the dark as I lie in my bunk. Enjoy? I cannot remember a single mouthful, but the taste of Mother's special recipe is on my lips, and my head still isn't quite right. But I feel good, comfortable and relieved of some unknown burden as I lie in my bunk. Rebekah's words repeat over and over in my head; the skin of my arm remembers her touch. And those eyes! I could drift away in her sky blue eyes and leave this grey existence behind forever. My pulse beats so hard in my ears I fear everyone will hear. But at least they can't see my face, guilty of showing my personal pleasure.

The buzzer hurts my ears. 'Noah!' Reuben calls over from his bunk. 'Your headset.'

'Sorry.' My bubble bursts. Back to reality and routine. I reach for the device and place it on my head. I don't want to add more fuel to the fire Barnabas has lit beneath me. I whisper to Reuben. 'Sorry. I was still thinking about the good news Mother said she—'

'Quiet, you two! Moses Day is over, now get some sleep.' Abraham puts a stop to my feeble excuse. Barnabas doesn't need to say anything—I can feel his suspicion scorching the wooden slats of my bed.

*We queue in long lines at the foot of the ladders. I tip my head back but my eyes cannot pierce the gloom obscuring the top of the exit. Mother stands at the front. She holds up her hands. 'My children. I am sorry but it is not good news. I have ventured to the upper levels and looked outside.' She shakes her head. 'I am afraid it is still too dangerous. The skies remain dark, too dark for the sun to shine, and the toxic rain still falls.' She tries to smile. 'But I promise you this. One day the clouds will clear, The New Dawn will come and you will go outside. But until then, you will only be safe here with me.'*

*I sag as all the air leaves my body. A warm hand takes mine. I turn and find Rebekah stands by my side. She smiles and tugs me forward. I read her thoughts and we race to the front. Mother tries to stop us. 'No, you must wait.' But we run straight past her. I grasp a rung on the middle ladder with my free hand; Rebekah laughs as she takes the next. We climb, still holding hands.*

*Mother screams from below. 'No, you must stop! You do not know what you are doing. You have to stay with me.' But we ignore her plea. We climb higher, towards the surface, away from the world below that would keep us apart. We climb into darkness, but Rebekah's hand in mine gives me courage. Mother's cries fades. Her last words reaching only as far as the rungs beneath our feet. 'You do not understand. You are not ready to find out. You must not...' She's gone. For the first time in my life, she cannot tell me what to do.*

*We move faster, the chains gone from our ankles, I feel light; I feel free!*

*A breeze blows into my face. I look up and am blinded by a bright light.*


'Five o'clock. Come on! Everyone up. It's Sunday, the second day of May. There's a stove to light, floors to clean and breakfast to be made. I want to see it on the table when I get back.' I blink into the glare of the lamp inches from my nose as Abraham strides through. My head hurts.

The night's events come to mind. Rebekah and I had defied Mother! My heart hammers into my ribs and vibrates in my skull. We had ignored Mother—and it felt good. I sit and look over the Reuben. He's already out of his bunk, stretching the stiffness from his muscles. He smiles. 'Shame we couldn't go up the ladders, but it was good when Mother let us take a look at the upper level.' I yawn to give myself time to think. My night story had a different ending. The others clamber from their beds, all speaking at the same time. I say nothing. I climb out of my bunk and almost trip over David scrubbing the floor. *Why did I not share the story?*

The crate with the bread and milk sits in the same place outside our dormitory. *Had Rebekah shared it too?* I take hold of the crate and lift. I don't understand—my headset was attached when I woke.

'What color is the sky today, Noah?' Seth looks up from the stove as I enter.

'Sorry?'

Seth frowns and lowers his voice. 'The sky?'

The sky. I hadn't noticed! I'm grateful Seth appreciates my lack of attention could land me in trouble. But Caleb has already heard Seth's question. He pipes up. 'Is it blue? Is today the good news day?' The others look over.

*Think fast.* 'Guess. What color do you think it is today?'

But Barnabas isn't playing along with my game. 'Stop this nonsense! Just tell them so they can get back to their duties.'

'Blue.' I speak without thinking and hope I'm right. If I had delayed, Barnabas would be on my back all day. If I'm wrong, I can argue I was trying to cheer them up.

I take the milk from the crate and place it on the table. I try to act as if nothing is out of the ordinary, but I can't get the thought of Rebekah and the ladders out of my head. Seth is watching me. He can see. I avoid his gaze as I return to the stove to toast the bread. The pot feels lighter this morning and I wonder whether Amos has filled it properly. But it's full to the line and nearly slops over the side as I move it to the rack.

'Everyone to the table!' Abraham returns from reporting to Mother. 'It's a blue sky day, so let's make it a good one.'

Barnabas turns to face me as I silently exhale. He speaks only to me. 'We already know.'


I must see Rebekah. My eyes jump from one approaching face to the next in the sea of jiggling heads of the morning rush. I have to know if she shared the same experience last night. Are we somehow connected? If so, we could be together every sleeping moment. That would be perfect. I could work each day as if nothing has changed, perhaps even break the record set by Moses, because the nights would belong to us. Alone together— no one could keep us apart. We would go to the surface. Just the two of us, strolling for hours holding hands under the real blue sky and warm Sun. We could find the tree from my book, sit in its branches and look out for the bird.

A girl from the farm smiles briefly then looks away. *Stop!* My face must be revealing my thoughts again. I shut off the flow, but I cannot hold the flood back for long as I see Rebekah. Her blue eyes shine through the grey crowd; they're looking straight at me. As she draws level, they flick towards me and I know. She knows. We are meant to be together.

Seth tugs at my arm. 'Who's that girl?'

'Wh… what girl?' But he's not fooled.

'The one who just looked at you.'

'I don't know her name. She works at the laboratory. We were at the production meeting last year, she had some ideas about—'

'She looks nice.' He grins. I shoot him a look to be quiet. He nods and closes his mouth. But not for long. He checks Abraham and Barnabas are engaged in conversation before he asks, 'Have you spoken to her yet?'

'No! And that's none of your business.'

Reuben bumps into me. 'Move along, lazy bones.' I mumble an apology, I think it includes a reference to Moses, but my mind is whirring. *How could I get to speak to her?* Reuben sees my expression. 'Are you tired, Noah?' Before I can speak, Seth answers.

'We were just wondering—' I catch his eye. He obliges. 'We were just wondering how many times Moses must have walked this way.'

Reuben makes a face. I cannot tell if he's disappointed about the subject, or doesn't believe Seth. He sighs. 'Oh, I see. Well I guess it must have been at least…' I care not for his view, and I can tell he doesn't either. I glance back to the blue sky—no it's not the sky, it's a dome, a roof. But what lies above it?.

# 9

'Good work, Seth. You've met your first target in quick time.' Barnabas looks up from Seth's shelf. He watches me as he lifts the first batch onto his trolley. 'I see we have a contender to replace Noah as the most productive member on the team.' I have no problem keeping my calm face showing, because I don't care. Odd. Only a few days ago I would have shuddered at the thought. But I realize it no longer matters now I have Rebekah.

For the sake of keeping Barnabas off my back, I smile and reply. 'He learns fast. Thanks to Mother of course. She knew he would thrive on our—'

'And thanks to Noah's guidance.' Seth shoots me a look once Barnabas turns to stack his trolley. With a slight shake of my head I let him know that he should stay silent.

Barnabas turns just as I stop. He looks first to Seth, and then to me. 'Noah is performing his duty and nothing more. We work together, we succeed together.'

We nod and repeat the words. Barnabas checks my tray of completed work; I sense he's disappointed that I'm on target. He collects the units without another word and moves onto Reuben. I hear them exchange a few words but cannot make out what they say. As Barnabas proceeds to deliver the result of our morning's work to Lydia's team, I glance to Reuben; he smiles briefly then looks back to his workstation.

The queue shuffles forward half a step, but apart from the odd sigh, no one wants to say anything. Mother says productivity is up, so the queue must be moving faster, it's just that we don't notice. My stomach rumbles. Shame I have no memory of the meal I ate on Moses Day—it will be over seven months of tasteless mush before we eat meat again on Mother's Day.

In front of me, Barnabas takes another step. I must focus. I must not let my thoughts wander and bump into him again. But I cannot stop scanning the tables for Rebekah, even though I know the teams from the laboratory will not arrive for another thirty minutes—sadly after we have finished.

'Cake for you tomorrow!' Reuben nudges me with his elbow.

'What?' I turn. Reuben's grin looks different.

'Your birthday? Come on, Noah, you only get one birthday… and one cake!'

I don't care, but I smile. 'I know, and don't think you're getting any.' My attempt at a joke sounds more like a threat. I try to laugh, but it doesn't convince even me. Reuben steps closer.

'And, then it won't be long until,' he lowers his voice, 'you know what.'

Barnabas twists around. 'Reuben!' He glances down the line. David is staring at the floor, but Caleb, Amos and Seth are trying hard to look as if they're not listening. Barnabas speaks through clenched teeth. 'Not here.'

Reuben steps back. 'Sorry.' His shoulder sag and he looks to the floor. We take another step closer to the counter where we will thank the servers for food that will satisfy no one.

'What's a *third-timer*?' I just stop myself coming to a sudden halt. I cannot cause another collision on the bustling street. I glance to Seth.

'Where did you hear that?'

Seth lowers his voice. 'I heard Amos ask David. But he didn't seem to hear, or he ignored him.' His eyebrows rise. 'Amos thinks it's something to do with turning eighteen, or getting into Paradise.'

I sigh. 'You don't need to know. You'll find out soon enough, well, when you're eighteen.'

But Seth isn't put off by my dismissal. 'Are you a… you know?'

'No!' I fear my voice will carry to Abraham and Barnabas a little way ahead. But they're in a discussion, no doubt distracted by the upcoming production review. I grab Seth's arm and pull him closer. 'Look, you mustn't repeat what others say, it can get you in trouble. Now be quiet.' Seth drops his head. I've upset him, but I don't want him to speak out of turn.

The truth is I don't know the full story—no one is allowed to talk about it. All I know is that shortly after a worker turns eighteen, they're excused evening duties and are taken by a prefect to a building close to Re-Education called The Meeting Place. We secretly call it, *The Place of Knowing*. Reuben believes those who go, learn something new because after their third visit they come back changed, different.

I remember when Abraham returned. He stood at the entrance looking like a new arrival; his eyes appearing to see things that weren't in the room. He and Isaac exchanged a brief, knowing look before continuing their tasks. He went back to the building three more times before his visits stopped. But Barnabas went on six further occasions when it was his turn. His suspicion of my behavior when others haven't noticed, now makes me think it involves training to counter enemy agents. Maybe Mother saw something in Barnabas that she didn't in Abraham.

The pace slows a little. I check Seth. His glum face hangs forward as he watches his feet. I twist his cap back to front. 'I'm sorry, I didn't mean to snap. We're not supposed to know.'

He looks up. 'Never mind, but I guess you'll find out soon.'

# 10

Today is the third day of May. It's my birthday. I will celebrate the day of my birth eighteen years ago to the day, although I have no memory of being born. Mother tells us it's a special age—but I don't know why. I don't feel different. My first thought of the day is of Rebekah; the bird from my tree flutters its wings against my stomach.

I realize I've been awake for several minutes. I look around in the grey light—the others are still asleep. But I haven't had a story. I don't recall anything from the night, no sight of green grass, no tree, and no Rebekah. Do we not get a night story once we turn eighteen?

The light flickers above my nose. It glows a faint red, then orange before going through yellow to white. I shade my eyes and feel its heat on the back of my hand.

'It's five o'clock!' Abraham shakes Reuben's bunk. 'It's Monday on the third day of May. Awake! There's floors to clean, stoves to be lit, and breakfast to prepare.' He stops by my bunk. 'I want to see everyone at the table when I return,' he winks, 'we have something to celebrate.' I raise a smile but my spirits remain low.

The blankets on the other bunks stir, but I lie still. My limbs are heavy and I wish I could stay in bed a while longer.

'Happy Birthday, Noah!' I jump. Reuben stands by my bunk and beams. But I know the real reason behind that grin.

I check no one else is nearby before deflating his hopes. 'I won't tell you. You know I can't.' But I've missed David. His blanket moves and his face appears. He must have heard our conversation, but his dead eyes reveal nothing. He climbs out and walks past as if we don't exist.

Seth joins Reuben and is about to speak when Barnabas yells from the living quarters, 'Seth! Get the stove sorted. Now!' Seth's eyes roll up to the ceiling before answering Barnabas.

'Coming. I was just wishing—'

'And, Noah! Birthday or not, get out and fetch the breakfast crate.' I force my body to move and clamber down the ladder. I stand and stretch out the tightness in my lower back. I turn and trip over David's bucket.

'Sorry, I didn't see you—' but he doesn't even look up so I cut my apology short.

In the next room, Amos and Reuben are busy setting the table for breakfast. Caleb looks up from the bundle of wood in his arms and grins. 'Happy Birthday, Noah!' He nods to the table and I notice the special plate has been laid in my place. Caleb beams as if it's his birthday.

I try to look pleased. 'Thanks.' I step outside and remember to look up—Barnabas won't catch me out today. I freeze. The sky is... different. I don't recognize the color. *Is that a happy, angry, or sad sky?*

'Noah! We're ready for the bread.' Barnabas isn't giving me a spare minute today. I almost stumble as I carry the crate inside.

'So what color—?' Barnabas sees my face. 'Noah? What is it?' He almost seems concerned.

My voice shakes. 'I don't know, come and look.' The others stop.

Barnabas shouts. 'Get on with your duties!' But I can tell he looks unsettled by the change in our morning routine. He follows me outside and looks up. I watch as the blood drains from his face. His mouth moves but no words come. I feel guilt for causing this reaction.

I try to help. 'Have you seen this before? What do you think it means?'

He tries without success to regain his composure and

authority. He stammers while keeping his eyes on the sky, 'I… I…' he clears his throat, 'it must mean there's some news, or a special occasion.' He looks back to me. 'Surely it's not because of your birthday.'

My heart leaps in my chest. *Could it be for me?* It is a beautiful color, a sort of dark blue with another color mixed in. I look back to Barnabas. 'No, not for me. It must—'

'I see you've noticed.' We turn as Abraham returns from his morning report. He strolls past towards the entrance. 'Let's get breakfast going, we've got work to do.' We follow him inside. I'm desperate to ask if Mother has said anything, but don't want to undermine Barnabas.

The others stop their activities as we enter, but Abraham tries to act as if nothing is different. 'Don't stop, I see you're already behind schedule.' He turns. 'That includes you, Noah.' But all I can think about is the color of the sky. *What does it mean?* I place the bread on the rack, but it's not until I turn the slices over I realize the sky isn't the only surprise today.

'Abraham?' I point to the rack. 'There's only seven pieces of bread, we're one short.' Once more, I bring the morning routine to a halt. But Abraham laughs.

'Have you forgotten already?' He reaches into his pocket. 'You don't have toast on your birthday.' He pulls out a box from behind his back. 'You get cake!'

Despite my disquiet, I smile. A cake! My mouth tingles. Abraham places the brightly-colored box on my plate and beckons me to sit. 'Here. Caleb and Amos can finish the toast today.'

Now I feel different. I'm excused from duties and I get a blue plate. I sit and take a closer look at the box.

'Hey, no peeking.' Reuben grins as he sits opposite. Abraham and Barnabas pull up their chairs and I see them look briefly at each other, before they notice I'm looking.

Abraham calls over to David. 'You can leave that for now. Come and join us for a moment.' Caleb almost skips as he brings the toast for the others to the table. No one speaks as the chairs scrape across the floor, only the odd squeak escapes from Caleb as he fights to contain his excitement.

My heart beats faster as Abraham stands. 'As you know, it's Noah's birthday today. He is eighteen years old.' He gestures to the box on my plate and looks at me. 'And as a sign of her gratitude for your five years of service, Mother has made this special cake. She has asked me to pass on her thanks for all your hard work for the benefit of us all.' I've heard these words before, for both Abraham and Barnabas. I notice a small card on the table in front of Abraham—he's reading it. We're just going through the motions, following a script that's been acted hundreds of times before today. I look back to the box—at least no one has eaten this particular cake before today.

'So what are you waiting for?'

'Sorry?' I look up.

'Your present.' Abraham nods at the box. 'Go on, open it.'

No one makes a sound as I untie the string and open the box. My stomach flutters and my head feels light as the rich smell reaches my nostrils. I lean forward and feel the breath of the others as they stretch to peer at its contents. Inside, sits a white cake with a bright red ball perched on the top.

'It's called a cherry.' Abraham's voice sounds too loud. 'You can eat that as well.' Carefully, I reach inside and take the cake between my thumb and forefinger. I lift it from the box and hold it up for all to see. Saliva is soaking my mouth; we all lick our lips in unison. I turn it in my fingers, trying to make the moment last a little longer. For all I know, this could be the only time I ever get to taste one—

I may not make it to Paradise if my attention continues to slip. I open my mouth, along with everyone around the table, and carefully place it on my tongue.

Five years! That's one thousand, eight hundred and twenty-five days I have stood at this workstation. How many units have I made? I remember my targets for each year and do the calculation. I have made close to one hundred and eighty two thousand! And how many when you add up everyone else on my team, plus the other teams in the adjacent sections, and then times that over all the years we have been down here! *How many do we need?* When do we have enough for The New Dawn?

I stumble and steady myself with both hands on the desk. My head is still light from this morning. It took only a minute to eat my cake, yet the flavor still lingers on my tongue. I am not ashamed to admit tears ran down my face as Mother's love exploded in my mouth. She'd made it for me—just for me and no one else. It was if I'd never tasted anything before in my life, not even the Moses and Mother's Day meals come close. Sensations I didn't know were possible, flooded from my watering mouth to the rest of my tingling body. Then I thought of Rebekah. If I could put my mouth against hers and explore her with my tongue, would she taste the same?

I didn't care what the others thought when I sobbed with joy; not even Barnabas. But the joy was short-lived, and soon the tears were of sadness. I doubt I will ever taste anything like that ever again. Now I understand why Abraham had left the table on his birthday, but not Barnabas.

I fix the bracket and snap it shut. I think I'm on target but I haven't been counting today. I lick my lips. The sensation begins to slip away, and as hard as I try, I cannot remember the taste. Why does Mother give us a cake? Just one cake in all our time on The Workers Level. To awaken my mouth to what it has been missing all its life and then to snatch it away, is cruel. But nothing can stop me imagining what it would be like to press my lips against Rebekah's.

'It's still the same color.' I manage to suppress a sigh as Seth reminds me of the main issue of the day. My eyes are drawn to the skylight. Seth asks the same question for the twentieth time. 'What do you think it means?'

I make an effort to answer. 'I don't know. Mother has said nothing.' But he has a point. Not even the older workers can recall seeing a sky like this, yet we've had no word from Mother, or the prefects.

The bell chimes. I twist to check the clock—but it's still thirty-two minutes until lunch. It continues, ringing louder and louder. I turn to Reuben, then Barnabas, but they look just as puzzled. We all turn to Abraham. For a moment, he looks lost, then seems to recall an instruction. His eyes widen.

He jumps up from his desk and yells. 'To The Square! Mother needs us. To The Square!'

# 11

I stumble and bounce back off Abraham. I fear going down and being trampled under the hundreds of feet as we rush to Mother's aid. But I daren't take my eyes from the sky as surely the attack will begin any moment. I wince and grit my teeth, anticipating my ears bursting as the rocks rain down on our defenses. Sirens join the bells. They've done it! Our enemy has beaten us to the surface—and now they have found our hiding place. *Was it the smoke that gave us away?* Our worse fear has come true. Mother has failed to deliver on her promise. Or did we fail her?

We cry out for Mother. Surely she'll save us, she'll know what to do. We burst into The Square. We stream to find our places on the benches. I search the row for Rebekah, scanning the line of faces fixed in masks of terror. I find her. I want to call to her and tell her we'll be together at the end. But something isn't right. It takes a second to register—she looks calm.

The front wall glows. The siren and bell stop, only the sound of a few sobs hangs in the air. No attack, no rocks, the sky remains intact.

Mother enters. Her hands are pressed together with her chin resting on her fingertips as she walks slowly to the middle. She waits while the last of the sniffles die. Her stern eyes inspect the benches. But then her face softens as she lets her hands rest by her side. 'Why all the frightened faces?' She smiles. 'Oh, you think the call was for an enemy attack.' Silence. I cannot breathe. Then she laughs. Laughs like I've never heard her do so before. I glance to Reuben, he shrugs. Mother stops. 'Did you think I would ever let that happen?' I, along with everyone present, breathe out. 'Do you not remember my promise?' Her gaze drops to the floor. 'In fact, I'm a little offended. Do you doubt I can protect you?' She's right. We all expected the attack to begin. No one can speak. We would be lying if we denied our doubt. But then Mother smiles. 'No, don't blame yourselves, the alarm was my little trick, a game if you like. You should have seen the look on your faces when you came in.'

She tips her head back and raises her arms. 'Now you're probably wondering what I've done with the sky today.' We pause, not sure if we should agree and nod, or pretend we hadn't noticed. I nod but see many others choose to shake. If Mother noted our reactions, it doesn't show. She continues. 'Well, I'm sure you all remember my announcement on Moses Day.' This time we all nod. She beams. 'Yes! The good news.' I turn to Seth, then Reuben. Mother steps closer to the front bench. 'I hope you like the new color of the sky, it's called violet, named after my favorite flower,' she looks along the front row, 'but of course you all knew that.'

She stands straighter. 'I have been studying some interesting results from the laboratory. In fact, very interesting.' No one breathes. 'I have spent the day testing the readings of the air quality... from the surface.' Now we breathe, gasping at the very mention of that word. Mother waits as she scans our faces. 'And yes, they are encouraging.' Six hundred hearts beat faster, and I'm certain I can hear them echo back from the sky. 'So encouraging in fact, that I ventured to the upper level to take a look,' her eyes light up, 'outside.' Heads turn. *Does this mean—?*

Mother holds up her hands. 'And yes!' I grip the edge of the bench. 'The air is much better, the Sun is almost visible, and I estimate that if we hit all our targets, we will be ready to go outside in...' now even Mother can barely speak. She catches her breath. 'We can return to the surface in just twelve short months!' We leap up as one, throwing our caps into the air. Mother cheers with us. 'Yes, my children, this is it. The New Dawn is almost here!'

*We're going up!* I wrap my arms around Seth's shoulders, and find Reuben to my right. The whole team, even David, link arms as we spill off the benches into the open space before Mother. I'm deafened by cheers and whoops of delight never heard in The Ark before today. *She's done it! Mother has delivered on her promise.* We release arms and turn to her. Her eyes shine as she receives our thanks. I look for Rebekah. I long to go to her, to hold her close and whisper in her ear. Tell her of all the things we have to look forward to when we go outside, but I cannot see her amongst the jubilant mass of bodies.

'What a birthday!' Reuben slaps me on the back. He grins, 'And you thought getting a cake from Mother would be the highlight of the day.'

'But!' We stop as Mother speaks. 'Let us all remain vigilant for activity of the enemy agents. They will take every opportunity to distract and disrupt our work.' She sighs. 'For the good of us all, I may have to be a little… stricter. But all my actions are because I love you. Remember, I still have to find the unauthorized book, and if I find who is hiding it…' Her eyes sweep the rows—she doesn't need to finish the sentence.

A whole afternoon, that's four hours, with no work. For the first time ever, we are allowed to do nothing. No shift at the factory, no lectures, no meetings, no domestic duties, not even a story. We sit in The Square under a bright blue sky, bluer than any of us have ever seen. Mother has arranged for the soup to be brought to us in large bowls on trolleys. She said we could eat under clear skies every day when we return. We laughed at the funny word when she told us it's called a *picnic*. Reuben repeated it several times until tears ran down his cheeks. I have laughed so much my face aches and had to beg Reuben to stop his antics. But in the midst of my joy, one thing has puzzled me—Rebekah's reaction. She looks on edge.

For the first hour we sat and talked about all the things we would do on our return. Abraham said he wanted to climb the mountain Mother speaks of, and see the whole world from above. Barnabas will swim in the sea and ride the waves. Reuben can't wait to run across open fields until his lungs burst, and Seth wants to drive a tractor. The first thing I long to do, is find the hill from my book and climb the tree with Rebekah. I miss out the last part when telling the others. I think it's too early to reveal my feelings for her.

Rebekah's group sit talking nearby, but unfortunately we all stay with our teams so I have to be content with glancing over when I'm certain no one else is watching. I have caught her eye twice, but can't guess what she's thinking. She's laughing and engaging in the conversation, but still looks distracted.

'So what about you, Caleb? What will you do first?' I look back from Rebekah, aware that I have spent too long watching her. Caleb looks a little shocked to be asked his opinion by the team leader.

He clears his throat, looking to Amos. 'Err… I'd like to,' he blurts out, 'climb the mountain with you! Yes, climb a mountain, a big, tall mountain.'

Abraham smiles. 'Well you're welcome to join me.' He turns to Amos. 'And you?'

'Would it be okay if I came with you and Caleb?' Barnabas sighs, but Amos isn't put off by the dismissal. He speaks louder. 'And then, I'd really like to see the sea and, if I have time I would—'

'Let's not get too excited just yet.' Obviously, Barnabas

has had enough of the frivolous talk. I risk another look to Rebekah and catch her watching me. *Does she want to talk? Should I get up and go over?* Perhaps if I move, others will begin to mingle outside of their teams. I'm about to suggest we could go and talk to the team from the laboratory, when I notice the silence. No one is speaking—I guess we have run out of things to say after just one hour of freedom.

I stretch out my stiff legs, unaccustomed to sitting on the ground for so long. I notice the rest do the same. Abraham breaks the silence. He looks up to the sky and appears to ask the question to himself. 'I wonder what our new targets will be.'

I see a chance to win Barnabas over. 'No matter how challenging, I'm sure we can meet them.' I actually sound enthusiastic without having to try.

Barnabas eyes me briefly before answering. 'We have no choice, it's a race now.' He looks at our blank faces as if it's obvious. 'Do I have to spell it out? It's a race with the enemy. They'll have been monitoring the air quality and will be just as desperate as us to return—and you know what it means if they get to the surface first.'

'But why aren't we ready now?' We turn to David. It's the first words I think he's spoken since returning from Re-Education. He continues before anyone can speak. 'We've been down here for... how long? Mother says almost a hundred years. If the air is good and it's safe to return, why can't we go up this minute?' My mind whirs— why haven't Abraham or Barnabas interrupted? He must stop talking, but we sit in shocked silence as David asks his next question to his clasped hands. 'What more needs to be done that already hasn't been done in all the time we've been down here?' David closes his mouth and lets his head drop forward—but the damage has been done. He has a point. *Why aren't we ready?*

I look to Abraham. He must have an explanation. He leans closer so no one outside our team will hear. 'What are you saying, David? Do you think you know better than Mother?' Abraham's eyes shift from each of our faces in turn. *He's trying to buy time to think of an answer.* But Seth speaks first.

'Look, I know we're not supposed to ask questions about what we're making, but perhaps we make parts for a weapon?' I grasp his arm to stop him speaking before Abraham has had a chance to answer.

Abraham holds up his hand. 'It's okay, Noah. I believe Seth may be right. Perhaps the other teams make machines for building shelters, and tractors for food production, but we, as the top team... perhaps we're trusted to make components for the weapons. Then they go next door for Lydia's team to assemble.' Abraham sits straighter. 'Yes, yes, that makes sense. Mother tells us the enemy want to wipe us out, so it would be foolish to return without a means to defend ourselves.'

'Or destroy them.' We turn to Barnabas as he smashes his fist into an open hand. 'Why wait for them to come to us when we could reach them first?' I sigh. The thought of eating picnics beneath clear skies is snatched away; we won't see the sky for smoke.

David speaks again. 'But this doesn't explain why we're still not ready. How many weapons do we need?'

I turn back to Abraham but before he can speak, a prefect approaches. He waits for us to stand and addresses Abraham. 'Mother requires your presence at a meeting for the factory team leaders.'

Abraham nods and duly follows. We watch them leave The Square before sitting back on the floor. Barnabas wastes no time in assuming control. He looks to David and speaks softly, but his words are harsh. 'Abraham is too lenient. If I were in charge I wouldn't allow you to question Mother's judgement. If we're not ready to go up yet, then there is a reason.' He leans over and grabs David's overall, pulling him so his face is inches from his own. 'But I doubt you have the intelligence to understand.' Barnabas lets go. David rocks back; his mouth quivers in his pale face.

We sit in silence. The whole square now sits in silence until Seth stands and points to the sky. 'It's changing color again.' The dome darkens but remains blue.

# 12

'Looks like the picnic is over.' Reuben stands as the prefects enter the far side of The Square. Without being told, we return to our allocated places under a dark blue sky. Our brief taste of what life could be like on the surface is over—the work begins again, but at least we now have the end in sight. Abraham and the other team leaders enter after the prefects. I try to catch his eye, but he looks straight ahead and sits next to Barnabas.

The front wall glows. We straighten our backs as Mother enters. She is smiling—she must be happy and confident of returning first. 'I hope you enjoyed your picnic.' Reuben's shoulders shake. I nudge him with my knee. Mother looks to Reuben. 'Yes, Reuben, it is a funny word.' We giggle and Mother laughs with us. 'I'm sure you'll learn some more when we return. But!' She holds up her hand. 'On to the serious business of our final preparations.' I still find it hard to believe it will be our generation who will go up, but I'm grateful to hear Mother repeat the words.

Mother walks across the line of our bench with her chin resting on her fingertips. 'I know some of you are thinking *why can't we go up this minute.*' David's words exactly! She stops and turns, returning the way she came. 'And I don't blame you, I know you're desperate to go outside, but we have to be patient. We still have more machines and equipment to make.' She turns again. 'Getting the raw materials for the factory is not easy. They have to be mined from deep beneath the lower levels. Work in The Mine is difficult and unpleasant work...' *There's something lower than The Trench?* Mother continues. 'We have to drill deep, it's the only way I can be sure I

80

don't bring contaminated material into The Ark.'

She stops opposite our team. 'So you see, David.' My heart stops. 'That is why it will take a while longer. The miners risk their lives every day, the very real danger of being buried alive in the tunnels is not something you would want hanging over *your* head.' She walks away. Abraham risks a glance at David with her back turned. I catch his eye—we both know there'll be a new miner starting the next shift.

'He had to go.' I look at the faces around our dormitory table and see we're all in agreement with Abraham. Two prefects were waiting for David as we returned from The Square. They took him straight away, he wasn't even allowed to collect his book—he has forfeited the right to Mother's gift. The prefects each took an arm and marched him out, head bowed as he avoided looking any of his team in the eye.

Abraham continues. 'He had his chance but he obviously wasn't interested in seeing this work through to the end. We couldn't have him bringing down the team.' He places the spoon next to his empty bowl. 'And listen to this. The prefect says Mother is so impressed with our team, and,' he turns to Seth, 'how quickly our new member has met his target, she doesn't think we need a replacement.'

Seth beams but Barnabas quickly puts his pride in its place. 'Let's remember we're just doing our duty, and now it's safe to return, it's even more important we work as a team until we're ready.'

Abraham nods. 'Barnabas is right, we must not get carried away with thoughts of finishing the work,' he looks to the entrance and lowers his voice, 'I did ask about… you know, what we spoke about at the *picnic.*' I stop chewing. 'And yes, Seth, you were right. The prefect confirmed we make parts for the weapons, but he couldn't tell me what sort.'

I have to ask. 'Has David been sent to The Mine?'

Abraham checks the entrance once more and looks back to me. 'I believe he has.' His head drops as he speaks to his chest. 'I also learned that many don't return.' I see David's face peeping over his blanket the morning I first noticed his weakening—could I have done more to help?

I speak to stop the guilt. 'Did you know about The Mine, Abraham?'

He shakes his head. 'It sounds like valuable but dangerous work, but it doesn't concern us, so long as we get the materials on time.' Abraham sighs. 'Anyway, it could have been worse,' he lowers his voice, 'it could have been The Trench.'

I shudder and hope for David's sake he's not *there*— anything but *the stench of The Trench*. I scrape the last of the potato from the bottom of my bowl and place it in my mouth; nothing. I taste nothing. Although I cannot recall the flavor of the cake, it awakened a dormant longing that surely can't belong to me alone.

'Oh, before I forget.' Abraham turns to me. 'We have an interim production review planned soon in view of the new development, I'll ask if you can come and put forward your process for improving efficiency. I'm sure it will go down very well with Mother.' My heart pauses. The others turn to me. I will get to suggest my idea to Mother. I run the calculations through my mind once more. They still add up. She will be impressed. Abraham turns to the clock. 'Right, ten minutes to get this cleaned up before Mother's evening address.'

What a day. My birthday, a taste of cake, and of course, the news generations of those who have gone before have yearned to hear: the imminent arrival of The New Dawn. I stare at the light above my bunk. Where will I be sleeping in a year's time? Will I see stars in the night sky? I think back to the nursery when Mother first showed us pictures of dark skies speckled with thousands of small brilliant lights. When she explained they were suns like our own, but far, far away; even at the young age of six, I was in awe of the wide universe out there and felt trapped in this small world of ours.

But a year still seems far into the future. Eighteen long years I have lived in The Ark, the last five working almost every waking hour. I will be nineteen before we finally go outside. But how long will I have to enjoy life under the open skies? How many years do I have left? I have never thought about death before today; it didn't seem important.

I turn to look out of the window as the light goes out. Mother tells us we live three score and ten years before our own light fails, but I'd always thought I would be ready to die, to do my duty and make way for the next generation of workers. I could see the end of my days out in Paradise if chosen, and be satisfied in the knowledge I had done my part. But now? Would my life last long enough to do everything I've ached to do once outside?

I attach the headset and roll onto my back. The ceiling looks suddenly very close in the grey light. I think of the hundreds of feet of steel and earth above, pressing down on my frail body. I have to get out—now. I push my hands to the ceiling and start to claw at its hard surface. I have to get out!

My heart thumps loudly in my ears and I gasp for air, clean air. *Stop!* I must stop. If I lose control, I will be reassigned to The Mine, be sent deeper into this prison and never make it to the surface. I close my eyes and imagine climbing my tree. I must focus on the goal and keep the lid on the panic rising in my chest. I see the blue sky through the upper branches and feel my body grow lighter. I climb until the sunlight grows brighter, but my head strikes something hard. I cannot go any further. Something blocks my way.

I open my eyes. A tear runs down to my pillow. The ceiling looks different. *Is it moving?* I raise my hands and push up—they sink into the soft surface. It draws me in. I rise from my bunk and pass through the roof of the dormitory. Higher still I float, through the dome of the sky, through the rocks until I reach the rich soil Mother says will help feed us when we're free. I break through the earth and drift up to the real sky. *It is soft!* I feel its warmth caress my skin. I roll over to gaze down upon the green fields below. I laugh and stretch out my hands to squish the stuff of the sky through my fingers. The whole world is mine to explore; no timetable, no rules and no Mother. But Rebekah is not here.

I feel heavy. My body sinks as something beneath tugs at my legs. I look down. My stomach churns. A large, gaping hole has rent the once green field. It's sucking me into its mouth. I claw at the sky, but it offers no help, or it doesn't want to save me. I plummet into the darkness. I tumble over and over and crash onto my back. The sky explodes.

The light above my bunk is on. 'Awake, awake!' Jared strides into our dormitory, banging our beds with a stick. 'Awake and come with me.' I groan and blink in the sudden light.

I hear Abraham. 'But it's still night. What is the meaning of this? We have work in—'

'Silence! Come with me now. All of you. Mother is very angry.'

# 13

We stumble in the gloomy walkways. No one speaks, but we must be all thinking the same—what have we done wrong? Does this mean we are not going up? Jared marches us towards the factory. My blood freezes. *Has Mother discovered the scratch?* No, surely she wouldn't wake every worker just for that.

Jared stops. He twists around and spits out his command. 'Join the end of this queue. Face forward and no talking!' He turns and looks down the line before calling back. 'Don't move until I call you.' Jared marches around the corner. I hear another prefect shouting, but cannot make out the words.

We shiver in the grey air. We stamp our feet and rub our hands on our thin undergarments to keep out the cold, hoping we're not making a noise to anger Jared.

I hear someone weep. A prefect appears from around the corner followed by a line of workers from the farm. I risk a sideways glance and catch the red eyes of one of the girls—she quickly looks away. Our line moves forward twelve paces and then stops. More shouting but now I can hear gasps and sobs. *What is it?* In front, Barnabas's shoulders are clenched, almost touching his ears. *What have we done?* I hear footsteps—it must be our turn.

Jared comes to a halt by our line. His eyes hold each of us for a few seconds as if looking for an answer. He straightens, and when he speaks, I detect contempt. 'Workers. Follow me. Keep your eyes in front until I give the order to turn.'

Abraham falls in behind Jared and we march towards the side wall of the factory. 'Halt!' I keep my eyes fixed on the back of Barnabas, not daring to disobey Jared. He moves to our right and stops—he's standing beside the wall. My legs feel heavy. I don't want to turn, I don't want to see what has angered Mother. Jared clears his throat. 'Right turn!'

We turn as one, we gasp as one. I cannot believe what I'm seeing. *Someone has scrawled on the factory wall!* It takes a few seconds for the shock to pass before I can bring myself to read the four short words. It takes longer for the meaning to sink in.

Jared glares at us and speaks through his tight jaw. 'I don't need to tell you how serious this is.' He steps forward and for a moment I think he's going to strike Abraham. But he stops short and waves his arm back to the wall. He shouts, 'These despicable words are the work of an agent! And someone on this level has done this, or must know who has written…' his lips curl, 'written this disgusting nonsense.' Jared's voice drops. He forces out his words through gritted teeth. 'Now back to your beds. No talking. Mother will speak to you in the morning.'

I don't know what to think. I attach my headset and stare at the ceiling. An agent is active in The Ark, but it's not just that that worries me. The prefects have always been here to guide and keep our minds focused on the work, but tonight I thought Jared could have hurt Abraham, or any of our team. When we left, we passed Rebekah's team at the corner. The look Jared gave her, froze the blood in my veins. He wants her for himself. I can see it in his eyes but I cannot let that happen. I have to find a way to protect her. But how? After tonight, the prefects will be watching us all very closely.

Then there's the damage to the factory. I see the writing on the wall—the harsh words attacking Mother's authority leave a nasty scar on her immaculate brickwork. When did an agent have the time to write those words?

They didn't rush; they even had time to draw a bird in flight for the full stop.

A bird to punctuate the sentence: '*Mother is a liar.*'

# 14

No story, not even an appearance from Rebekah, and yet again, I'm awake before the light. But today my first thought is not of her red hair but of the words on the wall. What could they mean? Of course, Mother is not a liar, but what does it imply that the enemy's agents can do this right in the heart of The Workers Level, and at the very place where we make the biggest contribution to getting out. Are they about to defeat us? To be this close to The New Dawn only to fail would be unbearable. The light blazes in my face.

Abraham announces the new day with less than his usual enthusiasm. 'Everyone up. It's Tuesday, the fourth day of May and,' he speaks under his breath, 'it's not going to be an easy one.' I rise to see the same fear on the faces of the team. No one else speaks—this morning, doubt keeps our mouths shut.

I walk like a machine to fetch the bread and milk. Outside, the sky is grey, a dark, menacing grey as if the enemy had chosen today's color. I bend to collect the crate. I stumble. The ground is bare! It's not there? I check the other side—nothing. I wander back inside and almost fall to the floor as I bump into Caleb coming the other way. My voice shakes. 'There's nothing out there. No bread, milk, or fuel for the stove.'

He blinks and whispers. 'No fuel? But what do I do?'

I shrug and open my mouth, but before I can speak, Abraham appears around the corner and answers Caleb's question. 'Everyone to the table.' We stand and gape at his unrecognizable stern face. He doesn't slow as he pushes past and bellows, 'Now! This minute.' He strides through the entrance. I follow Caleb and join the others as they take their positions, even Barnabas looks shocked by our team leader's anger.

Abraham waits for us to settle. He stands at the head of the table and takes a deep breath, then sighs. 'Breakfast will be delivered shortly, but before then…' he rubs the back of his neck, suddenly looking uncomfortable in his commanding role, 'I have… have to ask if any of you know anything about the act of vandalism on the factory wall.' He looks at each of us in turn. 'It doesn't matter how trivial it might seem, you must tell me.' I glance at the other faces around the table. Abraham continues. 'After breakfast I am to report to Jared, all the team leaders will do the same and then Mother will speak to us in The Square.' Seth shuffles in his seat and catches my eye. Abraham looks to him. 'Do you have anything to say, Seth?'

Seth sits forward. 'There's something that I don't understand. Who are—?'

'This isn't the time!' I jump at Abraham's outburst. 'Don't you get it? Don't you understand what this means? That agents can do this… now, right under Mother's nose.' His shoulders sag and he leans on the table as if he might fall. Abraham lowers his voice. 'Not now, Seth. I'm asking the questions.' But Seth isn't done.

Seth stands. 'This is important!' Abraham looks stunned, Barnabas moves to intervene, but Seth speaks first, rushing out his words before anyone can interrupt. 'Who are these agents? How did they get in?' Both Barnabas and I try to answer, but Abraham holds up his hands.

'This is my fault. I was angry and haven't thought this through properly.' He sits down and he looks more like the Abraham we know. 'So let's calm down.' I relax back into my chair. Abraham looks to Seth. 'Please sit. I'll try to explain.' He waits for Seth to get comfortable and takes a breath before speaking. 'Mother says they got amongst our people when we first came down. They—'

Seth straightens. 'But Mother says we've been here almost one hundred years. If they live to seventy like us, then they would be dead by now, wouldn't they?' No one answers, Seth continues. 'Can they live as long as Mother?'

We look to Abraham, but he looks confused like the rest of us. I will him to answer, to put a stop to the doubt spreading through our team. He opens and closes his mouth several times before speaking. 'Perhaps they've come here since then. Perhaps—'

Again, Seth interrupts our leader. 'But that's not possible, we're sealed from the outside world, aren't we?'

Now Amos breaks ranks. 'Or they have broken in, but that… that would…' He stops as the rest of us turn to him.

Seth finishes Amos's line of thought. 'That would mean they are already on the surface and,' his voice wavers, 'and they've found us.'

Caleb blurts out. 'I'm scared. Are we trapped?' He searches our faces as tears fill his eyes. 'Are we? Abraham? Is it okay?'

'Stop!' Barnabas bursts into life, slamming both fists on the table. 'This is exactly what the enemy wants. Can't you see? All it takes is one scrawled sentence on a wall and you all fall apart.' For once, I'm glad Barnabas has spoken. He looks to Amos and Caleb. 'Think it through.' He speaks slowly as if delivering a lecture to the new arrivals. 'If the enemy have already reached the surface, they wouldn't need to send their agents down here, they would only have to blast a hole in the dome and rain their fire down on us, and I'm sure even you two dimwits would have noticed that happen.'

He turns his attention next to Seth. 'And if Mother says there are agents at work, then there are agents at work. Her word is good enough for me, so it should be good enough for you.' He maintains eye contact until Seth looks away. Barnabas scans our faces. 'Don't you think the timing is the answer? Why wait until now to act?' He looks back to Seth, but Seth remains quiet. Barnabas taps the table as he speaks. 'It's because Mother has announced the good news.' I nod. He's right.

Abraham finds his voice. 'Exactly. The very moment our spirits are lifted and we know the end of the work is in sight, their agents do this.' He stands. 'And I'm very disappointed to see their tactics seem to have worked on some of us around this table.' Abraham looks to the entrance. 'The breakfast and fuel have arrived, if none of you have anything *useful* to say, I'm off to report to Jared. I expect breakfast to be ready when I return. And remember, we have a meeting with Mother at The Square before work.'

Another day without routine; the last three days have been challenging for us all. I check the walkway ahead for Abraham and Barnabas before turning to Seth—he knows my question is coming. 'What were you thinking back there? Do you want to be sent down The Mine?'

He scans the crowd before speaking. 'I don't care what Abraham says, it still doesn't explain how enemy agents could be operating in here.'

I raise my eyes to the sky. 'But how else could that wall have been vandalized?'

Seth leans closer. 'Haven't you considered it might not be an agent who wrote it?'

My mouth drops open. 'But that would mean one of us! Who here would write that Mother is a... that she's... No, I can't even bring myself to say it.'

Seth tries to keep a blank face for anyone watching. 'But why write it? If you can agree it's not possible for enemy agents still to be down here, and I know you do in your heart, then it has to be someone on this level.' He rubs his cheek to hide his mouth. 'And why would Mother get the prefects to show us? Why not get them to scrub it off the wall before we wake? If she's so concerned about morale, then it doesn't make sense to drag us from our beds and march us to the very scene of the crime.'

I have no answer. My eyes are drawn to the arch as we enter The Square. '*We work together. We succeed together.*' But if Mother is not telling the truth, what is she keeping from us? Is the surface still too dangerous? Or is there something else she doesn't want us to know?

I take my seat next to Reuben. He looks over but says nothing. The lights glow. Mother enters.

# 15

I will admit that I've had thoughts of what life would be like without Mother. Without her rules and routine, Rebekah and I could be together. I don't care what other hardships we could suffer because, with her by my side, I can face anything. But as I sit here this morning, I long for Mother to be happy again and reassure us that everything is normal and we can get back to work. Yet I'm not so sure that's going to happen. I can't tell from her stance.

Mother stands in the middle, her head bowed. We sit in silence for what seems like an hour with all eyes and hopes resting on her slender shoulders. Slowly, she looks up. My stomach knots. She has been crying! Her red-rimmed eyes are clear for all to see. If I knew anything about the writing on the factory wall, I would jump up this minute and denounce the perpetrator to make her happy again.

She takes another step forward. She speaks softly and I strain to hear her pained words. 'You know, I have always tried to protect you, to shelter you from certain truths and activities outside of our home.' I've not heard her describe The Ark as 'home' before, but she's right, it is our home no matter how much we desire to leave.

Mother looks up to the grey sky and blinks away a tear. Still her voice barely carries to our benches. 'With great reluctance, I asked the prefects to raise you from your beds last night. I dearly wish I didn't have to, but I felt I had to show you the wall and those...' her head drops forward, 'and those dreadful words.' Her gaze lifts to take in the front row. 'You see, you have to be made aware of the activities of the enemy, to know what lengths they will go to in order to crush us.' She sighs and turns to walk along the front row. 'I owe you all an apology.' Heads turn. Surely not. What could Mother have done to be sorry for? She stops and looks across our faces. 'As you know, the enemy did infiltrate our people. Before I had even built The Ark, they had moved among us and planted their vile seeds. And…' She looks down to her clasped hands, 'and to my great regret, in the rush to escape the devastation, I unknowingly brought this poison into our home.' I hear Seth's heartbeat. 'You know this, but what I haven't told you is this malicious seed passes across generations. It could be any one of you,' she stops opposite our team, 'and you wouldn't know it.'

My neck stiffens. Do I have this foul seed in my head? I did wake before the others and didn't share their story. Could I have written the words on the wall while under their control?

Mother turns. 'So you see, it doesn't matter if we're… sealed from the outside world.' Hadn't Seth used those words? Mother turns and her voice begins to rise. 'The enemy have their ways. It could be an act of vandalism spreading *their* lies. It might be a few words whispered here, and a few questions asked there, all to cast doubt in your minds.'

The muscles in my legs knot. It's Seth! I should report him right now. Both Abraham and Barnabas go to move, but before either stand, I hear Seth. 'Mother?' All heads turn. He's standing. Tears stream down his face as his weak voice confesses. 'I think it might be me. I… think it could have been me who wrote those words.'

Gasps fill The Square, and amongst them I hear some hiss and boo. 'Silence!' Mother holds out her hand, then lowers her voice and turns to Seth. 'Come and join me, Seth.' I watch, fixed to the bench, as he steps over the front row. Mother gestures with her fingers. 'Come here, here, in front of me.' Her voice carries no wrath. Seth stops a few respectable paces from her. Mother smiles. 'Now turn and face your colleagues.' He obliges. He looks so small, standing in the empty space in front of Mother. She leans forward and whispers loudly in his ear. 'Now tell them what you have done.' Seth twists around to face her, but she twirls her finger in the air. 'Go on, to them, not me.' Now she sounds annoyed. 'Tell everyone how you have tried to undermine our work, and...' her voice softens, 'remove your cap.'

Seth's pale face comes back into view. His hand goes to his cap and he slides it slowly off his head. A murmur rises as his white hair is revealed. I see his mouth open and close but no words reach our ears. Mother prompts him. 'Louder please, Seth. I'm sure everyone wants to hear what you have to say.'

'I... I'm...' He stands straighter. 'I'm sorry for what I have done.' He looks to me. 'I have let down my mentor, my team and,' he turns around but Mother holds up her hand and repeats the finger twirl. Seth follows her direction and continues his confession. 'And you, Mother.' He stops and looks to the floor as if his words have exposed the seriousness of his crime to him for the first time. Mother says nothing. The Square remains in shocked silence. Seth stands before us, an agent of the enemy trying to bring us down, but somehow, I feel sorry for him.

Seth stammers. 'I... I have been having thoughts... doubts about what we're doing.' I catch his eye. He seems to need help with what to say. It's too painful to watch but I find I can't look away. His voice breaks up. 'I want to go up... I really do... but... I have done wrong and...' Tears now roll down his cheeks and he cannot continue. I grasp the material on the legs of my overalls and squeeze tighter. I want to stand up, to defend him, to say it's not his fault, but then everyone will think I am also an agent.

Mother speaks, ending his pain. 'That will do. Thank you, Seth.' She takes a few paces forward and stands to one side to address The Square. 'I don't want you to feel anger towards young Seth.' This catches me by surprise. Mother paces towards to front row. 'It is not his fault. He didn't ask to be infected by the enemy. But thankfully due to my vigilance and my tireless work, it has grown weaker, and…' she looks back to Seth, 'I believe the seed of the enemy can now be removed.'

Seth's red eyes find me. I try to smile, to reassure him, to let him know I'm on his side. Mother almost laughs as she says, 'Don't worry, it doesn't hurt.' She straightens. 'Now! Is there anyone else who thinks they may be infected by this insidious disease?' Her watchful eyes search the benches. 'Are you having doubts about our work here? Come now, I will not be angry. I will help you.'

I quickly find Rebekah. Will she stand? Is that why she's been acting strange lately? Thankfully, she doesn't move—but others do. I count four. Gaps open around them as their neighbors on the bench slide away.

Mother beckons them forward. 'Thank you. Your honesty is testament to the goodness that still lies within you, despite the enemy's poison.' The four walk slowly forward and line up with Seth; they are all recent arrivals from the lower level. Mother moves to stand behind the guilty. 'Now please remove your caps.' A line of light-haired heads bow before us. Mother looks along the line. 'Good. As you can see, my efforts to strengthen our people has worked. The agent's seed cannot endure long in these *purer* individuals.' I glance to Abraham. Is that why they have the same color hair as Mother? She looks back to the benches, maintaining her smile. 'Are there any more? Come now.' Her mouth straightens. 'Do not make me have to find you.'

I look around as much as my tight neck will allow. Two more stand and join the line; two more white heads appear.

'What do you think will happen to Seth?' I turn to see Reuben. Already it seems odd not to have Seth in my ear as we make our way to the factory.

I can't think, my head is too full. I stammer. 'I… I don't know. Mother says she can cure them but...' I look around for Rebekah, hoping her face will give me a clue to what just happened.

'But what?' Reuben tugs at my sleeve to slow my pace. 'Do you think Seth wrote those words?'

'I… I suppose he must have. He did say he—'

'Did he do it alone, or do you think he had help?'

'I guess there could have been—' I catch Reuben glance to Barnabas. He looks back and must know I saw his telling act. I try to sound unconcerned. 'I don't know. I have no idea.' I turn away from Reuben and pretend to study the grey sky. But he persists.

'Oh come on, Noah. You knew him better than the rest of us, you must know if he was capable of acting alone.'

We stop as the line queues at the factory entrance. I lean in close and whisper. 'Look, I didn't suspect he was an agent until Mother spoke just now.' I check for prying ears. 'And if you think I was involved, you're wrong.' Reuben steps back. He knows that I know he's trying to look shocked at my disgust of his accusation.

'To work!' Abraham calls from the front. I step ahead of Reuben and turn my back on him.

'Today is a great day!' Abraham stands in front of the workstations. I can see he's shaken by Seth's confession. He stands taller, putting on his brave face. His chest rises.

'In the years to come, we will celebrate the fourth day of May when Mother finally rid us of enemy agents.' He clasps his hands together, pumping them up and down to the beat of his deliberate words. 'We now have a clear way ahead. A clear way to The New Dawn. Nothing can stop us now.' He folds his arms and looks along our line. 'We have a good team, the best team.' He nods and smiles, repeating his words. 'Nothing can stop us now,' he claps his hands together, 'so let's get down to the work!'

# 16

I'm on target, yet I have no memory of the afternoon shift. My mind has been everywhere except at my workstation. The hands busily assembling the parts under my nose, don't belong to me; they're obeying orders from somewhere within while I try to figure out if I'm happy, sad or frightened. I should be happy. As Abraham said, we have nothing to fear from the enemy inside The Ark, and we'll be ready to leave in a year. But I feel I've lost an arm. Seth had only been with us a few days, but in that short time we had connected in a way I have not felt with the others, not even Reuben. Seth's questions made me think about things I'd never considered before his arrival. At times I found him hard work, but now he's gone I miss him.

In the silent routine of the shift, I've had time to run the last few days through my mind—and I'm frightened. How could Mother have allowed so many agents to come through the Education Level? And all at once. Has she kept something from us? Have the enemy arrived in force? I also fear that Mother could punish me for Seth's actions. But if she hadn't seen it coming, it would be unfair to blame me. My stomach trembles. Do I have their seed? If she'd failed to detect Seth, had she missed me? I have shared some of his views. Does the evil of our enemy grow inside me?

'Noah!' I realize Abraham has spoken my name more than once.

'Sorry, pardon?' What is he doing on the production line before the end of the shift?

He leans over my workstation. 'Are you tired?'

I know what he implies. 'No, I'm fine.' I force a smile. 'I was so absorbed in the work, you know, with the end in sight, and all that's happened.'

He looks to my shelf. 'I can see. You've almost completed your quota.' He pats me on the back. 'Good work.' He straightens his spine and raises his voice—this is to be an official announcement. 'I've had word from Mother. You're not be held responsible for Seth's actions, this was beyond your control.' He turns to leave, then stops; his clenched fist taps the end of my workstation. 'And,' Abraham edges closer and speaks behind a raised hand, 'you're excused this evening's duties. You're to shower and report to the Place of... to The Meeting Place.' His eyes wander up to the wall behind me, 'At eight.' I look to Seth's empty desk and see the expectant look that would have been on his face. Abraham clears his throat. 'So be ready for the prefect at ten minutes to eight.' He turns smartly but walks away slower than his preparation suggested.

# 17

The Place of Knowing. What secrets will I learn now I'm eighteen? I'd always thought I'd be excited, or at least nervous. What happens in that place changed Abraham and Barnabas. How will it change me? But in a way I'm relieved that Mother has selected me—I would not have been invited if she suspected I was an agent.

The grey water from the shower swirls, briefly defying the pull of the plughole, before disappearing down into the dark. Will I become like Abraham, or... I shudder, Barnabas? Abraham became distracted following his third visit, almost sad at times. Barnabas, frustrated, more driven and angrier. Isaac had completed his visits before I joined the team, so I don't know what effect his time there had on him.

I reach for the towel and wipe away the cold water clinging to my skin, escaping its fate in The Trench. I turn and rest my hand on the cubicle door that will open to an uncertain future. Since I saw Abraham return from his visits, I have been curious, but now I'm not so sure if I want to know.

'Noah!' Barnabas yells through the door. 'The prefect is here. Why aren't you ready?' *Dear Moses!* How long have I been in the shower? I stumble through to the living area, trip over my towel and sprawl naked onto the floor. My face stares back from a pair of polished boots under my nose.

I look up to see Jared; his mouth curls up at the corner. 'I see you're not quite ready yet, *boy*.'

Barnabas grabs my overalls from the drying rack and thrusts them at me. 'Quick, cover yourself! Don't keep the prefect waiting.'

What a start. My overall trousers rub on the damp skin on the inside of my thighs. I struggle to keep up with Jared. He called me, 'boy'! I recall we're almost the same age, yet he looks older and taller as he marches confidently in his pristine uniform. I should have been a prefect. It should be me in front marching him to The Meeting Place.

I had asked to see Mother when he was selected instead of me. My eight-year-old mind could not understand why it was Jared and not me marching straight-backed off to prefect's school. My memory had been of sitting on Mother's knee as she consoled me, telling me I would get my chance one day. But now I think of it, I had stood fidgeting in front of a screen with tears in my eyes, pleading with her to let me go. Her blurred face had told me to *pull myself together* and accept I was to become a worker—a valued worker, but a worker all the same, a worker in a dull grey overall while the prefects wore smart, black uniforms and had an important job to do.

I trip. Jared sniggers. I recover my step and notice the empty walkways. Everyone will be going about their evening duties, leaving the path clear and... so wide. So wide I fear I could lose my way in the emptiness and low light. I fix my eyes on Jared's back. Focus! I am on my way to find out the secret that Mother and the other seniors have kept from the younger workers. I straighten my tight back and try to walk taller. I must look my best for Mother, show her I'm ready to be included, and fit for the new challenges that await.

We pass the deserted benches lining The Square. I recall Isaac, dressed in his light blue clothes. What has he learned on the upper level? Are there more secrets? I look up to the sky. It appears lower in the dark; ever-present and reassuring. My knees almost buckle. Before long we'll be on the surface, and no longer under the protection of the dome. It will take time to adjust to the expanse of the new world. But I will be with Isaac again, and have Rebekah by my side.

Jared stops. We've arrived. He spins around. 'Report… ' he pauses. He sees me standing straighter; it seems to amuse him. He smirks. 'Report to the prefect inside.' But he's half-blocking the narrow entrance and I can see he's not in a hurry to move.

I nod. 'Thank you, Prefect.' I'm not going to let him think he's better than me. I look him in the eye as I squeeze past him.

As I draw level, he whispers. 'Forget her.' I spin around. Jared grins and I feel his breath on my face as he delights in telling me, 'she's mine.' He turns and marches away before I can answer. An icy hand grips my insides and twists. I see Jared holding Rebekah's hand, dragging her away from our tree. Her pale face turns, imploring me to rescue her, but I cannot move.

'What are you waiting for?' I look up to see a prefect sitting behind a desk inside a small room. I gasp, letting go of the air trapped in my lungs. A metal band tightens around my chest. How does Jared know? My face must have betrayed me. What else has it given away?

The prefect stands. 'Are you unwell?' I fight to control my panic.

'No, I'm… fine. Just a little nervous.'

He speaks as if he hasn't heard my answer. 'Go straight through and take the seat nearest to the door.' He sits and picks up a pencil. His hand hovers over a sheet of paper—it is empty except for two blank boxes and a few words. One box is next to my name, but I cannot read the other word beneath. He frowns. 'Did you hear me?' He waves his hand holding the pencil. 'Go in. Take a seat. And close the door behind you.'

My stiff legs move. I take three steps to the door, take a deep breath and open it. I hear the pencil scratch across the paper. I step inside.

I blink as I enter a brightly-lit, white-walled room. I step back and push the door shut with my back and bring my hand up to shield my eyes. A table and two chairs look lost in the room—in the middle of the table sits a small box. As my eyes adjust, I notice a door on the opposite side.

'Take a seat, Noah.' I jump as the flat voice of the prefect sitting outside fills the room. The chair legs scrape across the floor as I make space to sit. 'Good. Now place the earpiece from the box in front of you into your right ear.' He can see me? How? I follow the instructions and fit the device. His voice crackles in my ear. '*Make yourself comfortable. You will be joined shortly.*'

By whom? I thought I would meet Mother, but I cannot think she would grace a room like this with her presence. Again, the prefect speaks. '*Straighten your hair, Noah. There is a comb in the drawer under the table.*' My hand reaches forward and opens the drawer; a comb, small cloth and a pair of scissors sit inside. I pick up the comb and run it through my still wet hair.

Muffled voices come from behind the other door—a low, flat tone like the prefect who met me, followed by a girl's. I stop breathing as the handle turns. The door swings slowly open. A girl I recognize from the farm steps in—she's not wearing a headscarf! Her long, brown hair flows down to her shoulders and curls at the ends. Her skin is darker than Rebekah's, but the same as Abraham's. My mouth drops open.

'*Stand.*' I wonder what her hair would feel like if I could stroke it. I rub my fingers into my palms. '*Noah! You must stand.*'

'Oh. Sorry.' The girl frowns. I close my mouth and obey the earpiece and wince as the chair once more scrapes across the floor. '*Now say hello, tell her your name and shake hands.*' I hold out my hand.

'Err… hello. My name…' My mouth is dry. 'My name is Noah.' Her eyes dart around the room, then come back to me. She smiles and takes my hand—it feels warm in my clammy palm. My face grows hot as her fingers wrap around mine.

'*Tell her to attach the earpiece on the table.*'

I point the table. 'You need to put that in your right ear.'

'*You can let go of her hand now.*'

'Sorry.' I release my grip and immediately miss the warmth. She picks up the earpiece and flicks her hair behind her ear. She tips her head to one side revealing the skin on her slender neck—my face grows hotter. Her trembling fingers fumble with the device and after two failed attempts, she secures it into place.

I hear it buzz. She jumps, then looks back to me. 'Oh! Hello. My name is Naomi.'

I smile and follow my instruction. 'Naomi. That's a pretty name.' Is it? I guess it sounds okay, but it doesn't flow like 'Rebekah'.

She smiles. 'Thank you.' She looks down to the table, places her hand to her ear, then looks me in the eye. 'Noah is a nice name too.'

I speak before the prefect. 'Thank you. I like the name Mother—'

'*Ask her what her favorite color is.*' He sounds impatient.

'Oh, right. What's your favorite color?'

'*Nod as she speaks… and smile.*'

Naomi places her finger to the earpiece. She looks up. 'Blue,' she sits straighter, 'like the sky… and your eyes.'

'My eyes are blue?' No one has ever told me that. I grin. My eyes are blue—just like Mother's.

She nods. 'Yes! What color are mine?'

'*Noah! You must follow the instructions.*'

I look closer. 'Yours are brown. Like the color of...' Think! I look up, 'Gravy! Just like on Mother's Day.'

She laughs, then stops to listen to her prefect. 'So, what's yours?'

'What?'

'Color, what's your favorite color?'

'*Say bl—*'

'Red. Like the color of...' Rebekah's hair, 'of a dying fire.'

She claps her hands. 'Yes, that is nice. I like to look at the fire when we have the evening story.'

'That's my favorite time of the—'

'*Wait for my instructions! Now ask her where she works.*'

'But I know where she—'

'*Ask her!*'

I soften my jaw. 'Where do you work?'

Naomi sighs, then stops herself. 'The farm.'

'Do you make the food?'

'No, I grow trees.'

I clap my hands, almost jumping from my chair. 'Trees!'

'*Now ask her where—*'

'How do you do that? How big do they grow? When do the leaves—'

'*Noah! Ask her—*' I pull the annoying voice from my ear.

'When do the leaves start to grow? Can I come and see them?'

Naomi laughs and also removes her earpiece. 'I would really like to show you, but we've never had a visitor.' She leans closer and places her hands on the table close to mine. Her fingers stroke the surface next to my hand. 'But I'll ask if you can come. If you want me to.'

Both discarded earpieces on the table squeak, but I'm not interested in what they have to say. I've never been this close to a girl before for so long. The curve of her face would fit perfectly in my palm. I should speak. 'Yes… yes, I would like that.'

The smile stays on her mouth. Her eyes light up. 'I will.' Her sweet breath brushes my lips. I notice my hands have moved onto hers, and she hasn't pulled them away. I watch her lips move; it takes a moment for her words to sink in. 'Can I come and see what you do in the factory?' She knows where I work!

'Of course. But it's not as interesting as growing trees.' I hear raised voices from the connecting rooms, but Naomi laughs and I laugh with her.

'But it must be. The factory is so big, it must be really important what you do in there.'

'Yes, I guess it is. Abraham tells us we're making the—'

The doors burst open. The two prefects speak as one. 'That will be all for this evening.' My body sinks into my chair. I don't want to leave, but the prefect grips my upper arm and helps me change my mind. I glance to Naomi and catch her eye just as we are led through our respective doors. We exchange smiles when the prefects aren't looking and I let her face imprint in my memory.

The prefect closes the door and stands with his back against it. He exhales. 'You are not allowed to remove the earpiece, we are here to help you.'

Help? I stammer. 'I'm sorry, I didn't realize.'

The prefect moves around to his chair and holds my gaze as he sits. 'Well, you do now. Mother will let you know if you're needed again.' He picks up his pencil.

'Needed again? For wh—?'

'That will be all.' He looks down to his desk, his pencil hovering over the sheet. 'The prefect is waiting outside. Don't keep him waiting.'

I open the door to the sound of his pencil scratching once more across the paper. To my relief it's not Jared waiting to escort me back to the dormitory.

# 18

Thankfully, the ceiling above my bunk looks the same. So much has changed over the last week, I find comfort in the familiar stains and cracks I've come to know so well. But if they're looking back, they will see a different face. Life had seemed so simple. I woke; I worked; I slept. I knew what I had to do, and I could do it well. Mother made the plans and we followed without question. But now? I see things I hadn't noticed before. I have feelings that I don't know how to handle. I have lost Seth, and Jared threatens to take Rebekah from me. And what was the purpose of tonight's meeting with Naomi?

Life has become complicated.

I should be excited about the challenges awaiting us on the surface. I should be invigorated and working harder than ever. But my head is full of doubts and fears of the unknown. Before tonight, Rebekah was my anchor in these unpredictable days. She'd become the reason to work towards bringing in The New Dawn. I had only spent seconds in her company, but I knew she felt the same—I'd seen it in her eyes. But it's Naomi's face before me now.

The buzzer instructs me to fit my headset. I reach behind, lift it from the hook and let my head sink deeper into my pillow. The light fades, but tonight I don't look out of the window. I let sleep take me and hope the story will let me feel like the old me again.

I blink into the light, confused. Is it morning already? I had barely closed my eyes. But my stiff muscles and aching joints confirm I've slept for my allotted seven hours; but again no story.

'It's five o'clock on Wednesday the fifth day of May. Everyone up!' Abraham starts the morning routine. 'I want to see breakfast on the table when I return.' I wrench my body out of bed and see Reuben watching me. We haven't spoken since our disagreement outside the factory. I know he longs to ask me about yesterday evening, but even if I wanted to tell him, I would find it difficult to explain what happened on my first visit.

I jump to the floor, arch my back and sigh as it clicks. Naomi's smile crosses my lips but it feels wrong—it used to be Rebekah's face I saw first in the morning. I leave without a second glance to Reuben to fetch the bread and milk.

Outside, I look up. Blue! I expected grey. I must focus. Everything is going to plan. Mother has captured the agents, so nothing can stop the work now. I bend to pick up the delivery. I freeze. Poking out of the top of the packages, is a piece of folded paper. I check no one is watching and carefully lift it out. A note for me? It has to be. No one else but me collects the crate. Whoever placed it there has taken a huge risk. Written communication between teams is strictly forbidden. Even speaking to other workers is kept to a minimum. Mother says we'll too easily become distracted by idle talk outside of formal meetings.

Footsteps approach. I stuff the note into the top pocket of my overalls just as Abraham returns. He frowns. 'Everything okay, Noah? It looks like you've seen an agent.'

I laugh. 'I'm fine. I was just admiring the sky.'

He looks up. 'Yes, it's…' his voice trails off as his gaze wanders across the dome, 'beautiful.' His eyes drop to the floor before he remembers I'm there. Abraham straightens. 'Yes, it's going to be a good day today.' He pats me on the back, inviting me to go first. 'After you. I'm hungry and looking forward to breakfast.'

I pause. I want to ask him about his first visit to The Meeting Place, but now isn't the time. Besides, I have a new distraction. My heart beats against the paper in my breast pocket. It will spend all day teasing me, but I have to wait until I'm back in my bunk before I can discover its secrets.

Concentrate! Barnabas is due to make his collection in ten minutes and I know he will take great pleasure if I am below target. The burden of the note weighs heavy in my pocket, pulling me down towards my workstation. Surely Barnabas will detect its presence and report me to Mother. *You fool!* It's just a piece of paper. *Concentrate.*

I check my shelf again for the third time in a minute— room for two more units to achieve my quota. I glance up to the clock. Exactly nine minutes and ten seconds to collection. *Good.* Time to make them with thirty-four seconds to spare. *Careful.* I must have slipped into my new procedure on at least three units to have time left over.

My hand touches my chest pocket. I pull it away, not realizing it had moved to the note. I catch Reuben's eye. I know the look on his face. He wants to tell me something, but this isn't the place.

The food counter was even slower today. By the time we had sat at our table, we had less than ten minutes before the start of the afternoon shift. I should ask Abraham to bring this up with Mother, but I doubt he would approach her.

I look up from the remains of my evening meal to the faces of my team around the dormitory table. What are they thinking? Everyone appears distracted. Leaving The Ark is on all our minds. We've thought about if for all our lives but it didn't seem real. Now the moment approaches, I think most of us are scared of what we will find on the surface—and of course, the inevitable confrontation with the enemy. But we must trust in Mother. She will protect us and know what to do on the outside.

Abraham stands. 'Well done, everyone. All targets achieved today and as a reward, Mother will deliver a special lecture this evening.' I mimic the excitement of the others and straighten my back. Abraham looks down to a note in his hand. I freeze. Is it mine? Did he find it? I twist in my chair and feel it move—it's still in my pocket.

Abraham reads the one in his hand. 'The lecture is on the new process used by the laboratory to improve air quality, and how teamwork has helped them achieve this success.' The backs around the table lose an inch as a collective sigh escapes—the smiles on our faces remain.

Abraham sits. The note in my pocket will have to wait.


I thought the lecture would never end. The effort of keeping my interested face showing while stopping my hand moving to my pocket has drained me. But now I have another problem. How am I going to take the note out of my overalls without the others seeing? But I have to read it now. I cannot go another hour not knowing its content.

I turn my back on the others as I climb out of my overalls and reach up to hang them on the hook. No one speaks. If I take the note out now, someone will hear the paper rustle in my hand. Slowly, I move my hand to the pocket and pretend to wipe out a crease. Amos coughs. That's all I need. I grab the note and scrunch it and drop my hand by my side.

I keep it in place with my forefinger as I hold onto the ladder and clamber into my bunk. Barnabas reminds us of the routine. 'Lights out in ten.' Plenty of time. I take out my book. Next, I roll onto my side to face away from the room and place the note inside my book. I open it, daring not to breathe. Inside, just a few words. It reads:

*'Leave your headset on the pillow.'*

I turn the paper over but that's it. What the—? Who sent it? *Leave your headset on the pillow?* But won't the alarm sound? I read it again, just to make sure I haven't misread the instruction. It reads the same. But for what purpose? I haven't had a story for several nights, so what difference would make? I re-fold the note and place it in the back of my book. I will have to burn it in the morning.

The light fades. My hand reaches for the headset before I can think. I stop. Within seconds the buzzer sounds. I lift it, but do as the note says and leave it by my head on the pillow. The buzzer stops. Interesting. I only have to take it off the hook to stop the alarm—I don't need to attach it. It feels strange to have my ear resting directly on the pillow. I would normally be asleep in minutes, but without the headset, what happens now?

I look out onto the empty walkway. Did Rebekah send the note? My heart stops. What if it was Jared? Is he trying to get me into trouble? My hand goes to the headset. It hangs in the air over my pillow. Surely Jared is the only person who could place the note in the crate. But if it's from Rebekah, it must be important. I leave the headset off. I'm prepared to take a risk if there's a chance the note is from Rebekah.

The dormitory is silent. I hear the others breathing slowly as they sleep. My eyes feel heavy and I let them close. I see Rebekah's face as she serves the Moses Day Supper. Her eyes are inches from mine. I smile and let myself be drawn into them. She leans closer. Her lips brush against my cheek. I jump and hit my head on the ceiling. No one stirs. I touch my cheek. It felt so real, as if

I was back at the celebrations. I close my eyes and hope to see her again.

# 19

*Noah.* I turn to see who called my name, but I'm alone in the field. 'Rebekah?' She doesn't answer. I'm sure she was by my side as we came through the gate. *Noah.* The voice is too deep to be a girl's. 'Reuben?' I squint as the sun appears over the hill.

'Noah!'

I twist around. 'What?' I blink in the harsh light. Reuben's bleary eyes meet mine. *Where's the field?*

'Get up! Barnabas will be after you if—' he looks at my pillow. 'What happened to your headset?' He leans over and whispers. 'What's it doing on your pillow?'

I don't understand. Minutes ago I was with Rebekah. I look to Reuben, then down to the headset. It must be morning, but I didn't hear Abraham announce the new day. I grope for the right words. 'Err… I just… I just took it off.' I reach over and place it back on the hook.

Reuben doesn't move. 'But you were asleep when I—'

I sit. 'But the alarm would have gone off if I wasn't wearing it.'

Reuben shrugs. 'I guess so.' He turns, but I can see he's unconvinced. *Leave your headset on the pillow.* I see the words from the night before. Is there another note waiting for me?

I leap from my bunk, grab my overalls and hop across the room as I try to get my feet through the leg holes. I leave Reuben standing dazed by my urgency, but I have to pick up the delivery before someone notices anything unusual. Barnabas's eyes follow me as I attempt to walk to the entrance as if it's a normal, routine morning. But something's different. It's me. I feel light, not stiff and heavy, as I leave the dormitory.

Outside, I still look up. Blue. Good, that's one thing I won't have to worry about today. The crate sits in its usual place. I squat to get my grip and my heart sinks with my body—no note awaits me today.

'Another blue day eh, Noah.' I stand, hugging the crate close to my body to see Abraham return—he looks happier than he has for several days. 'I can't remember the last time we had so many blue skies.'

I return his smile to hide my disappointment. 'She must be pleased with us, working so hard now The New Dawn is almost upon us.'

Abraham waits by the entrance, inviting me to go first. 'It's the production review this evening, so I'll put your idea to Mother.'

I stop. 'Oh, I thought I was to present it?'

He shakes his head. 'No, sorry, not tonight. You have a more important duty. You're excused duties again.' Abraham looks away. 'Be ready for the prefect to report to The Meeting Place at eight. Be showered and clean as before.'

Naomi. Her face pops into my head. Did Naomi send the note?

'Err, Noah?' Abraham touches my arm. 'You need to make a start on the breakfast.'

I stand firm. 'Can I ask you…?' I should go inside and stay quiet, but my curiosity won't allow it. I clear my throat. 'Can you tell me what last night was about?' Abraham's mouth drops open. I fill the gap. 'I thought I'd meet Mother, but instead it was Na—'

'Don't say her name.' Abraham tugs my elbow and steps away from the entrance. He whispers. 'We're not supposed to say the girl's name.'

'But..?' How did he know it was a girl?

Abraham sighs. 'Look, I can't say anything, you'll find out soon enough.' He rubs the back of my arm. 'Go along with what the prefects tell you to do and you'll be fine.' He looks away and blinks. His eyes glisten and I strain to hear his words. 'It's just something we have to do. We'll talk more after your third visit.'

'Noah!' Abraham jumps as Barnabas calls out. I catch his eye. I'm certain we share our annoyance but say nothing.

I call inside, 'Sorry, just coming.' I stroll through to the living area and address the room before Barnabas can speak again. 'It's blue today. Breakfast will be ready soon.' I put the crate down and check last night's note is in place. I take the bread and place the first slices on the rack, while dropping the note onto the fire beneath. I watch it burn with a mixture of relief and sadness at losing her words.

The units stack up along my shelf. I'm going too fast, I must slow down. I think about what happened while I slept. I had been in a field with Rebekah. I can't recall all of the details as I would one of Mother's sleep stories, but what I can remember felt… real. Was that the reason for the note? Did the sender want me to experience that? If so, once is not enough. I will leave it off again tonight. But I have to be careful. I hadn't woken with the others and I cannot afford to oversleep again. I stop. Has Reuben spoken to Barnabas about the headset? I glance to Reuben's desk but look away as he turns. No, he hasn't. Barnabas would have had something to say to me by now if he had. Perhaps we can be friends again—but he's not Seth.

I complete another unit and reach for two new plates. So much has happened over the last few days, but I must stay calm and prepare for our return to the surface. My fingers find the number six fastener to be attached to the—no!

I freeze. It cannot be. On the flat side of Plate B, the bird-like scratch is plain to see. My fingers tingle as I hold the offending plate—the evidence of my mistake of just a few days past exposed for everyone to see. I glance up. No one is watching. I turn the plate over. This is definitely the one I damaged. The unit must have been rejected and dismantled, but how did I escape punishment? Mother tells us how precious our limited resources are, and how difficult and dangerous they are to come by, so why have I not been chastised and taken to Re-Education?

I must do something. Barnabas will notice if I stand motionless any longer. But what? Should I reuse the plate? I have no choice. I can't hide it as I will be one short at the end of the shift. My stiff fingers flip the plate over and attach the fastener as if nothing is out of the ordinary. Perhaps it will turn up on another workstation and won't be noticed if it's rejected again.

I look up to the poster of Moses. His knowing eyes judge me. He would have reported the scratch straight away, but then he would never have allowed his mind to wander and let his fingers slip. I straighten my back to stand as Moses—in Mother's words, *a strong, upright pillar of The Ark*. He went selflessly about his duties, including, I imagine, his visits to The Meeting Place. He never questioned Mother. I take a deep breath. I must do as Mother says and do as Moses did. If I follow his example, our remaining days in The Ark will pass quickly and we will feel the fresh breeze on our faces before long.

I take encouragement from his strong jaw and determined look. Tonight, Abraham will present my idea to Mother and perhaps soon, it will be my face on the posters. In the years to come, Mother will speak of the moment my plan shortened our days in The Ark and gave us a head start on the enemy.

Yes. This is what I must do. If I get another note I will not read it. And when I go to bed, I will attach my headset and enjoy Mother's stories. I will be the new Moses. But then I have to let go of the thoughts of Rebekah. I will never get to meet her anyway—Mother wouldn't allow it. Jared has stated his intent for her and I won't stand a chance. I need to shed these improbable thoughts—then I cannot be disappointed.

# 20

'You may go through.' I take a step, but the prefect raises his hand to my chest, 'but remember, keep the earpiece secure for the whole of the meeting.' I nod; Moses would never have removed it. 'No wait!' The prefect steps in front. *What has he seen?* He leans forward. 'You have something on your cheek.' I check my urge to step back as my relief blows into his face. 'Here. Lick this and wipe that smudge off.' He passes me a small piece of cloth. I follow his instruction. The cloth has an odd taste but the prefect appears content that I am now presentable.

He takes a seat at his desk and looks up. 'What are you waiting for? In you go.' He waves his arm and ticks the box on his paper. I open the door but stop at the entrance, squinting into the bright light. The table and chairs have gone, replaced by an odd-looking piece of furniture. It looks a little like my bunk, but is thicker, wider and has two raised sides and a back.

'*Take a seat, Noah.*' The speaker on the wall is too loud, distorting the sound of the prefect's voice. '*Sit on the left side of the couch.*' It's a chair? It looks too big. The speaker becomes impatient. '*You must sit, your co-worker will join you shortly.*' I assume he means Naomi. I bend and push my hand into the flat part of the chair—it sinks into the soft cushion. A sigh escapes my lips as I sink into the seat. The speaker barks. '*And take that grin off your face! You're here to do your duty.*'

I hadn't realized my face had changed. I tighten my lips and lean back. The chair seems to surround my body, soothing its aches and pains, taking the weight of the work from my shoulders. I tilt my head back and close my eyes. This is what it must feel like to lie on grass under a blue sky. I wonder if this is what they sit on in Paradise—we'd never get any work done if we had one like this in our dormitory.

I sit up. I've let my thoughts drift again. I must be more like Moses. I shuffle to the front of the seat and sit straight-backed on the edge. I have my duty to perform, although as yet I don't know what that duty involves.

The speaker behind crackles again. *'Put in your earpiece.'* I look around. *'It's on the side of the chair.'* I locate it and fit the device in my left ear. The earpiece takes over. *'Good. Now stand as the door opens.'*

I do as Moses would have done and rise as Naomi enters. I gasp—her arms and legs are bare. She's wearing a blue dress, like Mother's, except this one is shorter, much shorter; it barely reaches her knees. It's also very thin, so thin I can see the shape of her body through the material. I notice Naomi has more curves than Mother.

*'Tell her how nice she looks.'*

'How,' my mouth fills with saliva, 'how nice she... you look.' I cannot take my eyes from her body.

She nods and tries to smile. 'Thank you.' I look up into her eyes. She seems uncomfortable with so much skin exposed to the light, and to my eyes. Naomi folds one arm across her chest and holds onto her elbow, then spreads her fingers and rubs her hand across her upper arm. My face grows hot. Now I feel uncomfortable.

*'Ask her to sit.'*

I step aside. 'Please, please take a seat.'

'Oh!' Naomi sees the chair for the first time, and I'm certain she had the same thought as when I first entered.

'Yes, it's a chair. And it's really soft!'

*'Noah! Wait for my instruction.'*

'Sorry.'

Naomi frowns. 'Sorry for what?'

'Oh not you. I was talking to,' I tilt my head to the door behind. She nods.

'*Ask her to fit her earpiece.*'

I point to my ear and motion to the other set by the chair. 'We have to put that in again.' I wait for Naomi to sit and notice her dress rides further up her legs. I swallow again, relieved she's reaching for her earpiece and hasn't noticed my attention.

'*Sit, Noah.*' She turns and smiles as I move to her side.

'Oh!' Naomi rolls toward me as I sink into the seat. Her leg brushes again mine—even against the thick material of my overall, it feels good. She laughs, edging away as she straightens. Her eyes look up as her finger moves to her ear. She flattens the dress on her legs. 'So, Noah. How are things at the factory?'

'*Tell her you're on target for The New Dawn.*'

I look into her brown eyes. 'Yes… good, it's all going very well.' But I can't help my eyes dropping back to her long legs. 'We're going to meet our targets.' Her hands go to the edge of her dress. 'The… targets for—'

'*The New Dawn!*'

I clear my throat. A bead of sweat runs down the side of my face. 'Yes! Ready for The New Dawn.' I sigh. 'Yes, we'll be ready for The New Dawn, very soon.'

Naomi gives up trying to cover her legs with the inadequate material. She leans forward and rests her hands over her skin. But now the top of her dress droops, revealing something much more interesting, more curves, more soft skin. I grip my knees as more sweat trickles down my neck and back.

Naomi sounds breathless. 'Oh, that's good.' She notices my new interest and clutches her right hand to her chest. 'It's good to know you're on target.' I force my eyes to look away. I want to apologize for looking, but the prefect has not given his permission.

The prefect feeds my line. I slow my breathing. 'And how is it going at the farm?'

'It's…' She tucks her chin in, glancing down to check her neckline. 'Yes, it's going very well.' Her eyes flit across the room, then back to me. 'We're growing more plants ready to cultivate on the surface.' I nod.

'*Sit closer, Noah.*'

'What?' We both speak at the same time.

'*Get closer.*' Naomi moves first. I follow and slide across until her legs and hips are touching mine. She laughs, looks away, but then leans stiffly over so her shoulder is resting next to mine.

'*Now put your arm around her shoulders.*' My heart races. I lift my arm and stretch towards the ceiling. '*Noah?*' I reach over and let my hand rest on her upper arm. Now, my heart is pounding. Her skin is so soft and warm. Her head rests again my neck and I breathe in the sweet scent of her hair.

'*Good work, Noah.*' This is work? '*Ask her what she wants to do when we get back to the surface.*'

I speak into her hair, but I cannot be sure I repeat the words exactly. Naomi turns and looks up. I'm so close to her face, I can feel her breath on my neck; her heart beats so strong, I can feel it through my overall. My groin grows hot. Am I unwell? I feel strange, but I don't think I'm ill. It feels somehow… good.

Naomi's earpiece squeaks. She looks into my eyes for a wonderful, un-interrupted moment, then her eyelids flutter and she lets her gaze drop.

She bites her bottom lip. 'I'm looking forward to planting the fields and…' she waits for her prefect, 'growing the crops that will feed us and keep us strong.' She shuffles under my arm. I realize I'm gripping too tight and relax my hand. Her eyes come back to mine. 'And what about you?'

'Sorry?'

'When we get back up. What are you going to do?'

'Oh, I don't—'

'*You'll build the shelters.*' Will I? I haven't thought about my duties once on the surface; Moses would have had it all planned at this stage.

'I'll be on the team building the shelters.' I see my tree, but push it from my mind—that will have to wait.

'Will you build one for me?' I pull her closer. Her earpiece squeals; those were not the words from the prefect. I see the two of us, sitting together on a chair like this in a small shelter. But what about Rebekah? My skin feels suddenly cold. *Is Rebekah sitting with another? Is Jared staring at her legs with his arm wrapped around her bare shoulders?* Naomi shuffles. 'I meant, will you build shelters for the farm workers?'

'*Noah!*' I look down to see Naomi's eyes waiting for her answer. I want to say *yes*, one for just the two of us, so as not to disappoint her, but go along with the prefect.

'I'll build shelters for every worker.' I feel her weight drop against my shoulder. I try to say something else with my eyes, but I don't think it works. I squeeze her arm and whisper close to her ear. 'Of course I will.' Her eyes light up and I make a silent vow to keep my promise.

'*Now sit and listen to the music.*' The Workers' Anthem bursts forth from the speaker on the wall. We instinctively go to stand, but the prefects tell us to stay on the chair and not to sing. I keep hold of her shoulder and she lets her hand rest on my leg. The taste of my birthday cake floods into my mouth. I long to push my lips against the skin of her cheek, but fear she won't like it. Instead, we look around the white room and say nothing as our earpieces remain silent.

The song ends and the doors open. Two prefects enter and stand before us. They look pleased and speak as one.

'Good work.' My prefect calls through the door. 'They're ready for you, Solomon.' Another enters with a clipboard. He looks older than anyone I've seen before, old enough to have been sent to Paradise. Solomon paces slowly around the room as he reads his notes.

After a minute, he stops in front of the others. My prefect gestures we should stand. We wriggle forward and struggle to get out of the soft chair. He waits for us to get to our feet, then rests the clipboard by his side. His lips attempt a smile, but they look unaccustomed to the position and instead he looks like Caleb as he's about to burp. The prefects behind stiffen as the older prefect speaks. His words are slow, but everyone in the room knows who is in charge. 'Yes. Good work.' His eyes stay on Naomi. His head nods as he speaks. 'I think they'll make,' his eyes drop to Naomi's legs, 'a suitable pairing.' He makes no effort to hide his appreciation. I want to step in front, but daren't block the senior's view. After a long pause, he seems to remember his purpose. Solomon looks up, speaking as if he's lost interest and has somewhere else he needs to be. 'You may go back to your dormitories. Mother will let you know when you're needed again.'

I turn to Naomi. Her fingertips linger briefly on the back of my hand. My skin tingles as we part and leave through our separate doors.

I follow the prefect assigned to escort me back to the dormitory. To only have a few minutes with Naomi is not nearly enough. I could have stayed all night, just sitting, talking and, of course, touching. I had a deep urge to do something more, something that felt instinctive but dangerous at the same time.

'You have forty minutes to lights out.' I look up to see the prefect standing outside my dormitory. *We're here already?* I wait by the entrance as Abraham signs the handover sheet. The prefect checks the signature against the specimen, nods to Abraham and leaves us standing in the low evening light.

It's quiet, too quiet for supper time. Abraham sees my confusion. 'The team are at a lecture in The Square.' He turns and leads me to the table in the living quarters. 'They'll be back soon, then we'll have a late supper.' He sits, leans forward and rests his chin in his hand, keeping his eyes on the table as he speaks. 'I've just got back myself,' he glances up, 'from the production review.'

I'd forgotten. I must know. I grasp the back of my chair. 'What did Mother think of my new procedure?'

Abraham leans back. 'Please sit.'

'Will we be using—?'

'Noah!' I freeze. Abraham softens his tone. 'Please sit, before the others return.' I pull out my chair and join him. He sighs and rubs the back of his neck. 'She didn't approve.'

'What!' I cannot believe she didn't like my idea. 'But… But why? Surely it will help to—'

Abraham raises both hands. 'I don't know. She didn't give a reason.'

My face flushes. 'I know it will work, we could increase production by over...' I slump. What's the point? But of course there's a point—returning to the surface before our enemy. He couldn't have got it right. I should have gone to the meeting. How can I replace Moses if Abraham can't convince Mother of my plan? I look him in the eye. 'Are you sure you gave her all the figures?'

He looks taken aback. 'Yes, all of them.'

'But surely she could see I'm right!' I rise and slap the table, stinging my palm but I want to feel pain.

Abraham jumps. I get a glimpse of the real Abraham as his mask slips; he looks lost, perhaps even afraid. He stiffens and regains control. He looks back. I know he knows what I saw. The muscles on his jaw stand out as he tries to reassert his command. But it doesn't work. He sighs. 'Mother knows best, she'll have her reasons.'

I collapse into my chair and gape at Abraham. I feel sick. This was to be my gift to Mother, to show my appreciation for her help and faith in me. This was going to bring forward the day of The New Dawn. I would be a hero, the new Moses. Mother would be proud, and Rebekah, and Naomi would be impressed by my achievement. Abraham tries to smile. 'Look. Maybe it's something to do with mining the raw materials? Or maybe Lydia's shift can't handle any more units.'

I run my fingers through my hair and scratch my head. I stare out of the window onto an empty walkway. 'But she could recruit more miners and... and give more workers to Lydia.' I stand. 'Yes, it would work. She could take some from the laboratory,' *Rebekah would work in the next room*, 'they don't need to worry about the air quality any more, down here or above. It doesn't matter now does it, we're going up soon, sooner if she puts my idea in place. Perhaps if I could—'

Abraham shakes his head. 'Mother has spoken, she's made up her mind.'

I slump back into the chair. 'But she could have given her reason.' I tighten my jaw. I don't want the tears of frustration breaking through just as the others return. 'Did she say anything? Even just a thank you?'

Abraham leans across and rubs my shoulder. 'Sorry, Noah, nothing. I know you mean well, but we cannot understand everything that goes on here. Let Mother take care of the big plan and we'll just get on with *our* work.' I bring my hands to my face and push my palms into my eyes. He lowers his voice. 'How was tonight?'

I drop my hands and look to Abraham. 'Pardon?'

He glances over my shoulder and then back to me. He whispers, 'Was everything okay?'

'I… don't know.' Was it? I turn to check the entrance. 'The senior prefect, Solomon seemed pleased.' I grasp his hand, suddenly feeling I can tell Abraham anything. 'Tell me. What *is* the purpose? What am I supposed to learn from these meetings? What should I do?'

Voices outside. I think Abraham may have been about to tell me, but he stands to greet the returning team. He pats my back. 'You'll find out. Next visit.'

# 21

I stare at my ceiling—the only piece of The Ark that no one else sees. I don't feel like reading my book, and I don't have a note to open. The ceiling closes in. If Mother doesn't need a *new* Moses, I will not try to be like him. I take the headset from the hook and leave it on my pillow.

The light dies and the familiar face of my old friend disappears. I try to imagine what it would be like to lie under a tree and gaze up at the sunlight through the leaves, instead of being trapped in this hole in the ground.

The hole grows darker, as one by one, the lamps outside go out. Reuben snores. The others are asleep and I am alone in the night with my thoughts. I wonder where I will be taken tonight without the headset. The stories are different. They jump from one moment to the next, and parts keep coming back during the day that I must have forgotten. But I prefer them to Mother's stories because they're mine.

'It's in the tree!' I jolt upright. Bright lights explode in my head. Sweat runs down my back but I'm shivering. *Where?* I rub my throbbing head. I'm back in my bunk. I must have banged into the ceiling as I woke. It's dark outside. My heart is still racing; is the creature in the room? A shadow with big eyes had lurked in the branches, waiting to pounce and take Rebekah from me. I slow my breathing and lie down. No, not Rebekah, it was Naomi under my arm as we leaned against the trunk.

'It came from over here.' I freeze. Voices. Outside!

'Do we have a walker?' That one is further away. I must have called out on waking. I turn to peer through the slit. Beams of light bounce off the buildings and along the walkway. Prefects. Only prefects are allowed torches—but to be out at night? I didn't think anyone was allowed on the walkways after lights out.

'Can't see anyone.' I shut my eyes. He's right outside my window, the back of his head is inches from my nose. I hold my breath.

'Must be a talker.' The other joins him by my window. 'Report it to Jared in the morning. Remember, talkers become walkers.'

'We should strap them all in.' The first snorts. 'That would make the night shift easier.'

'Yeah, but then we'd have no fun.'

They leave, their laughter echoing down the empty walkways. I let the air from my lungs. Talkers? Walkers? And prefects! I never knew prefects were up in the night. But I guess it makes sense to have them on patrol, just in case of an attack. But it didn't sound like they were taking their duty seriously. And they failed to catch the vandal—surely the words on the factory wall could only have been scrawled at night.

'It's five o'clock. Everyone up. Today is Thursday, the sixth day of May. Rise now. I want to see breakfast ready when I return.' I don't know why Abraham feels he has to say that every morning—he's always back before I've finished the toast. I roll onto my side, fighting against the damp blanket wrapped around my legs. My eyes are dry and my lids stick as I try to blink. Abraham stops by my bunk. 'Come on, Noah. The crate won't get in here all by itself.' He turns and heads off to deliver his morning report. But what does he say? We all slept well and nobody ran away? Where could we go?

My neck feels rigid, like one of the logs for the stove. I push back the blanket; the cold air gladly rushes in to lay claim to my exposed skin. I clamber down the ladder and reach for my uniform. The material feels rougher than usual against my body, offering little comfort against the morning.

'Are you okay?' Reuben looks up as I groan.

'Err… yes, just aching after yesterday's shift.'

He grins and I see the Reuben from our youth again. 'Or was it from your second visit to—'

'Reuben!' Barnabas wipes the grin from his lips. 'Get about your duties this minute.' He turns and glares at me. 'And, Noah. Stop your grumbling and fetch the crate.' Behind Barnabas I catch Reuben's eye. He winks. It looks like we're friends again.

In the next room, Caleb and Amos are already setting the table—I must get a move on. I step outside and look up. It's changed. What did Mother call it? Violet. The only time I've seen a violet sky was on my birthday, and the day of the special announcement. But why that color today?

I crouch to pick up the crate. My heart slams into my ribs. Another note! It sticks out between the bottles of milk. It's going to be another eventful day.

# 22

I slip the note up my sleeve just as Abraham returns. He's out of breath. 'Mother has a special announcement to make before the morning shift.'

'That explains that then.' I nod to the sky. 'What do you—?'

'Not now.' He eyes the crate. 'Get that inside. We'll discuss it over breakfast.' He turns and disappears into the dormitory. Special announcement? It should have been about my new process, and how we'd be ready to go up earlier. So what news today? It has to be good, otherwise we'd be looking at a grey dome.

'Noah!'

'Coming.'

I enter the bustle of the dormitory but feel as if I'm moving in a different time. I hear voices but they make no sense. My hands are numb and I cannot feel the bread as I place the slices onto the stove. But the pot feels heavier and I take extra care not to spill the water onto the stove.

'Bring the toast to the table, Caleb.' I look up to see everyone except Caleb and I are already sitting.

I find my voice. 'But it's not ready. I've not turned it yet.'

Barnabas slams his hand on the table. 'You heard Abraham. Bring it now.' He turns to the rest. 'What has happened to the discipline on this team?'

Abraham clears his throat. 'Thank you, Barnabas.' He looks to me. 'Just place the bread on the plate for Caleb, and come over.'

Caleb and I join them at the table as Abraham gives thanks to Mother for our food. 'Do start.' He passes the butter along the table, but it's not easy to spread on the cold bread. As tasteless as it is compared to my birthday cake, I miss the crunch of the toast. The soft bread sticks to the roof of my mouth and the lumps of butter make me feel sick. Now I know why we have it toasted.

Abraham opens his mouth to speak, but stops to finish chewing. He glances to Barnabas. I see his discomfort as he must realize the rest of us know his authority is in question. He swallows. 'Mother wants us all in The Square before the start of the shift.' He looks to me. 'She has an announcement about Seth and the... the other—'

'Agents.' Barnabas sits back and folds his arms. 'Let's face it, that's what they are.' Now he turns to me. 'Mother may say it's not their fault, but they're agents all the same and that makes them dangerous.'

Abraham pushes his plate away. 'Well, let's wait and see what she has to say. Hopefully she's cured them and Seth can come back.' I almost choke on my last mouthful. I have missed Seth and long to see him again.

'And if she hasn't?' Barnabas pushes back his chair and stands.

I speak my fear out loud. 'They'll be sent down The Mine.'

I find Reuben once more by my side—but we walk in silence. No one speaks. My head feels heavy and pulls my stiff neck forward, making it an effort to walk. I pass under the archway and glance up into the big expanse, but despite the violet sky, my spirits are low. I daren't get my hopes up for Seth.

The screen wall glows, yet today my heart doesn't race at the thought of seeing Mother. She enters and takes her time to walk to the center. Her head is bowed, resting on her fingertips held to her chin. I strain as far as I can without nudging Barnabas to look behind her, but see no sign of Seth or the others. Mother stops and slowly lifts her head. She smiles, but I don't feel her joy. Her words sound as if she's speaking directly into my head. 'My children, my hard-working children, my privileged children, how lucky you are to be the generation who will witness the first sunrise of The New Dawn.' She turns and speaks as she glides along the front row. 'I won't keep you from your vital tasks for long. I have called you here because I have some good news and,' she stops in front of our team, 'some bad news.' Her eyes come to rest on Abraham. 'What would you like to hear first?' I stop breathing. *What's the right answer?* She senses our dilemma. 'Let's have a vote, shall we?' We nod, relieved of having to guess. Mother takes a few paces back. 'So, who wants to hear the bad news first?' Her head lifts as she looks for a show of hands. 'Come on, raise your hand if you want the bad news.' I glance both ways; no one moves.

Mother laughs. 'Not one!' She claps her hands. She seems pleased. 'So let's check to be sure. Who wants the good news first?' As one, we raise our hands. 'The good news it is!' She raises her arms and tips back her head. 'As you can see, I have brought you a violet sky today,' she tilts her head to the benches on my right, 'which you know to be my favorite color.' She appears to grow taller as her voice rises. 'This is to celebrate the news that the threat from the enemy's agents has been extinguished for good!' We all stand to cheer. She must have cured Seth! Mother's voice booms louder than ever above our cheers. 'Never again can their seed infect our young. Never again will their filthy hands taint what I have made good. Nothing can stop us now!' But my cheers catch in my throat—what of the bad news?

Mother holds up her palms and we sit at her bidding. Her head drops. 'But now, for the bad.' Her voice shakes. 'I'm afraid,' she takes a deep breath, 'I'm afraid the dark art of our enemy was strong, too strong, and buried deep within your fellow workers.' My shoulders sink. Tears well up in Mother's eyes. My throat tightens. 'I tried,' she wrings her hands, 'I really tried, but I could not remove the disease completely.' She looks up and I see a tear roll down her cheek. Mother sighs. 'Not without permanent damage.' *Poor Seth! What has happened?* She stands taller. 'But. All is not lost. I have moved them to new duties, duties where they can do no harm, but still contribute to The Work.' She must mean The Mines. Or… please, not The Trench.

Mother reads our thoughts. 'Oh do not worry. They are in good health, and only too happy to continue their part in our grand and noble plan. They are also relieved to know they cannot disrupt your efforts and wish you all well.' She turns to the prefects. 'However, I have still to find that illegal book.' I glance to Reuben. Mother's attention moves back to our benches. 'Yes, it is still out there. Much has happened of late, and I have been busy with preparations for our big day.' Her eyes narrow and scan the rows. Will she see my note through my overall? Her voice hardens. 'I have removed the immediate threat of the agents, but that book could still spread its spiteful lies.' Mother folds her arms. 'But trust me. It will be found.'

Poor Seth. It's not his fault the enemy seed found its way into his body. It doesn't seem fair that he and the others are suffering. No matter how much Mother tries to claim otherwise, it was her fault, but is she paying a price for her failure? I look up to the skylight above my workstation, to the square of violet in the grey ceiling, and hope Mother is right and that nothing can stop us now. But what will happen to Seth when we reach the surface? If there is to be a war, won't the enemy still need them?

I place my thirty-fifth unit of the shift on my shelf, just three short of the revised morning target for the shorter shift. I pick up the next components and turn them over in my hand. What sort of weapon do these things make? The prefect said I would build shelters once on the surface, but who will fight the war? The prefects? I have to know. I must find a way to talk to Lydia—perhaps the prefects come to collect the finished weapons for training. My fingers fix the two plates and reach for the pins. I feel today's note in my pocket. Bedtime cannot come quick enough.

# 23

'*Meet me.*' I turn the paper over several times, but it's just two words and no more. Meet who? When? And perhaps more important, where? I don't know what to do. Is it urgent? But then it becomes obvious. The sender is rightly cautious. The message has to come in parts, then if one is discovered by the prefects, less information is revealed. I must wait for the next note before I can act. *Meet me.* It has to be Rebekah. I cannot bear the thought that it may be a trap.

'Ten minutes to lights out.' Abraham climbs into his bunk. Ten minutes. I have time to read but my mind is fixed on the sender of the message. I place my hands behind my head and stare at the ceiling—I see Rebekah's face, waiting for me in a dark place beyond the ever-watchful prefects.

'Dormitory inspection!' My body jolts clear from my bed. Two prefects storm through our sleeping quarters. 'Everyone up. Stand by your bunks.' I still have the note in my hands. They mustn't see it. I stuff it into my mouth and chew; luckily, my retches are masked by Abraham's protest.

'What are you doing at this hour? We need our rest.'

The prefect pushes him back. *Pushes Abraham!* 'Mother's orders. We have to find the book.' My stomach knots as I recognize the voice of Jared.

Barnabas sounds calm. 'You heard the prefect. Everyone up and get your books.'

I swallow. The half-chewed paper scrapes the sides of my throat, bringing tears to my eyes, but with one strained gulp I manage to eat Rebekah's words. I get my book, climb out and stand by my bunk. This isn't right. We've never had an inspection this late—and just before lights out. My fingers wrap around my book, relieved I'd had the sense to burn the first note, and remove the page with my pencil drawing of the tree.

I look across to Amos and Reuben clutching their books to their chests; Barnabas stands as if waiting in the queue at the canteen. To my right, Abraham snorts as he attempts to control his anger at the intrusion. Jared moves to Caleb on my left. He snatches the book from his hand. *Snatches!* A glare from Jared traps the protest from Caleb in his throat. I clench my fists. Caleb is a gentle worker and slow to anger. But he's very protective of his book. Jared flicks through the pages—the sound of the paper almost tearing is difficult to hear. I wince as Jared checks every page before snapping the book shut. He sneers as he reads the cover and sneers, '*Robinson Crusoe*. Have you read it?' I stiffen. Caleb finds words difficult and I've heard Abraham read it quietly to him some nights.

Caleb straightens, looking hurt by the question. 'Yes! Mother gave it to me when—'

'What's it about?' *Is this a test?*

Caleb speaks as fast as he can. I can tell he's desperate to get his book back from Jared's destructive hands. 'It's about a man lost on an island in the middle of the sea. He ran away from Mother,' Jared leans in close, Caleb stammers, 'he has to b… build his own home and…'

He walks around Caleb. 'Did I tell you to stop? What happens next?'

This is wrong. I can see Caleb's ample chest rise and fall in his tee-shirt. 'He… he meets another man, he… he calls him Friday. Friday tells him he should go back to Mother, but he—'

'Enough!' Jared thrusts the book back at Caleb. Opposite, Amos is suffering the same treatment. I bite my lip. This shouldn't be happening. If Mother finds out, she'd be angry with them for treating her cherished workers and their books in this way. I glance sideways to Abraham. The muscles on the side of his face and neck stand out likes cables. He's staring at Barnabas, who seems comfortable with the prefect's harsh discipline.

Jared's face fills my vision—his cold, blue stare seems to read my thoughts. His fingers grip my book and wrench it from my hands. 'So, Noah.' He steps back and tucks my book under his arm. He speaks for all to hear. 'Noah who wants so badly to be like Moses and break production records. Noah who craves Mother's love.' He opens my book. I sigh silently as his eyes drop to its pages. But he continues to mock me. 'Noah who thinks he's better than anyone else.'

I shake my head. What will the others think? I try to protest. 'No... no, I—'

His eyes bore back into mine. 'But! No. Our precious Noah was mentor to the traitor, a waster of Mother's time with his useless ideas, and,' he turns to his colleague, 'I hear has selfish thoughts about,' he leans closer and whispers, 'well, we know who, don't we.' My hands bunch into fists. He steps back; his attention goes back to my book. 'So! What do we have here? What did *Mother* give you?' Surely, Abraham will inform Mother of Jared's attitude.

I can only watch as Jared roughly turns my precious book over in his hands. No one has touched it since Mother presented it to me on leaving school. His fingers scrape across the paper as he turns the pages. I hold my breath—he will crease them! I must get it back.

I find my voice. 'I've read it all. I read it every night. It's about—'

He yells into my face, 'Did I ask you?' I wince as his malice spits in my eye. 'Do you think I care for...' he stops and grins, 'What's this?' My heart stops. *Did I leave the note inside?* He holds up the book and pushes it into my face. 'Have you damaged Mother's gift?' He lowers it. 'Well?' He must mean the missing page. My stomach churns. I feel its contents rise. I swallow hard; the note must stay hidden.

My dry mouth struggles with the words. 'No. I've always been very careful with Mother's gift.'

Jared pulls apart the pages and peers into the crease of the spine. His colleague calls over. 'Finished this side, Jared. Nothing suspicious.' Jared slams the book shut and shoves it back at me.

Jared turns to his colleague. 'Good.' Then steps forward so his nose almost touches mine. His mouth twists as he hisses his threat. 'Mother will get to hear of your carelessness.' He turns away. 'Now, all of you, into the other room. And no talking!'

I hug my book to my chest and feel its pain as I reluctantly place it back under my pillow. We walk as instructed and gather around the stove, feeling some comfort from its dying fire. I look to Abraham. He nods, trying, I believe, to assure us that Mother will hear of this travesty. But his wide eyes in his taut face weakens his attempt. Barnabas is the only one who appears in control. He watches us, his gaze passing from one face to the next. Jared's words play over in my mind. How did he know so much? Does my face give away my thoughts so easily? I hope the others were too absorbed in their own fears to have heard Jared's cruel jibes, no matter how much truth they contained.

Caleb flinches as something crashes in the other room. The prefects must be tearing off blankets and ripping out our thin bed rolls in search of the illegal book. I hear Jared laugh. What could he possibly find amusing in defiling our dormitory? I look down to the stove. The flickering embers are now the same red as Rebekah's hair. I think back to The Square when a curl had dropped onto her shoulder. What I would give now to brush it back and stroke her neck.

Barnabas snorts. He's watching me again. I stiffen my jaw but it's too late. I had smiled. My face does betray me. I have to save these thoughts for the privacy of the shower or my bunk.

The prefects enter. Jared looks disappointed. He sighs. 'All clear, so get back to bed. Your lights go out in five.'

Barnabas straightens. 'Thank you. We can take encouragement from your tireless vigilance and work to stop the agents.'

Jared nods to Barnabas. *He nods to him!* Abraham steps forward. Jared stops and frowns at him. 'Yes?'

Abraham pauses. 'The papers? I have to sign, to… to confirm we passed the inspection.'

Jared turns to his colleague and laughs as they leave. 'Paperwork? Don't waste my time.'

We turn and gape at Abraham, but he looks as shocked as we do. He says nothing. Barnabas seems happy to fill in the silence. 'You heard him. Five minutes. Get back to your bunks.'

Caleb gasps as he enters the sleeping quarters first. I follow and am not surprised to see our bedding and overalls strewn across the floor. But my blood freezes at their treatment of our books. Why do this? They'd already checked them! We stare in disbelief at the fate of our gifts from Mother. The prefects must have slung them against the wall, leaving them strewn with their covers open like dead birds fallen from the sky. Abraham kneels next to the pile and speaks through his gritted teeth. 'Mother will hear of this in the morning.'

I just had time to check my book before lights out. Two pages were creased by Jared's mishandling, but they should flatten out. Caleb wasn't so lucky. We all felt his pain as Abraham had lifted the book and several pages fell out. Caleb sobbed openly until lights out. Abraham has promised he will see what he can do to repair the damage. Yet it's not just the violation of our books that has stunned us—it was their departure from proper procedure. Even Barnabas looked briefly shocked at the attitude of Jared and his colleague as they left.

From our earliest memories in the nursery, we were taught to respect the prefects and the sacrifices they make in their line of duty. They protect us, ensure we follow the rules, and keep us focused on the goal. But tonight, they crossed a line. I had suspected a change in their conduct since the night of the vandalized factory wall. They'd began to treat us differently, with contempt even, but I'd never seen a prefect lay hands on a worker. And to push a team leader! That is unacceptable. But Mother will put it right. She won't tolerate the behavior we witnessed tonight. Jared will be disciplined. I hope I will get to witness his punishment.

I see his sneering face and hear his taunt, '*She's mine*'. My mouth fills with saliva. If he can enter any dormitory without justification or paperwork, he could pay a visit to Rebekah. I have to see her, to warn her. But what can I, a mere worker, do to stop a black-shirted prefect? I close my eyes and long for morning, hoping a new note awaits with instructions for our meeting.

# 24

My wish is answered! The edge of a folded note stands out between the slices of bread. I'm tempted to read it straight away, but know I could ruin Rebekah's careful planning with one such careless act. The sky. I'd been so absorbed by the promise of a note, I've not checked. I glance up. Blue. Some good news at least. Today is Friday, the seventh day of May. This time next year we will be on the surface. I turn to wait for Abraham, desperate to know if he'd had chance to report Jared.

'Noah!' Barnabas again. 'Bring in that crate and stop gawping at the sky.' Why can't he give me a moment's peace?

'Coming.' I delay. Abraham will be here soon. I peer down to the tiny triangle of white sticking out from my sleeve. Could I take a quick look? The white turns to grey. I look up. The sky is changing! I call through to Barnabas while not taking my eyes off the spectacle above.

'What's the matter?' He marches outside. 'Can't you do the one thing I—' he follows my gaze. His mouth drops open. The sky is growing darker before our eyes.

I turn to Barnabas. 'Have you ever seen it do that before?'

He shakes his head. His hand grips my shoulder. 'Quick, we better get inside.' I follow without question. The others have sensed the change in the light and have gathered by the windows. Our gasps fog the glass as we stare in silence.

Reuben is the first to speak. 'What do you think has happened?'

Caleb cries out, 'Are they attacking?' We crane our necks, searching for signs of the enemy crashing through the dome.

'Of course not!' Barnabas sounds annoyed, but his assured tone settles the team. 'We'd hear the alarm if we were under attack.'

'Where's Abraham?' I speak before thinking. 'He should be here by now.'

'Perhaps...' Amos stops as we turn to him. His hand hovers by his mouth. 'Perhaps he's telling Mother about those prefects. That's why the sky's changed. She must be angry with Jared.' His eyes dart across our faces, waiting for someone to belittle his theory. But we agree, even Barnabas.

'You may be right.' Barnabas turns to the room. 'But breakfast won't get itself ready. Come on, to work!'

We jump to our duties, happy for the comfort of our morning routine. I just have time to turn the bread when Abraham returns. We stop to face him. He leans against the wall next to the entrance; his dark skin looks pale. He looks up and seems surprised to see us watching him. His voice cracks up. 'Everyone to the table.'

I remove the bread from the rack and do as I'm told. Abraham waits for us to settle. His chest rises then falls as Abraham stutters, 'She... she didn't believe me.'

'What?' We speak as one, unable to comprehend his words.

His eyes remain fixed on the table. 'Mother didn't believe me. And she's angry with me for making up the story.' His hand clenches the edge of the table. 'Angry with me!' He looks outside. 'That's why it's grey. She said *her* prefects don't act in that way, and...' he looks up to Barnabas, 'there's no record they came here.'

'But, we know it happened.' I can see tears forming in Reuben's eyes. I don't think I've ever seen him like this.

Amos jumps up. 'We could show her Caleb's book? Mother knows that he'd never—'

'This isn't just about Caleb's book!' Barnabas turns on Amos. Amos backs away and slumps into his chair.

Abraham waves his hand towards Barnabas. 'Let's calm down.' His eyes stay on Barnabas. 'But Barnabas is right. This isn't about the books, bad as it is, it's about the prefects treating us workers as they please. And worse still, Mother taking their word over ours.' His shoulders drop. 'Jared was there. He stood before Mother and denied anything happened, even that they'd been here.' Abraham sighs. 'Things have changed, it looks like Mother is keen on—'

'More discipline.' We turn to Barnabas, still standing, looking more like the leader of the team with his straighter posture. 'But maybe it's not such a bad thing.' He looks at our faces in turn. 'We're so close now, she has to make sure nothing can sabotage our efforts. She's got rid of the agents, but this illegal book could still ruin everything. We have to look to the future.' Barnabas sits and picks up his toast. He takes a bite and speaks while he chews. 'I can put up with a few more months of stricter rule if it means getting to the surface first.' I glance at Abraham. Like me, I think he wants to believe Barnabas's logic, but something doesn't ring true. Abraham still looks lost in thought.

I speak for him. 'But how can she justify treating us, the very workers that will bring in The New Dawn, like naughty schoolchildren?' I unclench my fists. 'Is that supposed to make us work harder?'

Barnabas levels his eyes at me. 'Careful, Noah. You're in no position to question Mother's methods. After all, you failed to detect Seth's betrayal.'

'But no one—'

'Mother knows best, Noah. Remember that.' The others mumble the correct reply; I quickly join in but it's not heartfelt.

How did Moses keep going? How did he turn up to work every day and continue to break records when he knew he was unlikely see the real sky? His eyes look down from the poster. Did he work to forget? Did immersing himself in the drudgery of the work stop him going mad? I'm aware my hands are moving but they feel like they belong to another. At least I have my note. It has to suggest a time to meet. It has to! All day I have been wary of the sudden appearance of a prefect. A spot inspection now would discover my secret and put an end to ever seeing Rebekah. I must stop checking the clock before someone notices, but its hands are moving so slowly I fear the evening will never come, or the ink on my note will fade before I get a chance to read it.

My hands fumble with the plate. What if there are more night inspections? If Barnabas is right about stricter measures, will more prefects be out patrolling looking for walkers? If I'm caught out at night, I will be sent down below to new duties and may never get to climb a tree. Perhaps I should just get on with my work and endure the next few months as Barnabas suggests and ignore the note in my pocket. I see Rebekah's face... and hear Jared's threat. No, I cannot. I have to see her.

I press my little fingers into the paper and take hold of the ladder. In moments I will finally read the words I've ached to see all day. I can barely breathe as I anticipate the message.

'Lights out in fifteen.' My fingers twitch. The note escapes! I clutch at the ladder and watch as the bright, white slip of paper flutters to the floor like a tired bird.

The others are still talking and readying themselves for bed. I have to get it before it's discovered. I step down and cover it with my foot.

'Everything alright, Noah?' Abraham has seen me climb down. I stop breathing. I have to speak. *Sound normal!*

'Yes. I... I think I have something sticking in my foot.'

'Well sort it out and get to bed.' Now Barnabas is alert to my situation.

'Will do.' I crouch and slide the note out and scrunch it in my hand. I call out. 'It's a splinter. Must have trodden on it when getting undressed.'

'Amos! Caleb!' Barnabas sits up. 'Make sure you sweep the floor twice tomorrow.'

I stand. Amos watches me. I cannot tell if he's annoyed that I've got him in trouble, or whether he saw the note. He says nothing and rolls onto his side to read his tattered book. I climb into my bunk with my fist closed around the note—I won't get another chance.

I remove the headset and cough as I unwrap the paper. It reads, *'Tonight. R'* R? It is Rebekah! And she wants to meet tonight. I strive to quieten my breathing. We shall be alone at last. My heart is in my throat. Her feelings must be as strong as mine to take this risk—but I am only too happy to take it with her. If we're lucky we may have a few minutes together before anyone notices we're missing. But what can I say to her? I must focus. I don't want my feelings to spill out at once in the precious moments we'll share. She'll think I'm immature and just a boy fresh from the lower level. But I have no time to plan, I will—. My thoughts come to an abrupt halt. Where? Where do I meet her? I know she couldn't mention the location in case someone found the note, but it could take all night to find her. *Calm down.* She obviously knows my dormitory, perhaps she will come to me.

The light dies. This is it. But I must wait until the rest are sleeping; it would be impossible to come up with another excuse for getting out of my bunk again — especially after lights out. Be patient. I will be with her soon. Then what? Can we continue with these secret meetings? How cruel it would be if, like my cake, I finally get to meet her only to have her snatched away.

Jared. I see his sneering face from the inspection. I have to warn her of his intentions. I look out of the narrow window. Out there she'll know I have read her words. I send my thoughts to her. Soon, we'll be together. Soon, I can tell her how I feel and everything will change.

# 25

My limbs ache to move but I must wait. I peer through the slit to the walkway for prefects, but thankfully it's empty and quiet. The lamps go out. My heart stops. How will I find my way in the dark? What if I get lost? I could still be looking for her when the lights come back on in the morning. I listen to the breathing of my team. Is it safe yet? But I find I'm pushing back the blanket and climbing over the edge before I can stop.

Already, the air feels colder. I shiver as my feet touch the floor. I take two steps then stop. Should I put on my overalls and boots? I've been so caught up with the excitement of meeting Rebekah, I've not given any thought to this part. I decide to dress—I don't want to be shaking with the cold in her presence. But… it would be better if my thick overalls didn't come between us when I hold her soft body to mine. I'm getting ahead of myself. I decide to dress and pull on my clothes and boots. I'm ready to go. I've made my choice and have to see it through. Rebekah is out there waiting. I must not delay and let her down.

I take the biggest step of my life and leave the sleeping quarters. My heart beats loud in my ears as I enter the living area. I stop. The orange glow from the dying fire shimmers on the wall. It's beautiful! The bright light has kept the real beauty of the embers hidden all this time. I approach the stove and take the note from my sleeve. My eyes are drawn to the flickering red, orange and occasional yellow lights. I could happily stand in the dark and feel its warmth on my skin, and witness the last moments of its fading glory. But I remember the reason I'm out of bed. I drop the note into the fire and turn to leave.

I hit a glass wall at the entrance—my legs won't move! If I'm caught by a night patrol, there's no going back. Am I walking into a trap? This could all be a test of my loyalty to Mother. I'm stuck between two lives. What do I do? Go back, work hard, keep quiet and do as I'm told? Or go forward into… into what? The unknown, but also the possibility Rebekah is waiting. I step forward. My stomach flutters as it did on the factory roof all those years past.

Movement on the walkway! I freeze. Someone is out there. My eyes widen until I feel they will pop from my sockets. A tall figure stands opposite. Idiot. I almost laugh with relief as I realize it's my shadow cast by the burning note in the stove behind. But I have to move. A prefect standing at the end of the row will see the evidence of my crime flickering across the walkway. I step outside and move away from the light.

My breath becomes visible in the night air and I press back into the wall, my hands finding the smooth surface reassuring. I instinctively look up but can see nothing. Above the walls lit by the faint, orange glow, everything is black. I can see neither rooftops nor sky. My skin prickles. Mother's nursery stories of monsters lurking in the shadows fill my head. I should go back. It's wrong to be out. I take a sideways step, back towards the dormitory entrance.

'Noah!' My foot hangs above the floor. Did I hear that, or was it in my head? I hold my breath but can hear nothing above the shrieking silence. 'Noah!' It's barely a whisper but I can make out a girl's voice.

'Rebekah?' I wince as my reply bounces off the walls and down the walkway.

'Here.' She's to my right. I put my foot down and slide along the wall—desperate not to lose contact. 'A little further.' She's closer.

'Where are—?' My hand touches something soft and warm. It grips back. I've found her! Or she's found me. 'Rebek—'

'Shush. Not here.' She tugs at my hand, pulling me away from the wall into the dark gap by the next dormitory. I'm no longer afraid. Rebekah is by my side and together we can face anything. The black becomes grey, and now I can just make out the outline of her body in her overall. I see her flowing hair—she's not wearing her headscarf. My free hand itches to reach out and touch her hair, but not yet, I must wait a while longer. More of her face comes into view as she stands opposite with her finger on her lips. I nod. She leans forward and I feel her breath in my ear as she whispers, 'Follow me.'

She takes my hand and leads me back onto the walkway. We head off in the direction of the factory. But after a few steps she turns and points to my feet, pushing her palm down as if flattening a lump in her bedroll. I shake my head. *What does she want?* Again she points to my feet and then holds her finger to her lips. I understand and nod. She turns her back and sets off. But I don't know how to walk without making a noise. I can't move, worried I'll alert the prefects. But Rebekah is getting away and soon disappears into the shadows. I want to call out before the darkness snatches her from me. *Move!* I have to go now, or I have no other choice but to go back to my bunk—and then she'd never write another note. One knee bends. I hobble a few paces before my limbs loosen. I walk faster, my wide eyes peering ahead, aching for the sight of Rebekah's back. I see her! She glides silently across the hard slabs of the walkway—she must have done this many times before, but for what purpose? A sliver of red slices across our path, marking the position of the last dormitory in my sector. Rebekah steps into the light. My fears are forgotten as her hair falls across a slender shoulder as she glances back. She smiles, her eyes glisten for a second before she slips out of the glow and back into the night. That's all I need—I will follow her into whatever lies ahead. But my resolve is short-lived.

The factory rears up out of the dark. I freeze in the glare of its black windows—it knows we're here. I shrink back, fearful it will burst into life and expose our guilty act to Mother. Rebekah grabs my arm and drags me away before I cry out and confess my sin. She tucks her arm through mine and marches me in the direction of The Square; I can sense her disappointment. I have to be braver. I follow, trying to walk straighter and as quiet as possible as we pass the arch.

My shoulders relax as we enter the farm district. Rebekah releases my arm and leads me past the sleeping dormitories. I wonder what Naomi would think if she could see the two of us from her window. My body stiffens. It's been five minutes since we left the areas I'm authorized to walk without a prefect. I look to Rebekah. I want to ask where she's taking me, but I've already disappointed her once and I don't want her to think she's made a mistake sending the notes.

Voices! I clasp Rebekah's hand. Laughter and shouting. Prefects. She leans over—so close I can feel her hair on my cheek. I struggle to hear her frantic words above my pounding heart. 'They're early. We have no time.' She thrusts something into my hand. 'Quick, take this. Look after it. Go back. Meet me tomorrow… same place.'

'But—?'

'Go!' Rebekah spins on her heels and runs, leaving me standing alone in the dark a long way from home. I slip the package into my overalls and turn back. But again I find I cannot move. The prefects are closer. Torch beams pick out features on the building opposite. If I don't go now, their lights will find my pale, frozen face against the grey walls. I take a step, another, and break into a run, back past the sleeping quarters of the farm sector. The voices fade and I begin to breathe again. I slow to a walk and check my surroundings. I'm only a minute or two from my dormitory. What did Rebekah mean by 'early'? Does she go out every night?

The faint glow of our stove lights my way back to safety. I wait by the entrance to catch my breath. I reach inside my overall. Despite the cold, I'm sweating and the package from Rebekah feels damp. I step inside and approach the stove to examine the object. It's a book! It's *the* book—it has to be the one Mother is so keen to find and destroy. My fingers feels numb. In my hand, I hold what Mother fears could bring about the end of The Ark. To be found with it would mean a one-way trip to The Trench. And what was it doing in Rebekah's possession?

I turn to the entrance then stop. I should take the book to Mother this instant. But I would have to tell her how it came to be in my possession. In my heart, I know I could not do anything that would land Rebekah in trouble. But why did she give it to me? I enter the living quarters. But before I go to bed I have to know for sure what I have in my hand. I kneel next to the stove and open the first page. In the red light, I can just make out it's handwritten but cannot read the words. Did Rebekah write it?

# 26

'Five o'clock! Everyone up.' I stir. 'It's Saturday, the eighth day of May. I want to see breakfast on the table when I return.' Abraham's footsteps fade. Morning! Already? It seems I've hardly slept. It took what seemed like hours to settle on my return. My fear had turned to something new, something strong and energizing. Being out in the dark, along with the risk of being caught defying Mother's rules, ignited a fire in my stomach. I felt alive. Only the sight of Rebekah and the taste of my birthday cake have come close to what I felt surging through my body as I'd evaded the prefect's flickering torchlight. Something in me stirred last night, and I need to feel it again.

I wait for the others to leave the sleeping quarters and check Rebekah's book is still hidden. I'd pushed it as far down as it would go, into the gap between my bedroll and the wall—but how long before the next search? I hope Rebekah will have some answers tonight.

'Noah!'

'Coming.' If only I could report Barnabas to Mother on some charge and get him out of my face. The book! It would be the end of him if I could place it in his bunk and inform the prefects. But that would be wrong, and it would likely end up being traced back to Rebekah. I stroll through the living quarters—how different it looks in the morning. The rest of the team are busy about their tasks, oblivious to the world that exists outside while they sleep.

I look up to the dome out of habit, caring not for the color. It's blue, but it makes no difference to me now. I can only count the hours until it goes black so I can be with her in the dark, exciting world of the forbidden hours.

Today has been torture. I have toasted the bread, brewed the tasteless coffee, made another one hundred units, smiled and nodded at the right time, and eaten two bowls of greenish mush. I don't know how I managed to get through it without error. I've spent the last five years living the same, dull day over and over and over again. It has to end soon or I will break. My neck, back and shoulders are on fire—and for what? I would rather risk the dangers outside The Ark, fighting the elements and the enemy, than make another component for a weapon I'll never get to use in anger.

'Lights out in fifteen.' *I know!* Abraham says that every night at exactly the same time. It's not his fault. Like the rest of us, he's just following the routine laid down by Mother. But can we do anything to change it? Would Mother let us go up now if we asked?

I force my tired limbs up the ladder into my bunk and let my bones rest where they collapse. I wait for the others to settle. It takes an age for Barnabas to be satisfied we're all tucked up before he gets into his bunk. Finally, he's absorbed in his own thoughts. I come alive once more as my hand delves into the gap to find Rebekah's book. It slides out like the sword from the stone in one of Mother's stories. The plain, brown cover belies its power to destroy The Ark and all within.

I hold my breath as I prepare to commit an unforgivable act. What secret knowledge will be revealed? I flick through the first few pages and breathe out. It's a diary! Just like the one written by Moses that Mother reads to us on special occasions. This can't be the book. While it's against the rules to keep a private diary, this can't be a threat to our safety. Pages and pages of dates and what Rebekah had for breakfast doesn't make for dangerous reading. But, then again. Did she write anything about me?

I have only seconds left before lights out. I thumb to the last few pages. On the third day of May she writes,

*WE'RE GOING UP! Mother called us to The Square and told us it will be safe to return in a year. We'll have to work hard, but she gave us the afternoon off. No work! This is the best news we could have—*

The light fades. No mention of me. I should have looked at her entry for Moses Day. But it's wrong. Rebekah said '*look after it*', nothing about reading it. She must have known our dormitory had recently been searched and would be safe for at least a week before they return. I place the book back under my pillow, guilty for intruding on Rebekah's private thoughts. But I smile in the dark. We will speak again tonight.

The breathing slows to the night rhythm—they're asleep. I have to stop myself from leaping out of the bunk. My aches and pains have gone, healed by a rush of blood to my limbs and head. I pull on my clothes and make my way past the stove, through the entrance and onto the walkway. The night calls me. Bring it on. Bring on the shadows, bring on the silence, bring on the prefects, and bring Rebekah to me.

I step out of the glow spilling out from our dormitory and slide along the wall. I stop to wait, but my legs twitch with the urge to run. *Where is she?* I peer in the direction she will come, but I see nothing but the converging grey lines of the walkway leading down to The Square. I strain my ears for signs of her approach, but hear only the constant squeal of silence. *Where is she?* The fire in my body dies. What if she doesn't come? Should I go looking for her? What could have—?

'Noah!' She's to my left. I turn to see her slip past the dormitory entrance. She takes my hand, rekindling my fire.

We run the opposite way to the previous night. She calls softly over her shoulder. 'Never take the same route twice.' I look upon her with renewed admiration. She knows things that I want to know. Her knowledge gives her power, power to trick the prefects, power to do things of which Mother would not approve.

Still we run. If we keep going, we'll reach the perimeter, further from The Square than I've been for many years. My pace slows—it's too far. Rebekah gently pulls my hand. 'Almost there.' I smile bravely, but can think of nothing to say that wouldn't sound immature. We pass the outer buildings, buildings that look empty and unused. Did they used to be dormitories? Why aren't they full of workers, building, growing and researching our way to success?

Rebekah stops. We've arrived at the perimeter. The black wall brings our world to an end, slicing through the outer buildings like a gigantic blade, separating us from the foot of the dome. I've not been here since the induction tour. I step forward and slide my hand across its cold surface—but its purpose is not to keep us in. I think back to *that* day in the nursery. Mother sat before us and lowered her voice as she told us of The Outsiders living beyond the wall. My skin had crawled as I learned for the first time there were things in my world that would wish me harm. I look back to the wall. But it's not as tall as I remember—if I jump, I could easily touch the top. These Outsiders must be very small if this wall keeps them out.

I go to speak, but Rebekah places her finger on my lips. I wish she could leave it there longer, but she steps back and motions for me to wait. She turns to the empty building, climbs onto the window ledge and leaps up onto the top of the wall. *We're going over!* She waves me to the ledge. I try to protest but she raises her hand. I'm annoyed for hesitating. *Be brave.* With three steps, I climb onto the window and take Rebekah's hand and join her on the top. I ignore my pulse beating its warning in my ears and look beyond. But I can see nothing in the murk.

Rebekah twists and flips her legs over the edge. I grasp her arm and whisper as loud as I dare. 'Wait. What about,' I can't say their name here,' you know... the creatures.'

She stifles a laugh. 'You still believe that one? There's nothing to be afraid of, it's just a story Mother makes up to stop us going out.'

'But I'm sure I've seen one, last year.' Rebekah stares at me as if I'm mad. I protest. 'I did, honest. It bent over me as I lay in my bunk,' I shudder, 'ugh, it had black, shining eyes.'

She touches my shoulder. 'Trust me, they don't exist.'

'But Mother says—'

'It's not true, I've been out there and never seen one. Come on,' she loops her hand under my arm, 'Jump!' My stomach churns at the sudden drop. I cry out as pain shoots up my legs as if I landed onto sharp knives.

Rebekah covers my mouth. She whispers, 'Sorry. I should have told you to bend your knees.'

She removes her hand. I try hard not to grimace. 'I'm fine. Honest.'

'Can you walk?' I nod, hoping I don't fall over.

'Good. This way, it's not far.' I turn and forget the pain in my knees. An empty expanse, larger than The Square, lies between us and a dark line running as far as I can see to the left and right. Rebekah sees my face. 'It's a bit scary the first time, but you'll be fine.' She leads me away from the wall, away from everything I've known all my life, but I'd gladly follow her into the strange, new world that beckons. I shiver and worry my chattering teeth will alert the prefects. She squeezes my hand, seeing my glances behind. 'Don't worry. They don't come out here, Mother won't let them. She doesn't want them to see what's beyond the wall.' She giggles as my teeth won't stop. 'You'll be fine, it's warmer at the edge.'

'The edge?'

She beams. 'You have to see, it only takes a minute.' She breaks into a run. I match her pace, not wanting to lose sight of her outside the wall, just in case Mother was telling the truth about Outsiders.

Rebekah slows and comes to a stop. She turns but I cannot see her face, only her dark outline. 'We're here.' My eyes are drawn to the pale light behind. I follow the curve upwards. We're standing where the sky meets the ground! I step forward and, for the second time in my life, touch the sky. Instantly my fingertips recall its rough surface. 'Strange, isn't it,' Rebekah whispers close to my ear. I turn and see her face, lit by the soft glow of the dome. She smiles, and speaks a little louder. 'It's okay, it's safe to talk here. The sound won't carry back to the wall.' I watch her lips, entranced by her voice. She touches my shoulder and sighs. 'I thought we'd never get to be alone. I just had to—'

'Me too.' I cannot stop myself. Months of frustration are released. I step forward, run my hand across her smooth, red hair and take her in my arms. My body bursts with a passion I cannot contain. I press my lips to hers. She tastes so good. She clutches at my shoulders, pressing back against me—she feels it too. The heat I felt with Naomi rises in my groin, only this time it's more intense. I'm on fire. I'm in… agony! She pushes me away, her raised knee pulls back from the strike.

She gasps. 'What are you doing?'

My knees buckle. I double over, retching from the sickening ache rising up to my stomach, and spreading around my back. I roll onto my side, pulling my knees to my chest.

Rebekah looks aghast. 'What was that?' She wipes the back of her hand across her lips. 'Urgh. That was disgusting.'

'I… I don't understand.' I grunt. 'I thought—'

'No, you didn't think. I didn't bring you here for… for whatever that was!'

'I'm sorry.' I cannot look her in the eye. I turn away, still reeling from the pain and humiliation.

She kneels by my side and places a hand on my shoulder. 'Sorry. I… I didn't mean to hurt you. I just had to stop what you were doing.'

I roll onto my side but keep my eyes on the floor. 'It's okay, it doesn't matter. I deserved it.' The throbbing begins to subside, but the real hurt will take longer to heal. Rebekah leans over and strokes my arm.

'Are you okay? I didn't realize I'd hit you so hard.'

Still I can't face her. I cover my face and mumble into my hands, 'I'm fine, I'll be okay in a minute. It's just that it's very sensitive down there.'

'Sorry.'

I ease my body to face her and straighten my legs slowly. 'No please don't apologize, it was careless of me. When you looked at me at the Moses Day dinner I thought you… you felt the same way as I do.' My face grows hot. 'But I was wrong. I'm sorry.'

Rebekah sits back. 'Oh, I see.' She raises her hand to her mouth. 'I thought that look you gave me was because you'd seen the bird. That's why I brought you out here.'

'The what?'

'The bird. Oh dear.' She jumps to her feet. 'The book!' She steps away. 'I think I've made a mistake.' Rebekah glances over her shoulder. 'I… I shouldn't have brought you here, or given you the book.'

I climb to my feet, but cannot straighten fully upright yet. I wince. 'I… I won't tell them. I'd never do anything that would get you in trouble.'

She stares into my face as if trying to read a book in the dark. 'I guess I can trust you, otherwise you would have reported me by now.' She looks back to the perimeter wall. 'But Isaac said he thought you'd also seen it, and when I—'

'Isaac? What has he got to do with this?'

She crouches and beckons me to join her. 'I think I'd better explain.' I gratefully accept her invitation to sit, pulling my knees back to my chest as we rest against the edge of the world. She leans across. I flinch. She looks me in the eye. 'But first I need you to promise none of this will ever get back to the others.'

I nod. 'Of course.'

She holds my gaze. 'You have to say it.'

'Yes, I promise.'

Her head drops back. She sighs as she looks up to the dome. 'Thank you. Ever since Mother sent Isaac and Rachel away, I've been on my own. It's been…' she sobs once, suddenly into her hands, 'it's been so difficult.'

I move closer and lift my arm to put around her, but choose to let it drop by my side. 'It's okay, you've got me now.' As soon as I say it, I realize how pathetic my words of support sound. *How can I be of help? More of an unnecessary risk.*

She speaks to the ground. 'Thanks, that's… reassuring.'

I open my mouth, but stop. I need to think and say something that doesn't sound immature. I look to her. 'Did Isaac come here with you to the edge?'

Rebekah turns and rubs her hand across the surface of the dome. 'Oh yes. Isaac thinks there's a way up out here, we've been looking for months but found nothing.'

'Months! How many times have you been out here? And Rachel? What does she—?'

She holds up her hand. 'Slow down, too many questions.' I know how she feels. I'm acting like Seth.

'Sorry.'

'No need. I know what it's like. I felt the same when Isaac first showed me.' She places a hand on my knee. 'He saw the look, the one you gave me,' she glances away, 'the one that I thought meant you'd seen the bird.'

'You said that, but what... who is the bird?'

'The white bird. Isaac believes it's some sort of message, but only a few see it and we don't know where it comes from. I first saw it just after Mother's Day last year, every night in the sleep stories. But I soon realized no one else on my team had. Weeks later, Isaac approached me on the walkway and asked if I'd *seen the bird*.' She turns to face me. 'I must have had that look on my face. I thought I'd seen it in you, you know, the evening when Mother presented the chosen workers. I wanted to ask you at the Moses Day dinner, but the others would have heard. But when you looked at me like you did, I was certain you had *the look*.'

If only she knew why I had that *look* on my face. I shake my head. 'No, I haven't seen it. But I see strange things when I don't wear the headset.'

Rebekah smiles. 'They're called *dreams*. You can also have a sort of dream while awake, they're your own thoughts and no one else can share them. You call those a *daydream*. Rachel thinks it's where you can make things come true.' Her eyes wander up to the dome. I watch her mouth as she speaks. 'I dream of seeing the surface, but...' she sighs, 'Mother doesn't want us to dream, she must think they're dangerous.'

'Or a distraction. I think I've had those.' My face grows hot as I remember the Rebekah of my *dream*. I change the subject. 'You mentioned Rachel? How many others are there?'

Rebekah lets out a long sigh. 'Just us three, and now it's only me,' her eyes meet mine, 'oh, and now you.' She looks back to the perimeter wall. 'I keep checking on the walkways but I've not seen the *look* in other faces.' She twists towards me—this time I don't flinch. She grasps my hands. 'Did you read the diary?'

My face grows hot again. 'Yes, sorry, I had a quick look.'

She frowns. 'But that's why I gave it to you.'

'Oh, I thought it was to keep it safe. I didn't think you'd want me to read your diary.'

'Mine?' She shakes her head. 'It's not my diary.'

'So whose it?'

She looks at me as if it should be obvious. 'I thought you knew? It was written by Moses.'

I stare at her, my mouth and eyes wide open. 'But he... he said...'

Rebekah nods. 'Yes, Mother told them *they* were going up. The same date, your birthday, two days after Matthew's Day as it was called back then.'

'But,' I struggle to my feet. 'But what happened?'

Rebekah holds up a hand and I help her to her feet. 'I don't know. He ran out of pages and I don't know if he wrote another one. I guess Mother could have already destroyed it.'

I clasp my hand to my face. 'Was it agents?' *Dear Moses! Can they still stop us now?*

Rebekah shakes her head. 'No, that's the odd thing. He doesn't mention agents in the whole diary, and no word of The Mines, only The Trench.' She steps forward and places a hand on my shoulder. 'There's only one possible explanation. Mother is—'

'Lying.' My heart stops. I look up to the dome. 'So does this mean we're not going up?' I look at her through the tears I can't hold back. 'We're stuck down here forever.' My body sags. Rebekah grabs my arm to stop me falling. I turn to her. 'I don't think I can face another day if... if we...'

Rebekah wraps her arm around me. 'Let's sit.' I collapse against the edge and slide to the ground. 'I know how you feel. But you have to fight the despair.'

I bang my fists against the floor. 'But what have I got to fight with? If Mother doesn't want us to go up, what can we do? She has the prefects, she controls everything. We—'

'Outnumber them!' She grasps my hands. 'Isaac believed if we can find the way up and see for ourselves that it's safe, we can convince the others and maybe even Mother.'

'Mother? How?'

'Perhaps she fears we might come to harm on the surface. Or it could be she's scared of being captured by the enemy, but I'm prepared to take that risk, and I'm sure most of the others here would.' She looks up. 'If you and I can get out and prove to her it's safe, she *has* to listen. But if not, we only have one thing left to do.'

'And what's that?'

She sits straighter. 'We'd have to rebel.'

'Rebel? I don't know that word.'

Rebekah laughs; it seems out of place. 'You have a lot to learn. To rebel means to not have to do what Mother tells us.' She slides in front of me and takes both my hands and squeezes. 'It means *we* can take control, find a way up and get out of this pit!'

My stomach grows warm. I feel the embers of my hope rekindle. I smile. 'So it was you who wrote on the factory wall.'

She shrugs. 'I didn't know what else to do. If I spoke out, I'll be sent to Re-Education or worse. I had to get the message out somehow, maybe start people talking. Perhaps if—'

'Seth! What about Seth and the others? He confessed. They all did.'

'I'm sorry. I know he was... is your friend. I had to stop myself from standing and owning up, but if I went, how else could the truth come out?'

'But why did they confess?'

'They were just up from the lower level, I guess they felt somehow guilty. Who knows? Mother has a way of getting to us all.'

'But I don't—' Rebekah stands and glances back. A light streaks across the dome from behind the wall.

'Dear Moses! We've been here too long. We have to go, they've started the patrol.'

'But—?'

'We have to go now. I need my sleep, and, if we get caught...' I take her outstretched hand. I get up and look into her face.

'I really am sorry about what happened, you know... earlier.'

She shakes her head. 'Don't worry about it. This place gets to us all in one way or another. Is everything okay now,' her eyes drop, 'down there?'

I nod. 'Can we meet again tomorrow?'

'Not tomorrow. Things are going to be difficult for a little while. I think we should leave it for a few days.'

My heart sinks. 'A few days? But when?' I want to spend all my time in her company.

'I'll leave a blank note in your crate when I think it's safe, or at least safer.'

'Blank?'

She laughs. 'So no one knows it's from me to you. How many notes do you get?'

'Yes, of course.' I still have a lot to learn.

She grabs my hand and pulls. 'Come on, we really should go.'

We set off to the wall. She turns back and puts her finger to her lips again. 'Remember. No speaking once we get close to the wall, the prefects might be at the perimeter.'

My eyes are wide open. I watch light from prefects' torches jump across my ceiling, making strange, elongated shapes as the patrol passes our dormitory. My hand rests on the diary, the diary that has been in the hands of Moses. I feel its power. Now I know why Mother is so keen to stop its message spreading through The Ark. I breathe out as the voices fade—another team will feel the bitterness of their disdain tonight.

The journey back was uneventful, but in an odd way I felt disappointment. Only a few days ago, I would have been destroyed by the thought that we'd never surface. But now? I feel Mother's chains binding me to the cause have been loosened. We've always believed that the day would come when our hard work paid off. The New Dawn was the sunlight at the top of our deep hole; the goal we strove to achieve, if not for ourselves, but for those who came after. But with the revelation that Mother appears to not want us to return, it seems pointless to continue. What have we got to lose if we rebel? But we must be patient. We need to choose our friends carefully to build our numbers. One wrong decision before we're strong enough can only end in disaster.

I see Rebekah's face and hear her voice. Is she thinking of me? I've never spent so much time with just one person alone—not even Naomi. I roll onto my side and look out onto the walkway. How many others have discovered the truth? Has Mother plucked them out one by one, removing the seeds of rebellion before they could sprout?

*Mother knows best.* I stop. Am I missing something? Could there be a reason she's not letting us leave? I grit my teeth. No! This is how she's controlled thousands of us for years. Mother has been with me all my life, filling my head with stories, stories she's made up, stories I've never had any reason to question—until now.

I find I'm smiling. Although I was wrong to think Rebekah felt the same way about me, we'll still be together. We'll stand alone for now and plan our return to the surface. Perhaps with time she will come around to think of me as I do of her. Then we could start a new life under the real sky.

# 27

'Five o'clock! Today is Sunday, the ninth day of May and one day closer to The New Dawn. Rise up. I want breakfast to be ready when I return.' Abraham announces the start of another pointless day, but at least he said something different. But it's the thought of meeting Rebekah to discuss our new plan that gets me out of bed. I look to Reuben. He grins and I grin back. I know something they don't, but I daren't say a word. Barnabas leers at me as I enter the living quarters, but I'm big enough now to take it—I smile back.

Outside, I glance up and am relieved to see it's blue; Mother doesn't suspect anything. I have to stop myself laughing. We're planning an uprising against her, but she doesn't have a clue. I bend to pick up the crate and turn to see Abraham return. Good. It looks like it will be a routine day. But Abraham stops; his face dashes my hopes of just another dull day. I can tell he has something to say, but seems reluctant to open his mouth.

I wait by the entrance. 'What is it, Abraham?'

He tries to smile. 'I've just had word from Mother. We're to report to The Square immediately after breakfast.'

I run my tongue around my dry mouth. 'Do you know why?'

He shakes his head. 'She didn't say. But I guess it can't be serious.' He glances to the dome. 'Just look at that sky. Have you ever seen anything quite so beautiful?'

I'm pleased to find Reuben by my side again as we walk to The Square. He speaks as if we've never had a disagreement. 'Do you remember the day when we stood on the roof?'

I smile. A real smile as I think back to our childish antic. 'Of course. How could—?'

'You said you'd touched it.'

The smile leaves my face. What is he getting at? 'Yes, I did.'

'But you couldn't have.'

'What? Of course I did. It felt—'

'Look.' Reuben raises his eyebrows towards the factory. 'You couldn't possibly have. It's too high.'

I follow his gaze. Caleb bumps into my back.

'Hey, keep moving.' Barnabas glares but I'm struggling to believe my eyes. Even if the whole team had stood beneath me on the roof, I still couldn't have reached the dome.

'But... I did. It felt rough, it scratched my fingers.' I look back to him. 'You saw the gap. You were going to have a go after me, so you must have seen it was close enough to touch.' Reuben shrugs. I glance back to the roof. 'Mother must have raised the roof to stop anyone else trying.' *Or lowered the factory.* Is there anything she can't do?

Barnabas turns to check our progress. Reuben's smiling face doesn't match his words. 'But wouldn't we have noticed?'

'Quiet, you two!' Barnabas announces our arrival. 'Get into line.'

I exchange one more look with Reuben. I think he believes me, but it doesn't really matter. I have more important things to worry about than the height of the dome.

We sit at our designated position and watch as the other teams arrive. As much as I try, I cannot stop my eyes seeking out Rebekah. I see her. I'm relieved she looks relaxed; if Rebekah is concerned about our plot being discovered, she shows no sign. She takes her seat without looking in my direction. I feel chastised. I should follow her example and be more disciplined.

The prefects enter and form a line between the benches and Mother's stage. The wall glows. I turn to the front as Mother makes her entrance. Even now, knowing that she's not being entirely truthful with us, I cannot help but hold my breath. I wait until she stops in the middle before I release the air from my lungs. She opens her mouth, but pauses as her bright eyes take in the benches. But her face gives nothing away.

Mother brings her hands to under her nose and rubs her palms together. She lets them drop and looks up. 'I was young once.' She smiles. My shoulders relax. She's going to tell us a story. She laughs. 'Yes, I know you might find that hard to believe, but I can remember the days when the urge to do my own thing and go my own way was strong. I can remember the days when I wanted,' her head tilts forward, 'to defy my elders because I thought I knew better.' My shoulders rise.

Mother raises her chin. Her eyes wander above our heads as she seems to think back to another time. But the focus returns and I feel the full force of her gaze. She utters two words. 'The book.' Again her eyes scan our faces—I hope my tight muscles don't show. She speaks quietly. 'I have given you every opportunity to reveal the location of this evil book, but no one has come forward.' She turns and walks towards Rebekah and the laboratory teams. 'Someone here knows.' Her voice rises. 'Someone here is hiding it. Someone here is willing to put all of our futures at risk.' She twists back to the front. 'And I will not stand for it!' We recoil as her words slam into the benches. But then she softens. 'And neither should you.' She sighs. 'You know that I love you.' I find myself nodding along with everyone in The Square. 'So you know that I would not do anything to hurt or cause you pain.' Again, we agree. 'But this book presents the biggest threat to our safety I have ever known. I have kept our presence here hidden from the enemy, I have defeated the agents they sent down amongst us, and I have prepared you all for our glorious New Dawn.' I see the words of Moses. Did he hear a similar speech?

Reuben nudges my leg. The prefects are moving, taking up positions at the end of each row. Mother steps forward. 'There will be no work today.' A murmur rises from the benches. 'But this is not a holiday. This is to be no picnic. No. We will stay here until I have that book.' I shiver. Beads of cold sweat prickle on my scalp. If Mother sees them run down my face she'll know. But I could give myself away if she were to see me wiping my brow. I tighten my scalp, hoping against hope to hold the product of my fear to my skin.

Mother clears her throat. 'This is the last chance for whoever is hiding the book to come forward. You have one minute.' My bowels turn to water. I clench; an accident would announce my guilt in a most unfortunate manner. I think back to such an incident in the nursery, but then Mother had nothing but kind words of comfort—just as long as I didn't let it happen again.

A cough echoes in the expectant air. Every mind bar two must be willing the guilty to stand and speak of their crime. But only two know that isn't about to happen. Or should I? Am I putting everyone at risk? Doubt floods through my thoughts, dowsing the rebellious fire in my stomach. Does Mother have her reasons? I sense my body tilt forward an inch. I feel my toes spread as the weight passes into my feet. I hear the words I will speak, '*Mother, it's me. I have the book*'. But something stops the irretrievable action. My feet relax and my full weight sits back on the bench.

'Time up. Have it your way.' I glance back to Mother.

'Jared. Bring the first one to me.' Jared has moved to stand halfway between Mother and the bench to my right. He nods to the prefect positioned at the end of Rebekah's row. He moves to the first worker. She looks around before rising. The prefect leads her to Jared. He takes her by the arm and guides her to Mother, their footsteps echo in the silence. Jared handles her roughly in front of Mother. To our horror, he kicks her in the back of the leg so she drops to her knees. A few gasp but most are too shocked to react. Mother says nothing. Jared steps back, appearing satisfied with his work.

Mother looms over the girl, looking tall and stern. 'Tell me, Mary. Do you have the book?'

'No... No, Mother. I don't know what it looks like.'

Mother maintains eye contact. 'Have you ever seen this book?'

'No, Mother. I would have come to you straightaway if I had.'

Mother stands back. 'Thank you, Mary.' She looks to Jared. 'Next.'

Mary climbs to her feet and walks quickly back to the safety of the bench. Jared meets the next worker, Bethany. She stands before Mother, and again, Jared forces her to kneel with his boot. Mother repeats the questions.

Rebekah is next. My chest heaves inside my overalls as I watch her calmly walk to the center. She kneels, but still Jared kicks her! My fists and jaw clench, but I can do nothing.

'Do you know who has the book, Rebekah?'

Her voice shakes. 'No, Mother.' I wonder if Rebekah is pretending to be nervous. I know when it comes to my turn, I won't have to fake my anxiety.

'Have you ever seen the book?'

'Never.' Mother watches Rebekah's face for what seems like minutes. I cannot breathe. Sweat trickles down my back. Mother steps back. 'Thank you, Rebekah.' She looks to Jared. 'Next.'

I look to the laboratory benches. I've already estimated it takes around forty seconds for each worker to be taken to Mother and questioned. That means almost two hours and fifteen minutes to complete just the lab teams. I am forty-eighth along the front of my row, so it will be at least another two hours and forty-five minutes before it's my turn. I groan inside. The whole process will take almost seven hours!

I recognize Levi from the production meeting as he approaches Mother. He repeats almost word for word Mary's first answers that pleased Mother.

Jude follows Levi, who's followed by Jacob, and then Jeremiah—all receive what now seems like a pointless gesture of the kick from Jared, all repeat the accepted answers. I hope Jared's foot is starting to hurt. I watch to see if he'll change foot, then I'll know he's suffering.

I look up to the blue dome—I wonder if it still looks quite so beautiful to Abraham. 'Eyes to the front!' I jump along with at least a dozen others. Luke now kneels before Mother. She looks up from his shaking body. 'Yes, I know this will take time, but I can do this all day if necessary.'

The procession continues until I no longer hear the interrogations. My eyes stay to the front, but I see green fields and my tree atop a low hill in the distance. I stroll through the grass towards my goal. This is why I have to stay silent; this is what I'm fighting for; this is what will make this all worthwhile. I rub my hand on my leg and imagine it's Rebekah's hand. We walk together, alone and free.

'Next row.' I check. The tall prefect has moved to the second bench of the lab workers. My stomach flutters. The tree. I have to go back to the field. If I think of my turn this early, I won't be able to walk.

We reach the tree. Rebekah is wearing the short, blue dress Naomi wore at our last meeting. I bend and interlock my fingers for Rebekah to place her foot. As I lift her to the lowest branch, her dress flutters in my face and I see a flash of her soft, inner thigh. I stop and check I'm not grinning. I'm safe. My tight face reveals nothing.

Rebekah sits on the branch and lets her long legs swing in the air. I jump, take her hand and join her. I'm wearing my undergarments and slide in close and brush my bare leg against hers. We look out on the field and let the clean air flow into our lungs. I hear her voice. '*I wish we could stay here forever, just the two of us.*' She leans over and I place my arm around her warm shoulders.

A cry from behind pulls me back to The Square. Several workers from our back bench jump up as a girl lies motionless on the floor. I turn to see how Mother will react. She calls to the prefect at the end of the row. 'Take Ruth away and splash some water on her face. I will deal with her later.' Mother's eyes widen. 'If anyone else feels like fainting... do not. You will not be spared this test.'

The next worker is brought forward. I'm surprised to see they are nearing the end of the laboratory benches. My waking *dream* has helped to pass the time, but more importantly, kept my mind from worrying about the ordeal to come. But I should prepare my answers. I repeat the replies everyone else has used in my head. If I can keep my face from revealing the truth, I will get through the interrogation.

Elijah, the first worker from our bench, is escorted to Mother and Jared repeats his part of the routine—with his left foot. I stifle a laugh; what will he do when they begin the farm benches?

My throat is dry. The clock's hands approach ten o'clock—the time we would get a cup of water at our workstations on a normal day. Others notice the time and begin to fidget. Mother rounds on them. 'Sit still! No one moves until I have finished.' Now I want to move. The dull ache in my back has turned into a hot knife twisting between my shoulder blades. I check Mother. Her attention is on the second worker from the factory. I tilt slowly forward to stretch the tight cables in my back and ease out the knife. It helps a little, but now my bones feel as if they're about to break through the skin and grind into the hard bench.

I try to imagine sitting on soft grass next to my tree with Rebekah resting her head against my neck. But the vision has gone—my burning muscles will no longer allow my mind to leave The Square. I look back to the clock. The big hand has barely crept past the hour. I let my eyes drift to the Metal Sun. But when I look at it now, I don't see the first sunrise on The New Dawn, I see a plughole. It no longer represents hope for me, it shows our future being flushed down the drain into the stench of The Trench below. Did Moses know when he made it? Was this an act of defiance?

The fourth member of our bench approaches Mother. I watch her face. What will she do when she doesn't find the culprit? She won't want to appear to be losing control, yet surely the failure will diminish her authority. Or does she have another plan? My pulse pounds in my ears. All of the workers are present, I could reveal the words of Moses. Tell everyone Mother had promised Moses and his generation that *they* would be the first to return. I could start the rebellion, here and now! I see myself refusing to kneel, turning on Jared and knocking him to the floor to the cheers of all those present. I raise my fist and call out, '*Arise, Workers, arise!*' With our superior numbers, we could easily overpower the dozen prefects. *We rebel together! We escape together!* I lead the factory teams to break down the doors and seize the hundreds of weapons that rightfully belong to us. We free the young, the weak and those deemed to be a threat to Mother from the levels below. We storm the perimeter, breaching the wall and streaming through before Mother can stop our march to freedom. Together we'd soon discover the way up.

Once back on the surface, our firepower and belief in our cause would destroy all who dare to stand in our way. Then, we could bury The Ark, trapping Mother and the prefects for good. The New Dawn would be truly new, a real beginning, a new day, a break from the years of rotting in this stinking hole that has become a prison.

My stomach rumbles. I look to the clock. Reuben stands. It's his turn already! And then it's me. What should I do? I've sat for all this time and now I don't know what to do. I look to Rebekah. But her eyes give me no sign. Reuben kneels before Mother but I don't hear his voice. Fresh droplets of sweat ooze from my scalp. Reuben stands. He turns and walks back to our bench. He looks pale, and he's innocent! How difficult will it be for me?

A prefect steps in front and clicks his fingers, gesturing for me to join him. My legs shake but I cannot delay. I somehow get to my feet and force my stiff legs to move. *Breathe!* I have to stay calm. Jared turns to me and grins. I won't let him win. I will show him. My back straightens as I approach Mother. She seems to grow as I draw near. Jared pushes out his hand into my chest bone. 'That's close enough.' I stop. Jared steps to the side as I kneel. The kick comes as predicted. Jared grunts. Good. His foot is hurting. I look up to Mother. Her bright eyes meet mine. I look into her fair face—how could I ever think of going against her will?

She pauses; I feel her mind reach into mine. 'Noah. Do you have the book?'

I breathe in, then out and speak clearly. 'No, Mother, I do not have the book.' *Stay strong.*

Still her eyes hold mine. 'Have you ever seen this book, Noah?'

My insides churn like the water boiling in a pot. 'No, Mother.' *Stay strong.* 'I would have come to you straightaway if I had seen it.'

Mother steps back. 'Thank you, Noah.' She looks to Jared. 'Next.' *I have passed the test! She looked into my mind and couldn't see the truth.* I keep the smile from my lips as I push back my knees to stand. As I turn, Jared glares. He's disappointed. I have faced Mother, answered her questions and passed. I walk tall back to the benches and pass Barnabas as he is summoned. I sit, suddenly the hard surface of the bench feels comfortable. Rebekah will be proud. I force my back to stay straight when all I want to do is collapse with relief and exhaustion.

Barnabas, Abraham and Amos return from their ordeals. All I have to do is see through the next three hours and forty-eight minutes, and I'll be safe.

'Yes... yes, I have seen it!' The whole square freezes. Tabitha from Lydia's team sobs into her hands, her pain and guilt spilling through her fingers. 'I'm so sorry, I couldn't help it.' Barnabas stiffens. I see his clenched fists. He shifts forward. I'm certain he's about to rush forward and beat Tabitha to the ground. Abraham catches my eye and we both grab his shoulders. He scowls at me, but we hold firm for his own good. Abraham hisses, 'No, let Mother deal with her.'

The gasps are brought to an end by Mother's raised hand. She speaks slowly, but her anger is obvious. 'I have had my doubts about you, Tabitha.' Her body quivers as she steps closer. 'But I have always given you the benefit of my doubt.' Tabitha tries to scramble away but Jared stands firm, preventing her escape. Mother bends over her crumpled body. 'And this is how you repay me?' Her voice booms. 'Look at me when I am speaking to you!' The bench vibrates, sending shivers through our backs.

Tabitha's hands remain clamped to her face. 'I can't.'

'You will look at me, or I will take off your hands.' Tabitha pushes herself up from the floor. Her hands fall from her face as if the arms of her overalls are empty. But Mother turns her back. 'No. I cannot look at you now. I am very, very disappointed.' Jared is almost jumping for joy, rubbing his hands together. Mother lets out a long sigh. 'Take her away, please. I will deal with her later.'

I watch, dumbstruck, as Jared grabs Tabitha's overalls and yanks her to her feet. Some boo and hiss as she is dragged from The Square, but most of us stay silent, stunned by her confession, no one more than I. My insides turn to ice. *Did Tabitha give the diary to Rebekah?* What can stop Mother getting that information from her? And then Rebekah will have no choice but to tell her it is in my care.

Mother turns and looks to the prefect at the end of our row. 'Next.' A few groans escape from the younger workers. Her eyebrows raise. 'Oh, do not think this finishes here. It takes more than one person to keep something this big a secret from me.'

I steel myself for what is going to be a hard afternoon. Are there more? Again, I seek Rebekah for guidance, but again her face remains a mask of indifference. As tired as I feel, my chest swells as I watch her sitting calm amongst the shocked and weakening workers of her team.

The last of our row returns. Halfway through the factory teams; halfway through the entire Workers Level. A few take the opportunity to shift their position, trying to move from one aching bone to another. Mother bellows. 'Sit still!' A worker behind me sobs. Mother twists towards them. 'Be quiet. This is for your own good. Do you think the enemy will take any notice of your sniveling once we return?' She softens. 'Trust me. I will do everything in my power to ensure you all get what you deserve.' She turns back to the prefect. 'Next.'

I sigh as I let my aching back rest against the chair. The faces around the table try hard to disguise the pain we're all feeling. I don't know how I managed to get through the afternoon's trial, but I made it—we all did. Naomi had stood tall and answered her questions without difficulty. She'd risked a glance in my direction as she returned to her seat and I'd returned a quick smile. I'd wondered if she could be trusted to join our rebellion, but now I'm not so sure. Abraham had seen our exchange and must know she's the one I see at The Meeting Place. A look like that could end in disaster for our cause.

Mother finished questioning every worker on our level but hadn't found the others she suspected of handling the book. She'd left The Square promising more thorough and *intrusive* searches. But I doubt if the new measures will be needed. How long before the prefects come for me? Tabitha had looked broken and in no state to resist the harsher questioning that must await behind the closed doors of Re-Education.

Abraham returns from his evening report—I can't think what he could have to say, seeing as we all spent the day together. He pulls his chair to the table as Amos retrieves his bowl we've kept warm for him. He looks up and smiles. 'Thank you.' We let him take a few mouthfuls before we cannot contain our questions any longer.

Barnabas rightly asks first. 'So, what news of the traitor, Tabitha?'

Abraham places his spoon on the table. He sighs. 'Who would have thought it, eh! All this time, the danger lay next door on Lydia's team.' He pushes his half-eaten supper away. 'Lydia has also been taken in for questioning.'

Barnabas nods. 'And quite right too.'

Abraham can't prevent a grimace. 'Yes, I guess it's only fair to give Lydia a chance to clear her name.'

'But what about Tabitha?' I hear my voice before I realize I'd made the decision to speak.

'Mother has given her time to think about her actions.' Abraham leans back. 'She'll be...' he glances to Barnabas, 'dealt with tomorrow.'

Reuben rubs his hands through his hair. 'But I thought Mother had got rid of all the agents, didn't she say—'

Abraham pushes his chair back and stands. 'Not now, Reuben. Let's wait until Mother has had a chance to speak with her properly.' He hovers by the table. He looks exhausted and slurs his words. 'Noah, could I have a word. The rest of you, please go about your evening duties.'

*Is this it?* I nod as if it means nothing. He motions for me to join him outside. I rise, but the others are too engrossed in their routine to pay much notice.

I find Abraham a few paces from the entrance. He looks up. 'Sorry to have to bring this up now after such a challenging day.' He rubs the back of his neck and speaks to the floor. 'Mother says you're to report to The Meeting Place tomorrow evening.' He turns and catches my eye. 'For your third visit.'

# 28

It's Monday. It's the tenth day of May. Would it be too much to hope for a normal day? This is my one thousandth, eight hundredth and thirty-second day on this level, and all but a handful have been exactly the same. But at least I have tonight's meeting with Rebekah to keep me going. I had to hold back my sigh of relief when I found the blank paper tucked in the crate. But I don't know whether she believes it's safe to meet, or if Tabitha's confession has triggered panic and we have no choice but to act now.

The clatter of the trolley and the imminent arrival of Barnabas draws my attention back to my workstation. My hands have completed another useless unit. It's been difficult trying to keep my hands moving this morning. All I wanted was an easy day at the factory, a quiet evening with a familiar story from Mother, before I could once more escape for a few precious moments with Rebekah.

But now I have the *honor* of becoming a third-timer. Ever since I saw my friends come back from their telling third visit, I've wanted to find out what mystery surrounds this milestone event. But now I have a greater calling. This evening's visit to The Meeting Place will be an unwanted distraction, and yet another duty I will have to fulfil without letting on my heart is no longer with the cause.

I stifle a yawn. Last night had been difficult. I dared not remove the diary from its hiding place, but it kept me awake, even with my headset attached. I slept deep and cannot recall any detail of Mother's story.

'I hear it's your third time tonight, Noah.' I look up to see Barnabas's stern face as he whispers, but I notice Reuben's smirk out of the corner of my eye.

'Yes. It is.' I set my face into its most sincere look.

'Just do your duty.' Barnabas collects my morning's work and stacks the total of my quota on his trolley. He speaks louder for the rest of the team to hear. 'Don't let Mother down. She has enough to think about at the moment with all this nonsense about that book.' His eyes fix on mine.

I move to deflect his suspicion. 'I will do my duty, and if I hear any more news about the book, I will go straight to the prefects.'

Barnabas studies my face. 'Good. Let's hope stepping up the rate of inspections will help find it soon.' He turns and moves on to Reuben, leaving me alone to think. What should I do with the diary? I cannot throw it on the stove. It would be a great loss to destroy the words of Moses, but it has value beyond the fact it belonged to him. If everyone reads it, they will know the truth about Mother. There can be no other explanation. She's either lying, or she's scared. Neither will help us get out of this dark place.

I look up to the poster. How did Moses feel when it first dawned on him that he wouldn't be leaving The Ark? What did that do to his mind when he realized all his efforts had been a waste of time? Did he rebel? There are only a few pages after the entry I had read. Did something happen to him? Or is there yet another diary?

My gasps bounce back from the hard, white tiles. The water seems colder today. But I have to get clean. The instructions from Mother made it very clear there is to be no grime on my body—I even have to scrub under my nails and wash parts we're not normally allowed to touch. The door rattles as someone hammers on the outside. 'Noah! You have two minutes. The prefect will be here in ten.' There he is. Good old Barnabas. I will enjoy telling him the truth, to see those hard-set lines of his absolute faith in the system fall from his face.

'Nearly done.' I pick up my overalls and slap them against the wall. I stop. It will be my third time, yet I've barely given it a thought all day. But now it's about to happen, I feel a knot in my stomach. I'm at a loss to know what is expected of me tonight. The first two visits have revealed nothing of the nature of the third, let alone its importance.

I get as dry as I can with the threadbare towel and turn to the door. My hand rests on the latch. I straighten my spine, pull back my rounded shoulders, lift the latch, and leave a trail of wet footprints on my way through to the living quarters.

Reuben steps forward. 'Here, I'll put them on the rack.' He takes my overalls, his face concealing nothing of his excitement. But if he thinks I'll tell him the secret of the third time tomorrow, he's mistaken.

I smile. 'Thanks.'

'He can do that himself.' Barnabas intervenes and pushes the overalls back into my arms. He turns. 'Abraham will be back soon. We have a lecture to attend so make sure the rest of you are ready.' Reuben raises his eyebrows behind Barnabas—he really should try harder to control his expressions. Until then, it would be a risk to confide in Reuben and bring him into our group. *Focus!* I must concentrate on tonight. I have to be prepared for the test Mother has set. To fail her now could result in a loss of faith in me and jeopardize Rebekah's plan.

I take a step and hold my hands out to the stove, welcoming the warmth seeping into the ends of my tingling fingers.

'Five minutes.' How does Barnabas do it? 'Get dressed. Don't make the prefect wait for you again.' How does he fulfil his duties and still manage to keep such a close eye on the whole team?

I swallow. 'Thank you, Barnabas.' My overalls are still damp, and scratch as I pull them over my clean skin. But I take some comfort from my warm boots that someone had kindly placed by the stove.

'Abraham's back.' Caleb almost skips through the entrance. He, like Barnabas, seems to thrive on the extra pressure we're now under. But Amos looks ready to break.

'Okay, listen up everyone.' Abraham bursts into the room, still breathless from his walk. 'Tonight's lecture will be held in The Square.'

Caleb can't contain his excitement. 'What's it about?'

Abraham looks amused. He smiles. 'You're lucky, we're in for a treat. The farm workers will show us how they grow cabbage without sunlight. That will be followed by a presentation from the team preparing the seeds for planting on the real farm once we surface.' I watch their faces. They're genuinely looking forward to the lecture, optimistic about the future, and have full faith in Mother to find the last of those who could yet sabotage our goal. I clench my teeth to stop my lips from blurting out the dreadful truth that Moses went through the exact same routine—and what happened to him? And the others?

'Noah!'

'Pardon?' I turn to Abraham and try to replay his words that must have been meant for me.

'I said, Amos will takes notes about the lecture for you.'

Amos is not the quickest writer, so perhaps it will be a short presentation. I turn to Amos and raise a half-smile. 'Thank you. I will look forward to hearing all about it.' His face lights up, looking pleased to have been given an important job by Abraham.

Abraham gestures for me to join him at the entrance. 'Come on. I'll sign for you outside.' My stomach flutters. *This is it!* The others stiffen as I walk past. Reuben nods a 'good luck' out of the sight of Barnabas.

The dome is an evening dark blue. Lights from the other dormitory windows paint the walkway with streaks of yellow, but it's not as beautiful as when lit by only the glimmering stoves at night. I flinch. Abraham has placed his arm around my shoulders. 'Don't look so worried.' I was unaware that I did. 'You'll be fine.' The boots of the prefect approach. I turn to the corner and breathe out as I see it's not Jared escorting me this evening.

The prefect halts. His flat tone belittles the occasion. 'Ready?'

'He is.' Abraham lifts his arm from my shoulders and lets it drop to his side.

The prefect thrusts the clipboard towards Abraham. 'Good. Sign for Noah and then take your team to The Square for the lecture.' I note the absence of a *please* or *thank you.* The prefect checks the signature with his copy and looks up to me. 'This way.' He twists on his heels and marches off, not waiting to see if I follow.

Abraham pats me on the back. 'Make Mother proud.' I want to say thanks, but he's already turned away and heading inside. The next time he sees me, I will be a third-timer.

The walkways are already busy with the teams making their way to the lecture. I watch with regret the eager faces of the younger workers. Part of me wishes I could be one of them, ignorant and happy to trust Mother. Some of the older ones catch my eye—they must know what awaits me.

'Wait here.' I just stop before I collide into the back of the prefect. We've arrived at The Meeting Place. He enters, leaving me standing by the door like a new arrival. I check my nails and see that I'm shaking. The door opens. I straighten as the prefect steps outside. He doesn't look at me as he speaks. 'You may enter.' He walks off, calling over his shoulder. 'The desk clerk will tell you what to do.' I watch the workers part as he strides down the walkway.

I do as I'm told and push the door open. I clench and then stretch my fingers to stop them trembling, but fail. The clerk looks up from his paperwork. 'Washed?'

'Yes.' My voices shakes. I clear my throat and speak louder. 'Yes.'

'*All* over.'

'Yes.'

'Under your nails?' He glances at my hands.

'Yes.'

He leans over his desk. 'Down there.'

My face reddens. 'Yes.'

'Good.' He picks up his pencil and ticks the last box on his sheet. 'Go in. She's waiting for you.'

# 29

I have the look. I can feel it on my face as I wear the third-timer's mask. If the taste of my birthday cake lit a spark deep in my brain, tonight stoked a furnace that I know will never go out. I walk behind the prefect along the deserted walkway, but can feel or hear no steps. Something was taken from me in that room. Something I'd both wanted to give, but also keep at the same time. I can still see Naomi's face. I can still smell her body, feel her, and hear her. I've never seen a girl with a painted face before tonight, or wearing such bright colors. I felt scruffy and unworthy in my overalls, but then the earpieces told us to take off our clothes and get onto the large bed.

At first I thought I'd misheard the instruction—until Naomi removed her dress and stood naked, naked and embarrassed as her small hands failed to cover all she wanted to keep hidden from my eyes. But I saw. My mouth had dropped open as I'd gaped at her forbidden curves my fingers longed to explore, and the shadows whose secrets I was about to discover. And even though I knew it caused her discomfort, I couldn't take my eyes from her. Three times the earpiece blasted in my head before I could move my arms to undress.

I shudder as we near the dormitory. I couldn't tell what Naomi was feeling when we exchanged a last look before the prefects entered—but I guess she's wearing the same face as me now.

The prefect stops at the entrance. I glance back to the direction of Naomi's dormitory block. I dearly hope I didn't hurt her. At first, I thought she was in pain, but after a minute or two I couldn't be sure. But later, I'm ashamed to admit, it didn't matter to me; I would have found it difficult to stop, even if instructed by the prefect.

I want to see her again. I want to tell her I'm sorry for looking at her in the way I did; sorry for what happened next; sorry for losing control, but the voice told me I had to. I was just doing my duty and will happily do so again. But I have to see her, to somehow put into words what I'd felt. I want to say something to make up for my stunned silence when the prefects had entered.

Abraham meets us at the door and completes the paperwork. He waits for the prefect to leave. He checks we're out of earshot. 'Are you okay?'

I look away. 'I... think so.'

He rests his hand on my shoulder and squeezes. 'Good. You've done what was asked of you.'

'But what was the purpose of—?'

He shakes his head. 'Not now, we'll speak later. Times are tough at the moment, and many things may seem unfair, but Mother has a plan and we all have to play our part.' He turns, lets his arm slip around my back and guides me through the entrance. 'Come and get something to eat. The others are back from the lecture.'

The chatter around the supper table dies as we enter, even Barnabas looks briefly concerned. He turns to Amos. 'Don't just sit there, lad, get Noah's bowl.' Amos jumps but watches me closely. I take my place as he returns with my supper.

'Here you go. We've kept it warm.'

'Thanks.' I look down to the dried-out, green paste under my nose.

Abraham clears his throat. 'Well come on, who's going to tell Noah about the lecture?' Amos stands. I chew as he reads with pride from his clipboard. I try to show interest in his account, nodding in time with the others, but I feel sorry for them. I sense the anticipation around the table as

Amos describes how the collaboration of laboratory and farm workers resulted in new methods for cultivation of the soil above. I see them lick their lips at the part when Amos talks of what I know to be yet another one of Mother's empty promises. She says the proposed plan for farming will mean we will be eating meat once a week by the end of the first year. I look back to my bowl—this is what we'll be still be eating on the tenth day of May this time next year.

'Thank you, Amos. Good work.' Abraham stands and holds out his hand for the clipboard. 'I'm sure Noah found that useful.' He removes the paper, walks to the stove and drops it onto the fire.

I swallow. 'Yes. Thank you, Amos. That was very informative. I'm sure when we—'

'INSPECTION!' The lights flare. I turn and squint at the entrance. Jared and two other prefects stand rigid in their sharp black uniforms. My stomach drops through the floor. This is it—I am done for. Tabitha has betrayed Rebekah, and, Rebekah must have in turn betrayed me. The diary will be found in my bunk and I have no defense, and no reason to live.

Abraham steps forward. 'I must protest. We had an inspection only—'

'Silence! You heard Mother.' They march to the table. 'The book must be found.' Jared comes to a halt behind me. Surely he'll see my shoulders shaking.

Abraham stands his ground. 'But you didn't find it here before, what do you—'

'Forget it, Abe.' Barnabas rises and tugs at his arm. 'The prefects are right. They're only acting in our best interest.' Abraham's body slumps as his defiance wilts. He sits heavily but doesn't take his eyes from Jared.

'Thank you, Barnabas.' *Jared addresses him by name!* But his harsh tone returns as he speaks to the rest of us like infants. 'Stay here. Nobody moves. Nobody speaks.' I should confess now and prevent the carnage they will inflict on our room, but I cannot bring myself to do so. It takes all my effort to sit straight. I will be sent straight to The Trench for this. I have committed an act of treason and, once the diary is destroyed, I will have no evidence to lay bare Mother's lie. My protests will be dismissed as the words of a desperate agent, or the rants of an untrustworthy worker, mad and weak with exhaustion. It won't just be Enoch that will be the subject of Reuben's antics the next time they're treated to a mug of Mother's special recipe.

We sit still as instructed, exchanging glances and wincing as we listen to bed rolls being torn from bunks, and worse, books being slung at the walls. Tears brim in Caleb's eyes. Poor Caleb. His book cannot survive another inspection from Jared and his team. I wait for the moment. The moment silence will signal the book has been found in my bunk.

I tremble inside my overalls at the thought of my fate. I gag at the reek from the plugholes from up here. What must it be like in the bowels of The Ark? I catch Barnabas looking at me. He knows. I can tell from that look.

The crashing stops—they have found the book. My eyes dart around the faces of my team. The next time I see them, they will be full of disdain as I confess my crime before my peers in The Square. I could try to argue my reason, but it will be futile.

I can stand it no more. I shuffle in my seat, ready to stand and save Jared the pleasure of revealing my shame.

'All clear.' My mouth drops open as the prefects return. *How can they have missed it?* Has Tabitha stayed silent? That would mean Rebekah is still free. The taller prefect laughs. 'Now get in there and clear up the mess.' I take the opportunity to breathe out as the chairs scrape across the floor.

'No wait.' Jared's eyebrow raises. He must have seen my relief. 'All of you,' he waves his arm, 'stand over there by that wall.' Abraham's mouth opens, but he closes it with a look from Barnabas. Jared explodes. 'TODAY!' We all jump up. 'Get over by that wall and no one move a muscle.' We stand and form a line in order of seniority at the wall.

Jared nods to his colleagues. They grin, make their way to the entrance and take a position, facing out to the walkway. No one dares move. Jared stands at the head of the line with his hands tucked behind his back. He walks slowly past Abraham, then Barnabas, his shiny boots squeak as he rolls from heel to toe. He stops opposite me, seeming to take pleasure in delaying his next move. *Dear Moses. What now?* He turns and fixes his cold eyes on mine. His lip curls up on one side. 'Take off your overalls.'

'What?' I hear the others draw breath.

Abraham steps out of line. 'But he's just got back from... from his duty, he can't have anything hidden—'

'I SAID...' Jared doesn't take his eyes from me. He leans closer. 'Take off your overalls.' I turn to Abraham for help, but he's moved back into line. Jared steps back and smiles. 'This is part of our more rigorous inspection regime. Mother did warn you this would happen.' He looks across the line. 'From now on, there'll be random body searches.'

There's no point in protesting. I do as I'm told, my numb fingers struggling with the buttons. I shiver as I pull the overalls from my shoulders and let drop them to the floor. Jared's voice remains flat. 'Step forward.' I tread out of the crumpled clothes. 'Now your boots.' Amos sniffles. Reuben is breathing through clenched teeth, but no one speaks. I bend to undo my laces and stumble forward as I pull my left boot free. Jared laughs. I hop on the spot, trying to regain my balance. This is wrong, but I have to take it. I manage to remove the other boot and straighten as much as my tired body will allow—it's the last way I can show my defiance.

Jared's eyes move slowly up from my toes and come to rest on my face, sparing no effort to hide his disgust of my puny, stooped body. He steps up and tugs at my undergarment. 'And the rest.'

Now Abraham acts. 'No! Don't do it, Noah. This isn't right.' He glares at Jared. 'You don't have the authority.' Jared turns to face him, Abraham stammers on. 'Mother would never allow this, this is against all the rules. She... she...' His voice wavers under the prefect's glare.

Jared sighs. 'Have you finished?' Abraham has no answer. Jared snaps. 'I have every authority! Now get back in line with the others.' Barnabas reaches forward and pulls Abraham back to the wall. Jared turns back to me. 'What are you waiting for? Take them off.'

I try one more plea. 'But Mother says we shouldn't—'

'Take them off!' I pause. I want to scream what I know in his face, tell him we're stuck down here for good, and whatever he can do to me means nothing. But I have no choice. If I rebel now, all will be lost. I take a deep breath—at least I'm still clean from this evening's shower. Jared grins as I remove my undergarment. I stand naked for a second time this evening; a fact not lost on him. He sneers. 'You should be used to this by now.' Jared looks over his shoulder, then back to me, grinning. 'My colleagues tell me you cried this evening after doing your *duty*.' My insides clench, along with my fists. The others fidget. I flinch as Jared yells at the line, 'Stand still, or you're all next!' He comes closer. 'We've never seen anyone cry before.' His scorn blows right into my face. 'Well, not one of the boys.' The prefects by the door laugh.

I have nothing left of my dignity, even Mother with her mysterious ways never treated us like this. Humiliated in front of my team, with nothing left to hide behind, I stand exposed and vulnerable. But I must fight back. I think of Rebekah. She has stood alone since Isaac and Rachel left. I mustn't lose control and give Jared a reason to remove me from the team.

But the torture hasn't finished. Jared's left eyebrow rises and lifts the corner of his mouth. 'Mother lets us prefects choose our *friend* for The Meeting Place.' He kicks my undergarments across the room as he steps closer. 'And guess who'll be getting her birthday cake soon?' *No!* I tighten every muscle in my face, trying not to let my dismay surface. But I see Jared in the room with Rebekah, and the giant bed. She would have no choice but to perform her duty—her knee couldn't come to her rescue against a prefect. I cannot let that happen.

Jared turns to Abraham, still smirking. 'Okay. Inspection over, you've passed.' His sniggers. 'Well done. You're a credit to Mother. Fifteen minutes to lights out so you'd better clean up that mess in there.' He twists smartly on his heels towards his colleagues. 'I think it must be almost time for supper.' But Jared has one more message for Abraham. He stops by the entrance and delivers his threat through clenched teeth. 'And if you think I'm being unfair to your team, just try whining to Mother again. Then you'll discover the real meaning of unfair.'

The mocking laughter and clicking of boots echo down the walkway as I stoop and pull on my underclothes. Reuben picks up my overalls as Caleb gathers my boots. No one speaks. Jared's threat still hangs in the room. I climb back into my overalls, for once grateful for their protection. Amos places a chair beside the stove. 'Here, Noah. Have a seat.' I sit. Caleb kneels, pulls on my boots and takes his time to tie the laces. I want to weep but I have to hold firm. My face begins to cool but I cannot control the shivers spreading through my body.

Barnabas walks to the entrance and peers outside. 'They've gone.'

Abraham puts his hand on my shoulder and speaks so softly I barely hear his words. 'You didn't deserve that.' He looks to the others. 'Listen. Not a word of this to anyone. We don't speak of this outside of this room, in fact, let's not speak of this ever again.'

I want to thank them for their kindness, but I know I will not find my voice. The others pull up their chairs around me. Abraham's chest heaves. 'I guess we have no choice but to put up with this until we surface.' But I know different. I should tell them now, but I can't trust anyone yet not to go straight to Mother, especially Barnabas. Abraham stands. 'So let's keep our heads down, work hard and accept the stricter measures the prefects—'

Reuben jumps up. 'That wasn't *stricter* measures! That was cruel, and it was personal. Jared has something against Noah,' he glances towards me, 'yet you've done nothing to upset him.'

'Or has he?' Barnabas's calm voice gets everyone's attention. He looks to me. 'Why do you think Jared has it in for you?' All faces turn my way. But what can I say? Can it be just because of the way I looked at Rebekah?

'I don't know.'

'Come on. There *must* be a reason.' Barnabas isn't going to let me off lightly. 'Otherwise we're accusing a prefect *appointed by Mother,* of being cruel for no reason.'

I try to stand my ground. 'I said, I don't know. If I knew I'd—'

'So who's getting their birthday cake any day soon?' My blood stops. Barnabas's eyes probe my face. 'Is *she* the reason?' I have no choice.

'I... he...' it spills out, 'Jared saw me looking at a girl.'

Barnabas hasn't moved. 'Who?'

'I, she's from—' My mouth snaps shut. I can't tell them. I must not reveal her name.

Abraham places his hand on my shoulder. 'You don't have to tell us.' He turns to the Barnabas. 'Give him a break. You know what it's like once... well you know.' Now my mouth opens. So I'm not alone in having these thoughts? Abraham stands. 'Come on. The lights go out soon and we have to tidy the mess next door, and more work to do tomorrow.' He sighs as he looks through to the sleeping quarters. 'We'll talk another time.'

The mess next door. The diary! I must go in and see for myself, but I have to hold back from rushing in, not wishing to give Barnabas ideas on why I should appear so keen.

I enter last. Our bed rolls lie in a heap in the center. Before I can look for the books, Barnabas calls us one at a time to pick up our rolls and place them on our bunks. Once cleared, Abraham stoops to recover the books from the pile by the wall. I count six. That's a good sign. Caleb fidgets as he waits to see if his damaged book survived the search. But his hope is misplaced. Abraham rescues *Robinson Crusoe* from the tangled mess. He shakes his head. 'I'm so sorry, Caleb. It's going to need another repair.' Caleb takes the book and hugs it to his chest. His face screws up as he tries to hold back the tears. He walks to his bunk. I try to catch his eye to give him my support, but he stares straight ahead and gets silently into his bed.

I climb into my bunk. What happened to the diary? My roll had been thrown to the floor like the rest, exposing the slats beneath, so it would have been impossible not to find the book. I have to speak to Rebekah. The only explanation is Jared has taken it. But for what purpose? He could easily have marched me straight to Mother and taken all the praise, so why keep it to himself?

I look out onto the lights on the walkway as they go out. Jared must have his own plan for me. If he does, I don't have much time. I cannot risk losing everything. We have to act soon. We have to find the way up to see what it's like outside—then perhaps we could convince Mother it's safe, but if not her, the other workers.

I roll onto my side. The weapons. If I can discover where they're kept, Rebekah and I could learn how to fire them. Then Mother would have to listen. If our enemy is outside already, we'd have the means to fight them. Or, if necessary, we could force Mother and the prefects to let those who want to go, leave The Ark. But not before I've made Jared suffer for his actions tonight. I want to see him grovel, see him humiliated in front of everyone, stripped of his uniform and sent to The Trench.

But first, I need to talk to Lydia about the weapons without raising suspicion. But how? Perhaps Rebekah will know.

For the third time in my life, I creep out of bed after dark. But I mustn't become complacent. I wait by the entrance and listen. All quiet, all clear. I venture into the gloom and slide along the wall. Rebekah is already waiting. She takes my hand and leads me down the side alley to the outer walkway.

She turns. I can just see the creases in her forehead as she whispers, 'We don't have long. I passed a patrol on the way, they'll be here soon to search the dorms in this sector. You must—'

I take her hand. 'But they already searched ours this evening, and—' Her fingers tighten. I clear my throat. 'I'm afraid it's gone.'

Her eyes widen. 'What do you mean, gone? Where?'

My head drops. I've failed her. 'The thing is, I don't know. When the search was over, it wasn't there. A prefect must have taken it.'

'Prefect? Who?'

'It could only have been Jared.'

Rebekah's shoulders sag. She sighs. 'Him.' The creases return. 'What's he up to?'

I see the smirk on Jared's face. 'He's got it in for me, he...' I look back to Rebekah. 'Has he searched your dorm?'

She shakes her head slowly. 'No, not yet, but he's always looking at me,' she shudders, 'and I don't like what's behind those eyes.' She glances over my shoulder. 'You must go back, I'll let you know when to meet again.'

But it's not enough. I want to stay with her longer. I try to buy a little time. 'I meant to ask you last time. How do you get the note into our crate?'

She answers while scanning the alleys. 'I go out most nights. The delivery is made an hour before everyone else wakes.'

'But I thought you said it wasn't safe to be out.'

She looks me in the eye. 'Well not for you. I'm used to it,' she sees my face drop, 'but you're getting better, you'll be ready soon to go out on your own.' She turns to leave.

I grasp her wrist. 'No, wait. I've got an idea.'

She looks down to my hand; I let go. 'Go on, but make it quick.'

'I'm going to find out where the weapons are stored. I'll find a way to speak to Lydia.' She looks confused. I continue. 'I'm sure I can do it in a way that won't make her suspicious. Then if we need to, we can take control.'

She speaks slowly. 'Oh, okay. I suppose that could be useful.' She pulls me closer; I feel her warm breath on my lips. 'But be careful. Don't give her any reason to suspect you.'

'Don't worry. I won't.' But she's already slipped away, leaving me alone in the dark.

# 30

'Five o'clock. Everyone up. It's Tuesday on the eleventh day of May. There's a stove to light, floors to clean, breakfast to be made, and targets to be met. I want to see breakfast on the table when I get back.' My eyes sting. I blink, bleary-eyed in the light. Abraham strides out of the sleeping quarters. How does he keep going?

I have no memory of the night. I didn't have a dream such as Rebekah spoke of. I bring my hand to my head and find I'm wearing the headset, but I have no memory of attaching it when I returned. But it couldn't have worked.

I clamber from my bunk. Today will be a long day if Rebekah believes it's not safe to meet. I pass Reuben. He goes to speak, but I pretend to be preoccupied with what's outside.

I lift the crate as Abraham returns from his morning report. But he wouldn't have dared mention the nature of last night's inspection. Abraham looks up. 'Grey again.' I hadn't noticed, but it's no surprise. His hand goes to my shoulder. 'Come on, I have some—'

'What was last night about?' I had no idea I was about to ask. He steps back. I can see he's preoccupied with Jared. I try again. 'No, not the inspection, my... you know, my third visit.'

His eyes dart to the entrance. 'Not now.'

'But—?'

'Noah!' Barnabas has noticed the delay. 'We need the crate in here, now!'

Abraham calls through. 'He's coming.' Then leans over. 'We'll talk later, I'll find an excuse.'

'Any news on the search?' Barnabas looks up from the table as we enter.

'Everyone sit. Breakfast can wait. I have something to report.' I place the crate by the stove.

We take our places. Abraham remains standing and clears his throat. 'Mother questioned Tabitha yesterday evening.' I glance at Reuben; we both know questioned is probably too lenient a word.

'Good. I hope she got what she deserved.' I join in the nods of agreement with Barnabas, perhaps a little too late, but I don't think anyone notices.

Abraham raises his hand. 'All in good time, Barnabas. But Mother says she found something,' his voice falters, 'something she hadn't expected.' Amos groans. Abraham sits down and sighs. 'I'm afraid it's not good news.' He pulls his chair forward and rests his hands on the table. His hands clench and unclench as if he's trying to work up the courage to speak. He looks up. 'It turns out that Tabitha is a new kind of agent.' Amos cries out.

'What?' Reuben jumps to his feet. 'But I thought she'd got rid of them all.'

Barnabas slaps the table. 'Get a grip. All of you! Have faith in Mother. Let Abraham finish the report.'

Abraham motions Reuben to sit. 'Thank you. Barnabas is right, have faith in Mother. Yes, it's a new threat, but Mother says she can deal with it, but...' he looks around the table, 'it will mean even tougher measures.' I force my back to stay straight. 'Mother cannot allow this to spread. It has to be stopped before it can get worse. If more of these new agents appear she'll have to resort to the emergency measures.'

That's new. I ask before anyone else can call their open mouths into action. 'What emergency measures?'

Abraham's head drops. 'A total shutdown.' He waits for us to take in the meaning of the words. 'Then, we all have to go below and—'

Amos cannot hold his tongue. 'But that will delay the day we—'

'If we don't,' Abraham cuts him short, 'it won't be a delay, it will be the end.' Again he has to clear his throat. 'There'll be no going up, we'll be trapped down here for good.' We sit in silence. I don't know what to think. Is this true? Is Tabitha a new threat?

Barnabas is the first to speak. 'So what happens if we go below?'

Abraham takes a deep breath and blows out. 'Mother called it a purge.' I look to Reuben, but he's not laughing at the sound of this new word.

Barnabas shakes his head. 'And what is this purge?'

Abraham's lips tighten. He swallows. 'It means she'll remove anyone she suspects of being an agent, or even has doubts about her methods.' My blood stops. He continues in a whisper. 'We stay below until she's satisfied we're completely free of this new threat and everyone is committed to the cause.'

'And,' Barnabas clears his throat, 'how does she do that?'

Abraham keeps his head bowed. 'She has her ways to test our resolve.'

I glance to Barnabas; he doesn't have anything more to say. For a second, I see a flicker of doubt pass across his face.

Abraham pushes back his chair and stands. 'Mother doesn't want to have to do that. She's asked us all to keep our eyes and ears open and report any suspicious behavior immediately to the prefects.' He claps his hands together. 'Right! Let's get breakfast. At least we know we're all in the clear. So as long as we keep our heads down and get on with our work, we'll be fine. If we do have to shut down, I can be sure everyone on this team will survive this purge.' But I'm not so confident.

The buzz on the walkways of the last few days was absent this morning. We made our way to our places of work in silence, each deep in thought or perhaps keeping mouths shut, not trusting what might spill out. Faces were fixed ahead, no eye contact made, marching in step as we streamed in long lines through doorways to work another day.

How I long for the day of the rebellion. We will smash the workstations, tear down the factory, storm The Square and demand an audience with Mother—and if Jared just happens to stand in our way, I will bring him down with a swift knee to the place he deserves it most. We'll strip the prefects of their uniforms, line them up and humiliate them as they have us. But I am getting ahead of myself.

I turn from my workstation and up to the poster of Moses. His stern face is the very picture of determination and loyalty. I will have to be like him until we're ready. Wear his face, work like him, speak his words and be the machine Mother desires.

I place the ninth unit on my shelf. I hadn't seen Rebekah this morning and my stomach clenches at the thought she might have been a victim of an over-zealous worker trying to impress Mother. I have to stop myself snorting—not too long ago, I was that over-zealous worker ready to inform Mother about David.

My eyes wander to the empty workstation to my right. I try to picture Seth. Where is he now? Is he working in The Mine? Or has he been sent to The Trench? I hope he's still the curious boy full of questions and not taking any answers for granted. But that's unlikely. It's been days since he and the others were taken—Mother must have broken his spirit by now.

But how things have changed. To have to go below for this purge Mother speaks of, is a blow to the stomach. All these years we've dreamed, yes dreamed is the right word, of going up. Whether it's to live in Paradise, or all the way to the surface, it was always up and away from here. But now? To be forced down to the lower levels is a defeat, adding one more level in the struggle back to the sunlight. I have to speak to Lydia and find the location of the weapon store. Then we'll have the power, we'll have options, we'll have a plan. Up, not down. Up, not down!

'Noah!' I don't have to turn to know Barnabas is striding towards my bench. He stops opposite. 'There's a prefect here to see you.' My rebellion collapses.

If my jaw hadn't been so tight, I think my confession would have poured out, there and then to Barnabas. The fear of discovery has weighed heavily on my shoulders for days now. It feels so real I fear my back will break under the pressure—I'm not sure if I can bear it for much longer.

I follow the prefect up the stairs to the factory office, my numb feet incapable of feeling the floor. This is the first time I've walked up this flight of stairs—I didn't know we had an office. The prefect stops at a door at the back of the building. He knocks. A voice inside calls out, 'Come in.'

The prefect turns and raises his eyebrows. 'Well, he's not talking to me.' He shoves my shoulder. 'Go on.' My stiff fingers grip the cold handle. But I'm not quick enough as another push from behind crushes my face against the door. He laughs. 'You'll find it easier if you open it first.' I daren't answer back. I take his advice before he finds another reason to strike.

I stand in the open doorway. Inside, I recognize Solomon, the senior prefect from The Meeting Place, sitting behind a small desk. He grins to his colleague over my shoulder. 'That's a good one, I'll remember to use that next time.' The corners of his mouth turn down as he looks to me. He jabs with a pencil at the empty chair. 'Sit.'

I step through and see the back of another worker's overall. It's Lydia! My heart races. The meeting must be about Tabitha. Lydia remains facing the front as I pull the chair from under the desk and sit; both must hear my heart pounding in my chest. I force my eyes to look to the front. The prefect waits for me to settle, then reaches inside the top drawer and takes out a brown folder and a flat box. His gray eyes stay fixed on my face as he opens the folder and then pushes the box across the desktop. Again he points with the pencil. 'Open it.'

Now I look to Lydia. Her eyes have dropped to the box on the table—she's not breathing. I lean forward and take hold of the box. My tight fingers struggle with the lid. It has to be the diary. But why now? What plan does Jared have for me?

My dry lips stick and I have to push my tongue forward to force open my mouth. 'I, I don't know where it—'

He leans over the desk. 'Shut up and open it.'

I lift the lid and peer inside. I have to stop the sigh of relief ready to burst from my lungs. A metal plate gleams under the buzzing light bulb; the bird scratch has no place to hide. At first I'm pleased to see it again as it takes flight to freedom. I freeze the smile ready to spread on my face and push it down to my stomach. But the bird is not free. It's trapped in a box, unable to fly from the metal that gives it form.

'Lydia?' I look up to see the prefect has turned.

She coughs. 'We, err... found this damaged plate this morning.' I sit up. Only this morning? But it's been days since it had passed across my workstation. Lydia continues. 'Sarah saw the scratch just before she packed it away for—'

'Yes, yes, thank you. That will do!' He softens his voice. 'Please pass on Mother's gratitude to Sarah for spotting this example of,' his dark eyes look back to me from under his heavy brow, 'poor workmanship.' He sits forward, placing his elbows on the desk and resting his chin on his fists. 'Enlighten me, Noah. Why did you think it wasn't necessary to report this accident immediately to your team leader?'

I have no answer except the truth. 'I'm sorry, Prefect. I didn't think it mattered, and,' I look down at my hands clenched in my lap, 'I didn't want to get Abraham's team into trouble.'

He slaps the desk. Both Lydia and I jump. 'You mean, you didn't want to get yourself into trouble!' He snorts loudly. 'I believe your reason for not reporting your,' he jabs an index finger at the plate, 'your carelessness was purely selfish. It was you, not your team you were protecting.'

'No, I would never—'

'Don't interrupt me when I'm speaking!' He sits back and strokes his chin. 'Or perhaps it wasn't an accident. How do we know this wasn't an act of vandalism?' My mouth drops open. I shake my head.

'No, it was an accident, it just—.' His scowl shuts my throat.

He places his hands on the table. 'We cannot have this. Any inattention to detail could jeopardize our whole plan! You're lucky Mother doesn't send you straight to Re-Education. If it were up to me, I wouldn't take the risk. I'd throw you straight into The Trench.'

He turns over the first page in the folder and slides his pencil across the neat lines, but too quick to be taking in the words. He sighs and snatches at the sheet, flicking it over and repeating the same ridiculous routine with the next page. He finishes and puts the pencil back in his pocket. 'But Mother says you're one of her best workers.' He shakes his head. 'Yet I cannot think why she would value your contribution so much judging by this example of your shoddy workmanship.' She values my contribution? A week ago I would have rejoiced at those words. But now, I wonder how she'll react if Rebekah and I can prove it's safe outside.

The prefect closes the folder. 'Take this as a warning. Abraham has been informed. If it happens again there won't be another, you'll be taken off factory duty and reassigned.' He looks up. 'Now, both of you return to your duties. I hope I can trust you to do so alone, us prefects have more important duties than to lead you lot around by the hand.'

I stand with Lydia. She nods. 'Yes, of course, Prefect.'

I can't believe I've got off with just a warning. I reply with a little too much enthusiasm. 'Thank you, Prefect. I promise it won't happen again.'

He replaces the folder and box into the drawer and speaks without looking up. 'Be sure that it doesn't.' I catch Lydia's eye. She turns and I reach forward to open the door. As we leave, I hear the drawer shut. I wonder what will happen to my scratched plate.

I close the door. We both set off, keen to put some distance between us and the office. Lydia frowns. She glances over her shoulder and whispers, 'You wouldn't think they would make such a fuss about a tiny scratch.' She tries to smile. 'Just as well Mother thinks highly of you.'

I blow air between my lips. 'Thank Moses, for a moment I thought—' Before I can think, I stop and grab her wrist. Her eyes widen as she stares down at my hand. I let go. 'I'm sorry, it's just that...' can I ask? I have to. I may never get a better chance. 'Can you tell me,' I check the corridor—it's safe. 'Do you know where they store the weapons?'

She steps back. 'Weapons?'

I can see she's pretending. I reassure her. 'It's okay, you can tell me. I know that you assemble the units to make them. A prefect told us.'

She shakes her head. 'I don't understand. Is this a test?' She turns, checking if we're alone. 'We don't make anything. We're the recovery team.' She spells it out as if lecturing a new arrival. 'We recover the components from the old, spent machines you send us so they can be recycled. We have to report damaged parts to ensure they're not sent for re-assembly.' She leans closer. 'Do you know what the machines are used for? There are thousands of them.'

My mouth gapes. I try to speak, but no words get past my lips. Lydia puts a hand on my shoulder. 'What is it? You've gone very pale.'

I can't unclench my jaw, but my eyes must be bulging from my head. Recycled! Can it be true? Everything I have made has been unmade. I look up to Moses. Did he know? I place the completed unit on my shelf. In a day or two, Lydia's team will dismantle it and send the parts back to our workshop so I can put them together again. I have spent the last five years toiling for hours at this workstation—and for what purpose? We have no weapons. We've made nothing in all these years. And what about the farm and laboratory workers? Are we doing anything to prepare to leave?

I attach the two plates together with the number six fastener. My fingers wrap around the metal. I'm seconds away from bending it in two and hurling it across the workshop. Breathe! I soften my face and feel the muscles of my neck release. I loosen my grip and check for the groove as I reach for the bracket. I cannot let my disgust, shock and disappointment show. I have to meet my target. I have to carry on. But the strength that has kept me going when I've been ready to drop, has drained away with my hope.

I must see Rebekah tonight; she has to know the truth. Our only hope now is to make our own way to the surface. Then if it's safe, we can reveal Mother's secret and lead the people of The Ark to freedom. We'll be defenseless against the enemy, but I'd rather take my chances outside than spend another day at my workstation. Perhaps our enemy has changed after a hundred years below. Perhaps we could work together to build a new world. Perhaps if we could all—

'Noah, can I see you for a moment?' Abraham stands opposite. I must pay more attention—I hadn't notice him approach.

'Err... yes, of course.' He turns and walks back to his desk at the other end of the room. He sits and waves his hand to the chair opposite. 'I'm sorry, but I should have made time to speak to you earlier.'

I pull up a chair, pushing my revulsion at Lydia's revelation deep into my stomach. 'If it's about that scratch, I promise it won't happen again.'

He shakes his head. 'No, it's not,' he glances over my shoulder to Barnabas's station, 'but he'll think it is.'

'Oh, I see.' But I'm not sure if I do.

Abraham leans across the desk. 'I wanted to talk to you about your third visit.'

I remain sitting upright for the benefit of Barnabas. And even with other more pressing thoughts, I'm curious to hear what Abraham has to say. I repeat my words. 'Oh, I see.'

'It does get easier with each visit, even for your partner.' Abraham's eyes wander up to the grey skylight. 'I came to look forward to those visits, even counting down the days to the next time.' He smiles and appears to talk to himself. 'It has to be the most rewarding of all our duties.'

'But—' Abraham's eyes stare through me as if I'm no longer there. I lean forward. 'But why? What's the purpose?'

He looks back to me and blinks away a tear and frowns. 'I don't know, Mother never told me.' His eyes drop to his clasped hands in his lap. 'I miss her.' He speaks so quietly it takes a few seconds for me to understand.

'Who?'

He sighs. 'Her name was Abigail.' His fingers unclench and he rubs his palms together. 'She was so, so clean, soft... and warm. She could make me feel like it was my birthday all over again, she looked...' His lips quiver. He tightens his jaw and breaths out. 'But then the visits suddenly stopped, I asked if I could see her again, but the prefects said the objective had been met.' He leans back in his chair. 'I'd do anything to see her just one more time.'

I see Naomi's smile. 'Where did she go?'

'I don't know, the prefect didn't say. Isaac said she'd probably gone up to Paradise as her reward.' He laughs, quickly cutting it short. 'But then he also believed the whole thing was about making more workers.' He shakes his head. 'Can you imagine anything more absurd?'

I agree. 'No.' But at least we'd be making something.

Abraham stands. 'So, I just wanted to let you know I'm here if you need to talk.'

I push my chair back. 'Thanks.' I stand and turn to go, but stop and look back, realizing what he'd just offered. 'Thank you, I appreciate your... help.'

Abraham nods. 'It's the least I can do for one of my team.' He looks over to Barnabas. 'Oh, and don't forget to look upset when you walk back to your workstation.'

'I will.' I turn to see Barnabas watching. I make the required face and return to my place. Did Isaac ever speak to Abraham about his plan? I know I can trust him, but with Barnabas as second in command, I'm not sure I can speak openly to him.

I pick up the unfinished unit, snap the bracket shut and place it on my shelf.

# 31

'I would like to thank Barnabas for suggesting I make this apology to you all and to give me a chance to explain my actions.' I let my head drop forward in mock shame, avoiding the eyes of my team sitting around the dormitory table.

'Thank you, Noah.' Abraham prompts me to sit; Barnabas nods in response to my gratitude—*if only he knew.* Abraham folds his arms and leans back. 'Now I'm sure Noah only had our best interests at heart, but this must be a lesson for us all. If you make a mistake, you must report it straight away. Most other workers would have been sent for Re-Education, but if you work hard like Noah, Mother will give you the benefit of her doubt.' He pushes back his chair and claps his hands. 'Now let's have supper.'

I stand to fetch the bowls and try to look guilty, but only Barnabas watches me closely; the others keep one eye on the entrance expecting another snap inspection at any minute.

I lay the bowls on the table as Caleb places the spoons. Reuben pulls up his chair and looks to Abraham. 'Do you think Mother will enforce a total shutdown and invoke this *purge*?' The crash sends us all leaping from our seats.

Amos groans. He stands, hands clasped to his forehead, gawping at the green lines streaked across the floor as still more seeps from the upturned pot.

'Don't just stand there! Scoop it back into the pot.' Barnabas glares at Reuben and forces out his words through clenched teeth. 'Could you have at least waited until he'd put it down? You know how jumpy he is at the moment.'

Reuben mumbles his apology. We take our spoons and rescue what we can. Abraham sighs. 'At least we can thank Caleb for doing such a thorough job keeping the floor clean.' Once done, we sit back at the table and start our late supper—it tastes no worse than usual.

# 32

I have to tell Rebekah we have no means to defend ourselves against our enemy. Lydia's revelation changes everything. Either Mother never intends to deliver on her promise of The New Dawn, or there is no enemy. Both explanations appear to call Mother's intentions into question.

I check the headset is safely in place on my pillow and pull back the blanket. The others lie asleep, oblivious to the big lie as Mother pipes another story into their heads. I ease down the ladder and can just see the face of Caleb above the covers. The glow from the stove flickers on his face—he's smiling. Tonight's story must be his favorite; the tale of the tall ship Mother sailed across the seven seas on her epic voyage of discovery. Caleb gets excited when Abraham reads the part in his book about the wide, blue waters going on forever in all directions. In his sleep, he'll be on deck besides Mother as she tells him stories of the ocean and curious beasts that lurk in the dark waters—I too, enjoy that one.

I stop. Am I wrong to rebel against Mother? Yes, the days are hard, and, as I'm now aware, pointless, but at least the nights bring some freedom, even if it is Mother's choice. I turn away, knowing if I stay longer I will be tempted to join them on the ship.

I pull on my overalls, knowing it will be cold outside. I enter the living quarters. The stove warms my face. I stop once more. It would be the easiest thing to sit by its comforting glow and let my mind wander and maybe dream. Then I'd go back to my bunk, live out the rest of my days leaving Mother to worry about the wider world. But my feet have other ideas.

Once outside my resolve returns. Close to six hundred workers lie asleep in ignorance to the stark truth. Then there are countless more elsewhere in The Ark striving towards the day that may never come. Tomorrow they'll rise and complete another wasted day of back-breaking work for nothing. I stretch my arms and legs. We are right to challenge Mother. We have to find the way up and end this misery. Then at least we can become masters of our own fate—once we've learned how to fend for ourselves.

I edge along the wall to get out of the light of the stove streaming from our entrance. My heartbeat quickens at the thought of seeing Rebekah again. Tonight we'll look for the way out at the edge and form our plans for the rebellion; tonight I can gaze into those eyes again.

My heart stops. How do I find her? I've been so obsessed with delivering my message, I've given no thought of how to find her dormitory. I know the location of the laboratory sector, but there are twenty-five teams. It could take all night to find the right one. And, she could already be out.

Footsteps! More than one person. I slide away from the approaching prefects and slip around the corner, pushing my body as far as it will go into the wall. If they search our dormitory and find an empty bed... My mouth fills with saliva. I have to hope they'll be satisfied they've already inspected us twice in recent days and will move onto some other unfortunate team.

'She's turning on the lights tonight.' Jared! I swallow, trying to push the rising fear back down my throat.

'She's not done that for ages.' I recognize the voice of the tall prefect. 'She must be desperate to get her hands on this book.' *Has Tabitha spoken?*

Jared laughs. 'And it means we can have some fun.' They're close. I turn my head away and shut tight my eyes.

'Which one tonight?' They pass by our dormitory, so close I can hear Jared lick his lips.

'The lab sector.' My knees buckle. *No!* Jared sounds excited. 'Mother wants every dorm in that sector searched before morning.'

'We can't do all of them!'

'It's not just us, idiot, all the teams are assigned, and she'll give us all the time we need. But get a move on, I know where I want to start.'

I have to follow. The strength returns to my legs as the heat in my stomach burns away the doubt. I stay back from the light of their torch beams but needn't worry about being detected. Jared and his crew are making so much noise, they'll never hear the sound of my steps and thumping heart.

We leave my sector and enter Rebekah's. In a few minutes we'll be amongst the dormitories of the lab workers. What am I doing? What can I do to help her against the prefects? But I can't stop now and continue to follow in their shadow.

'Been a while since we've caught a walker.' The third prefect speaks for the first time.

Jared sighs. 'Shame, it's the look on their faces when we wake them in the middle of The Square that makes it worthwhile.'

They stop. I dash behind the corner of the first dormitory. 'Right, we're here.' Jared sounds like an enthusiastic new arrival. 'It's coming up to eleven, better put your goggles on.'

Goggles? The sky explodes. I cry out as hot blades stab through my eyes and into my skull. I fall to my knees, clasping my hands to my face, but still they burn. I scramble on all fours and find a wall, desperately hoping I'm not exposed out in the open. The others! Jared said more teams were coming. I have to get out of sight.

'Let's do a sleeper with this one.' Jared again. I must be safe, for now at least. I risk opening one eye, but the searing light is too painful. *Think!* I fumble with the buttons of my overall, loosen the top and free my arms. I pull my shirt off and wrap it over my face and open my eyes again, peering through the thin material. I blink away the tears and see my blurred, pink hand in front of my face. Turning, I see that I've crawled into a narrow gap between the dormitory blocks facing Rebekah's. Above, the dome is a brilliant white, exposing every inch of our level in a harsh light.

Jared's words come back. Sleeper? What did he mean by that? I shuffle to the edge of the alley. My heart sinks as I learn what he meant. The tall prefect drags one of the girls into the walkway, unconscious, still wearing her headset and dressed only in her thin undergarments. He leaves her sprawled on the ground and returns to get another. I can only watch in disgust as Jared brings out Rebekah slung over his shoulder with her long, red hair hanging limply down his back.

Soon, six lab workers lie in an undignified line— Rebekah is placed to one side. Jared grins at her prone body. He speaks to his colleagues without taking his eyes off her. 'You two do the search. I deserve some fun after my work in The Square. I want to see what I have to look forward to next month.' I twist away, screwing my eyes shut.

'Careful, Jared. Mother will find out. She won't like it.'

Jared sneers, 'Don't worry, I know exactly what I can get away with.'

My fingernails dig into my palms. This can't happen. I wait for the others to enter the dormitory and peer around the bend. Jared watches his colleagues go back into the dormitory. He kneels beside Rebekah and removes a glove. He strokes her hair then runs his fingertips across her cheek. I crouch, ready to rush out and drive my fists into his goggles. He looks up; two large, shiny black eyes search in my direction. I duck back behind the corner.

'Hey!' Jared calls into the dormitory. 'I think I heard something out here. We may have a walker.' I have to go. But I'm torn between escape and leaving Rebekah. I have seconds to think. If I try to stop him, the three prefects would easily overpower me.

'You go.' The tall prefect's voice. 'Some of us are working in here while you have your fun. Anyway, who cares? Mother wants the book, what difference does another walker make?' Footsteps. As hard as it is to accept, I have to leave. I vow to make him pay for this... somehow.

But as I turn to run, more prefects approach. One of them shouts. 'Hey, Jared! Mother wants to see you.' My fists unclench. I recognize the voice of Solomon.

'What? Now?'

'Yes, now! So you can forget your business with your girlfriend there.' Jared mumbles something I cannot hear. Solomon shouts, 'Now! And beware, she sounds angry so don't delay.' Perhaps Mother has heard of Jared's behavior at our dormitory. I hope he'll be reprimanded and made to suffer.

I wait until both Jared and the new team move on, then crawl to the end of the alley. The two prefects are busy with their search, judging by the noise coming from inside. I climb to my feet and check both ways on the walkway. Rebekah lies sprawled in the open. At any moment, more prefects could arrive but I have to reach her. It's now or not at all. I stoop and run, skid to a halt and drop to my knees beside her. I pull off her headset. She opens her eyes. I clasp my hand to her mouth to shut off her screams. She struggles.

I whisper as loudly as I dare. 'Rebekah. It's me.'

'Noah?'

'Quick, take my hand.' I pull her to her feet. 'Keep your eyes shut, I'll lead.' I stumble, but get her back to the safety of the alley. I guide her to lean against the wall.

She pushes her palms into her eyes and gasps. 'What's happened to the dome?'

I drop my head to whisper into her ear. 'It's Mother. But there's something else. I spoke to Lydia today.' I suddenly don't want to tell her the awful truth. She looks vulnerable and scared.

She tilts her head. 'And? What did she say?'

'Not here. I'll wait until we're safe,' I glance to the dome, 'safer.'

Rebekah removes her hands. 'But—arghh! How do you keep your eyes open?'

'I'm wearing my shirt over my head.' Despite her pain, she giggles. I laugh quietly with her. 'I guess I do look a bit... well, you know. But it works, try it.'

'I daren't move my hands. Can you pull it up for me?' I take hold of the thin shirt. I stop.

'No. Take mine. You've have nothing on under your shirt, and you'll be... you'll get cold.'

She smiles. 'Oh, yes, thanks. But what about your eyes?'

'I think I'm getting used to it now.' I wince as I remove my shirt. Squinting, I can just see to fold it neatly. 'Lean forward.' I place the shirt across her eyes. 'Now. Take your hands away.' I tie it at the back; her soft hair brushes my hand and I take longer than I should to secure the knot.

She straightens. 'Thanks. How are your eyes?'

I blink. 'Getting better, a little better.'

'Get them back in!' Solomon has returned. I pull Rebekah towards me and drop back to the wall. She buries her face into my shoulder. Solomon berates the rest of

Jared's crew. 'What would Mother think if she saw her precious workers treated like this?'

'Blame Jared,' the tall prefect grunts. 'It was his idea.'

'I don't care. Get them back in their bunks.' His voice fades. 'And, get on with your search.'

The third prefect speaks. 'Idiot. It's not our fault.' I hear the sound of a body being dragged across the walkway. 'You get that one, she looks heavier than the others, and you're the one who keeps saying how much stronger you are.'

He grunts. 'Dear Moses! You're right. This one must be getting second helpings.'

I wait until they've gone inside before I speak, but keep my arms around Rebekah. 'What happens now? They'll soon find out you're missing.'

She shakes her head. 'There's two empty bunks in our dorm, I doubt if they'll notice another. I don't think they were paying much attention when they came in. Too busy thinking about the *fun* they were going to have.'

My heart hammers against my ribs, but not from the thought of being discovered. Rebekah's body nestles against mine, and despite our situation, I wish we could stay like this all night.

The prefects return to the walkway. 'Shame Mother is in such a hurry, we could have had some fun of our own.' Two more workers are lifted.

I whisper close to Rebekah's ear. 'We have to get away from here, it's not safe.' She nods. Her silky hair strokes my cheek. I breathe in her scent and suddenly feel light-headed.

She pulls back. 'Where do we go?' I've not moved. *Think!*

'Err... away from here.' I put her headset into my pocket and step in front. I take her hand. 'Put your hand here, on my shoulder, I can see well enough to get to the other end of this alley.' I put my hand across my eyes and peek through my fingers. With my free hand, I feel along the wall and manage a slow pace. We make it to the end of the alley. I look back. 'Wait here. I'll check ahead.' But I can't resist. Her eyes are covered. I take the opportunity to study her face. Her lips look redder in the bright light, and I imagine what they must taste like. They move.

'Can you see anything?' If only she knew. I turn, trying to sound as if I'm further away.

'Not yet. Give me a second.' *What am I doing? Focus!*

I peer around the corner into the outer walkway that runs adjacent to the main route nearer to the center. It's empty. I return to Rebekah. 'It's safe. And they can't have noticed you're missing, they would have raised the alarm by now.' I retake her hand and put it on my shoulder. We cross the gap, staying low as if we suspect Mother is watching from above, and duck into the next alley. I take a few paces and find a recess in the wall. It's deep enough to offer some protection so at least we can't be seen from the main route. I guide Rebekah to the space. 'We can stay here until things have quietened down. Then you can get back to your bunk,' I pat my pocket, 'and don't forget your headset.' I glance back, just to be sure. 'Perhaps you can tell me more about what you and the others know.'

But she shakes her head; I can see her frown under my shirt. 'Not now. We don't want to waste a minute. This is the perfect time.'

'For what?'

'To find the way up! We couldn't see it in the dark, but with this,' she points to the dome, 'we *have* to find it.'

My head spins. 'You're right.' *Can we find it tonight?* We could be the first to see the world above for over a hundred years! 'But...' my shoulders sag, 'we'll have no cover in this light.'

She grasps my hands. 'It doesn't matter. They're all searching for the book, they won't be looking over the wall.' She's right again. I have to be more adventurous, take more risks. We have the light, the freedom, and have until morning. We can find the way up. Isaac believed it was at the edge. If he's right, we have all night to walk the whole way around and, in this light, we can't fail to find it.

The alley comes to an end. I stop at the corner and listen. Silence. I turn to Rebekah. 'We've reached the outer walkway. I can see the perimeter.' I look down the walkway once more. 'Take my hand.' We dash across the wide space and dive for the relative shelter of the next alley.

More shouts and laughter—it's coming from the laboratory dormitories. Rebekah's grip tightens. She speaks louder than I think is safe. 'We have to put a stop to this. When we get back, we must tell Mother what her prefects are doing.'

I stroke the back of her hand, trying to sound confident. 'We will,' I see Jared's grinning face, 'he can't be allowed to get away with this.' Her lips set into a straight line. My hand goes to her cheek. I stop it just before it rests on her skin—it wouldn't be easy climbing the wall after another blow to my groin.

I turn. 'This way.' I tug at her hand and run. The fire returns. I run taller, faster, and straight at the barrier between us and freedom. I call to Rebekah as loudly as I dare. 'We're nearly there.' I pull on Rebekah's hand to stop before we crash into its hard surface.

We stand, panting, our breath mingling in the cold air between. I look down. I cannot stop my eyes from resting in the curves revealed by her thin clothes clinging to her body. *Focus!* I lean closer. It's probably safe to talk out loud here at the wall, but I want to feel her hair on my skin. I whisper in her ear. 'There are no ledges here. I'll have to lift you.' She nods. I crouch and put my hand behind her knee. I pause.

'What is it?'

'I'm just working out the best way to do this.' I hope she doesn't guess the real reason. 'Here,' I lift her leg and cup my hands, 'put your foot on my hands and I'll push you up.' I straighten my legs and lift. Her thighs rest briefly against my cheek as she grasps the top of the wall. If we're caught now, at least I'd always have this memory for the dark days ahead. But my knees buckle and I almost lose my hold. I look up but the view from here doesn't help. 'Sorry. Lost my footing.' *Stop it!* I push my knees back to lift her higher, allowing her to step onto my shoulder and clamber onto the wall.

I take a few steps back and run. With one leap, I land with my chest across the top and pull myself level next to Rebekah. I squeeze her elbow. 'I'll go first.' I jump and land, remembering to bend my knees this time. I look back to Rebekah and hold up my hands. 'Okay, jump.' She slides off the wall and lands between my arms. I hold her for a moment, kidding myself it's to let her gain her balance. I step back and again my eyes are drawn down her neck and to her body.

I force myself to look away. 'Take my hand. I'll lead you to the edge.'

'It's okay. I can see now.'

I turn back. 'Oh. How, how long have—'

'Long enough.' Her face reddens as she smiles. 'Go on then, you lead,' she holds out her hand, 'take me to the edge.'

I oblige. 'But perhaps it's best to keep your eyes covered for a while longer.' I exaggerate a blink. 'I'm still finding it hard to see in this light.' I shield my eyes and turn to inspect our route.

Under the white dome, the edge looks closer, but the gap between looks too open and exposed. But we have to go—we may never get a better opportunity than tonight.

We leave the safety of the little cover we had from the wall. I crouch as I run, fearing I'll hear Mother's booming voice yelling at us to stop. But only our breath and footsteps disturb the eerie silence.

We make it, almost slamming into the edge of the dome as I misread the distance through half-open eyes. Now my head throbs, sending bolts of pain down my neck, back and into my legs. But my discomfort is a small price to pay if we can end the years of hardship we'd suffered down here for nothing.

I clasp my shoulder, digging my fingers into the tense muscles. I look to Rebekah. 'Which way?' I turn back to face the perimeter wall to get a bearing, surprising myself that I'm already planning our return journey. I gasp.

Rebekah tugs at my hand. 'What is it?'

Before us stands the only world I've known for most of my life. I speak more to myself. 'It doesn't look big enough. Everything. The Factory, Lab, Farm, The Square and all the dormitories, they all fit inside that wall. It looks too small in this light.'

Rebekah releases my hand and runs it across the surface of the dome. 'Well, let's hope we find the way up so we don't have to live another day here.'

I look for the gap between the factory and the dome. 'Reuben's right. Mother *must* have raised the dome.'

'Sorry?' She laughs. 'Oh, you mean when you climbed onto the roof.'

My mouth drops open. 'You know about that?'

'Everyone does. Mother told that story for a month, warning us we'd burn our fingers if we tried to do the same.'

In a way I'm relieved. 'Oh good. So I did touch it. But now it looks too high to reach. But when could she have raised it? Wouldn't we have noticed?'

Rebekah steps away and turns back to the dome. 'It's not important now. Come on, we're wasting time.'

We hold hands and turn left for no reason. We scan the bumpy surface for signs of an exit, but what would it look like, and how long will it take? It took twenty-six minutes to walk the length of the perimeter wall on my induction tour. I counted sixty-four paces from the wall to the edge, making the circumference of the dome just over four hundred paces further. But my legs are longer now, and we'll be walking slower as we search, plus my head feels as if it's about to split in two. I give up. If we're lucky, the exit could be on this side and we'll find it before we're spotted.

I whisper over my shoulder. 'I hope the prefects are occupied with their search, if they look over the wall...'

'They won't. We'll be fine. If Jared has the diary the others won't be finding it any day soon.' She pulls on my hand. 'So let's find the way up now,' she shivers, 'before Jared gets a chance to put *his* plan into action.'

I hear Jared's boast of his special birthday gift for Rebekah. I stop and look her in the eye. 'I promise I won't let him touch you again.'

For a moment, she looks as if she's about to cry. What did I say to upset her? But her quivering lips break into a broad smile as she steps up and throws her arms around me. She whispers. 'It's good to have you on my side.' I feel ten feet tall, but at the same time have doubts about how I can keep my promise.

Something behind her hair catches my eye. 'Is that it?'

She gasps. 'The way up?' A thin line runs up the surface of the dome from the ground up to just above my head. At the top, a horizontal line stretches about twice the length of my arm across to another vertical line, adjacent to the first.

I run my fingers along the line. 'It has to be.' I turn to Rebekah. 'But I can't see a handle or a way to open it. No wonder you couldn't find it in the dark. It feels completely flat.' I step closer and risk opening my eyes a little wider. 'Yes! It's here. I can see it.'

'What?' Rebekah pushes closer. 'What can you see?'

'There's a circle with a slight ridge in the middle. It could be some sort of handle.' I wrap my fingers around the ridge and push. It sinks into the door's surface then stops. 'It's not opening.'

Rebekah clutches at my arm. 'Try turning it.'

'It's not moving.' I twist harder; I feel it move. 'No, wait, it's...' A hiss followed by a clunk and the whole door drops back into the dome and slides to the left. On the other side, the air howls as if it's also desperate to escape. I stagger back and grab hold of Rebekah as my head spins. 'It's open!'

# 33

One step. With one step we can walk out of this level and enter a new world. I bend a knee and lift my foot, but it hangs in the air, refusing to come down. If we enter there'll be no going back to our old way of life. It would be impossible to return to the daily grind once we know what's outside. But if we stop now we may never get another chance.

A new world awaits. A new world without the old rules. Encouraged, I wrap my arm around Rebekah's waist. She looks back and grins. I pull her closer but neither of us speak as we pass into the black.

I gasp as a rush of air freezes my face like the water from our shower. Rebekah's mouth moves, but her words are lost in the gust. I shake my head. She points to the door and shouts into my ear, 'We'd better shut that. We don't want anyone to see we've opened it.'

I step over and put my shoulder to the rim and push. It slides silently shut. We stand, panting in the dark, relieved for the respite from the blinding light, only to be replaced by the chill.

Rebekah removes my shirt from her eyes. She yells, 'There's only one.'

'One what? I can't see anything.'

'One ladder. There were three in the sleep story.' I shuffle forward. Rebekah grabs my arm.

'Don't move!' The black turns to grey. I look down to see my feet teetering over a ledge. And just as Rebekah said, before us stands one ladder with three dim, glowing rungs providing the only source of light. I tip my head back, but the glow is too weak to reveal any more than a short distance up the narrow shaft housing the ladder.

Rebekah holds out my shirt. 'Here, you can have this back.' Her teeth chatter. 'You're going to need it out here.'

'Pity you couldn't get your... no wait.' I unbutton my overalls and climb out of the legs. I shiver and hold it up. 'You can have mine.' Rebekah stands for a moment, her eyes move down my body. I feel suddenly ashamed of my bent body and try to straighten.

Her eyes come back to meet mine. 'Oh, thank you.' She takes them and hands over my shirt. 'Are you sure?'

'Of course.' I pull my thin shirt over my head, but it offers little protection against the cold. 'I'll be fine once we get moving.' She bends to step into the legs of my overalls. I watch entranced as she wriggles her body to pull it up to her shoulders.

She laughs. 'It's a little long in the arms.' She holds them up with the ends of the sleeves hanging limp. I sigh. The curves have gone, but in a strange way it's good to see her wearing my clothes.

'Here.' I fold the sleeve back to her elbow, then repeat on the other side.

'Thank you.'

I move next to the buttons on the front. 'Shall I?'

Rebekah steps back. 'No, no that's okay. I can do those.' She fastens the front and hugs her arms around her body. 'That feels better.' I shiver. Her hands move towards me, but then drop to her side. She looks back to the ladder. 'Let me know if you get too cold, then we can swap back.'

I turn to face the cold air and shrug. 'Don't worry about me. I'll be fine. Let's hope it will be warmer once we're outside.'

She looks up. 'Outside,' then back to me, 'that sounds good.'

I lean over the ledge and grasp the ladder; more rungs glow brighter under my hands. 'Hey look, it's showing us the way.' I turn to Rebekah. Her lips tighten, creasing her skin with doubt. I feel her dilemma. My hand moves to her cheek but finds itself resting on her shoulder. I attempt to smile. 'This has to be the right thing to do. I'm sure Mother will reward us for our courage if we find it's safe outside.'

Rebekah frowns, adding to the lines on her face. 'And if she doesn't?'

'Then we start your rebellion.' I drop my hand. 'So who's going first?'

Rebekah grabs the rung and laughs. 'I will.' She steps onto the ladder and quickly takes the first four steps. I join her on our way to freedom. But as soon as I step onto the first rung, I feel the full force of the wind up my legs and back.

'Dear Moses!' I drop my head and stare between my feet. My head spins as I peer into the dark tube below.

Rebekah calls down, her voice fighting to reach me against the blast. 'What can you see?'

My eyes water as I blink into the air that wants to rip the skin from my face. 'Nothing. The light's not strong enough. I was wondering how far this goes down. Oh...' my stomach churns.

'What is it?'

I look up. 'How will we know where to get back in?'

I see her hand go to her face. She clicks her fingers. 'I've got an idea. Step down.' I'm only too pleased to get out of the cold and back to the limited protection of the ledge. Rebekah climbs back. I hold out my hand and help her down. She smiles. 'Thanks.' She looks to my shirt. 'We can mark this spot so we know when we're back at our level.' She grabs the sleeve and tears off a strip. My mouth drops open and she laughs at my reaction. 'See...' she leans over and loops it around the rung opposite, 'now we know where we came in.'

I finger the tear in my sleeve. 'Let's hope we don't have to mark too many more places.'

Her eyes widen. 'Oh I'm sorry, I should have used my shirt, seeing as I'm the one wearing the overall.'

'I wasn't complaining. I was trying to be funny.'

Rebekah rubs my shoulder. 'Oh I see. Sorry. Was I supposed to laugh?'

'Doesn't matter. Reuben, he's on my team, has a way of saying things that are funny. It helps when times are tough.' I look back to my torn sleeve. 'He would have said it better.'

Rebekah pats my exposed shoulder. Now she laughs, but we both know it's not genuine. 'I get it now. You're saying you wouldn't have a shirt left if...' she sighs, 'Sorry. We don't have anyone on my team that can say funny stuff.' She turns back to the door. 'I hope they're okay, my team. I don't like to think of them asleep while those prefects...' she looks up, 'we should go.'

Rebekah steps over and places her hand back on my shoulder. I watch her lips move in the glow of the ladder. She raises her voice above the din as we shuffle towards the edge. 'It's best if you go first, then at least I can give you some shelter from the cold.' She glances back to the floor. 'It must come up from The Mine.'

'Sorry... what?'

'The wind. Strange, though.' Her head tilts back as she peers into the gloom above. 'You'd think it would be coming from up there.'

'Lucky for us it doesn't. It would be harder climbing against that blast.'

She shrugs. 'I guess you're right.' Then she steps back. 'After you.'

I take the ladder and watch the next four rungs light up. 'I wonder how far we have to climb.'

'Let's find out.' I shudder as even just a few seconds of exposing my skin to the blast freezes my limbs. Rebekah takes her position below, giving me some protection.

I call down. 'If we keep moving we might stay warmer.' We begin our ascent. After a few steps the glow from the ladder turns red. 'Hey, look! What does that mean?'

'Perhaps it shows us when we're getting close to an exit.'

'Or the surface.' I climb faster as my heart races. I shout against the howling wind. 'We'll be the first!' The thought begins to sink in. We'll be the first people to come out of The Ark after... how long? Mother says we've been below for almost a century. What will it look like after all those years? I hope the Earth has had time to heal.

A cold sweat runs down my forehead, stinging my tired eyes, but still we climb. Around us, the glow from the ladder marks our progress. Rung after rung, my cold fingers wrap around the colder metal to pull as my numb toes push down. I stare up into the darkness. How much further? I try to move faster, but my muscles are on fire. I stop and rest my head on the ladder. I shout against the wind. 'Do you mind if we stop?'

Rebekah sounds weak. 'No, of course not.'

How far have we come? The further we climb, the further we have to fall. I clutch the ladder, wrapping my arms around the rung and rub my hands together. What if we fall? We'd bounce off the walls of the shaft all the way down to the bottom. Would anyone in The Mine find our broken bodies? We cannot let that happen—our discovery would be lost forever.

I groan. My head is ready to split in two and it feels like I've got a number six fastener stuck in my throat. Why didn't we think to bring water? Should we go back? Right now, the thought of the warmth of my bunk is tempting. For once I would welcome Abraham's monotonous tones as he repeats his routine greeting to the new day. At least then I could drink and quench my thirst. We should go back. Next, time we'll bring supplies and perhaps blankets against the cold.

Rebekah taps my foot. 'Move over. I'm coming up.' She climbs beside me and wraps her arm through the rung and around my shoulder. 'Here.' She unbuttons the overalls and pulls me close to her body. 'You're freezing.'

My numb lips struggle to speak. 'I'm, I'm so sorry. I can't move my feet, and...' the gale suddenly stops. I whisper in the silence. 'My head hurts.'

Rebekah looks down. 'Thank Moses, that's stopped.' Her moist breath against my neck feels comforting. 'We'll rest here a while to get warm.'

'Thank you.' The blood starts to seep back into my limbs and I feel her body through the two thin layers between us. 'It's, it's beginning to help.'

She rubs my back. 'I read about this in my book.'

'What? The ladder?'

'No. How to keep warm in the cold. Mine's about the first explorers who went to the ends of Earth on special ships Mother built. They found the best way to keep warm was to press their skin together.'

I cling tighter. 'I'm glad Mother gave you that one. I think they were right.'

Her hair moves across my neck as she looks into my eyes. 'That's what we are. Explorers!'

I speak my thoughts out loud. 'Let's hope we discover somewhere we want to live.'

Her grip tightens. 'Oh!'

'Oh, what?'

I feel her tremble. 'The top and bottom of the Earth are buried under thick ice. What if that's—?' She pulls away; her wide eyes hold mine. 'If that's where this ladder leads, how would we get out?'

I rest my numb hand on her cheek. 'I don't think Mother would have built The Ark under ice.' *Would she?* I shudder. It would make a good place to hide. But trees don't grow on ice, I know that much. I try to think positive and get Rebekah to do the same. 'What do you want to see when we get out?'

Her lips move but her answer barely makes it to my ears. 'The sea.'

'Oh.'

Rebekah frowns. 'What's the matter?

'It just that it seems so wide and dangerous.'

She shakes her head. 'Not if you respect it, then it's beautiful.' Her eyes wanders from mine and out to what her heart dearly wishes to see. 'I want to stroll across the beach and wade into the shallow water and wriggle my toes in the soft, wet sand.' As she speaks the image forms in my head. Her hands move to my face. 'Then I'll walk further out, into deeper water and let the waves wash over my head.' She stops and frowns. 'Why does Mother shows us these things in the stories, but then never lets us go in and play?' I see Rebekah, lying on the sand, her wet clothes clinging to her body. 'Noah?'

'What?'

'Are you okay? You look like you're about to pass out.'

'No, no, I'm fine. I was just hoping there'll be trees outside.'

She smiles. 'I'm sure we'll both find what we're looking for.' She loosens her hold. 'Are you warmer?'

I nod. 'I'm ready to go on. It can't be much further, we must have climbed past the top of the dome by now.'

Rebekah rubs my shoulder. 'We'll climb together. It will be slower, but you might fall if you get cold again.'

'That's fine with me. I think that—' My muscles knot. A shriek! From deep in the Earth. An ice-cold claw clasps at the base of my spine, crawling up until it wraps around my neck. 'What the—?'

Rebekah grips my arm. 'Is that an Outsider?'

My eyes bulge as I gawp down into the gloom. 'But you said they don't exist.'

She clasps onto my arm and whispers into my ear. 'I know, I did, but what makes a sound like that?' Another wail.

I let out my breath. 'Wait, that sounds like metal grinding against metal. It's something opening.'

'Are they coming for us?'

I catch her eye. 'No, listen.' Another clang, then a whoosh as a blast of cold air rushes past. I shout. 'It must be a vent, we have them in the factory.'

Rebekah lets go of my arm and laughs. 'I didn't think I'd be pleased to feel that again. For a moment there I thought...' she looks up, 'come on, let's get to the top.'

We move as one, slowly at first but increasing speed as we learn to work together. We climb in silence, preserving our energy by not shouting into the wind. It's hard going, but with each step we get nearer to the surface, and with each step I feel a little lighter as my hopes rise. Soon I will feel the warm sun on my face as it glistens between the green leaves of tall trees.

I look to Rebekah. Her eyes are fixed on our goal and is unaware I'm watching. No, not trees. I wish for her sake we come out by the sea. I want to see the lines on her face disappear as she wades into the blue water. We could run together into the foaming waves and wash away the grime, and then—

The wind stops. Rebekah catches me watching, but she smiles and I manage to force my frozen muscles to respond. She whispers in the renewed silence, 'It must be the system for recycling air.' She rubs my back as we continue to crawl our way up. 'In the lab, we only find ways to filter the air and test its quality, Mother takes care of everything else.' Her head tips back. 'But I wonder how far it goes before it comes back to our level?' She gasps. 'What if this funnel loops back over the dome and we end up back where we started?'

I mumble the words before I can think. 'Then we can get back to our bunks.'

'What?' Thankfully, she didn't hear me clearly. I grit my teeth to force myself to focus.

'If this is just a vent, why the ladder? It must go somewhere.'

She lets out a long sigh, filling the air with her white breath. 'I hope you're right.' We exchange a look and move on. But before long, the cold begins to creep back into my hands and feet, and my fingers fumble on the rungs.

Rebekah sees my difficulty. 'Let's stop.' She unbuttons the overall—I hope the grin on my frozen lips doesn't show in the low light. 'Here,' she wraps her free arm around me, 'this helped last time.' I gladly cling onto her and hope my chattering teeth stop soon. 'Noah?' Her voice sounds different. *Has she seen something?*

My numb lips move. 'What is it?'

'Are you a,' she swallows, 'no, it doesn't matter.'

'Yes it does, or you wouldn't want to ask.'

She turns away and blurts out her question. 'Are you a third-timer?' I choke as I laugh with relief, suddenly feeling the warmth from her body flooding through mine. She pulls back. She looks hurt by my response.

I manage to stop. 'Oh, no I didn't mean to... I'm not laughing at you. It's because why ask me now?'

She looks up the ladder then back to me. 'It's important. I want to know what happens. It's my birthday next week, and I know I'll be asked to go to *you know you where.*'

A shiver, but this time it's not due to the cold. I see Jared's smirk. I have little time to stop his dream coming true. Her eyes meet mine. I stutter. 'It's... it's difficult to explain. I had to shower and go to *you know where.* There I met... someone, and we had to speak for a while,' no, I can't say it, 'look, we're not supposed to discuss it.'

Now it's Rebekah's turn to laugh. 'We're stuck up a ladder in the middle of the night, breaking all the other rules set by Mother, surely you can *discuss* it with me?'

I see her point. I nod. 'Okay, but not now.' I glance up. 'Let's get to the top first, I think I'm ready to go on.'

Rebekah follows my gaze. 'Alright, but you should have the overalls.'

I shake my head as far as my stiff neck allows. 'No. You keep them. There's no point both of us freezing, and what if we drop them?'

'Okay, but you must tell me if you get cold again.' I agree and grasp the next rung—it glows white. Rebekah gasps. 'Does that mean—?'

I squint into the grey above. 'I can see some sort of vent, and,' I look back to Rebekah, 'a ceiling. This must be it!'

Rebekah cries out, 'We're at the surface?'

I feel her warm tears run down my neck. I hug her tight. 'We have to be.' I release my grip and look around. 'Look! There's a door.'

Without a word, Rebekah steps off the ladder onto the ledge. I pry my fingers from the rung and collapse beside her. Every muscle in my body aches. She lies down and wraps herself around my shivering bones. 'Dear Moses, you're worse than I thought. I hope it's warmer,' her eyes light up and she claps her hands, 'outside!'

I grab her wrist. 'Wait.' Her shoulders drop. 'We don't know what's out there. We could be walking into a trap.'

Rebekah sighs. 'Would you prefer to spend the rest of your life down there in the dark, doing the same thing every day? Or...' she looks around to the door, 'walk through that door and into a new world?'

'You're right. But there's something you should know.' She frowns. I almost can't tell her. 'If it is safe to live on the surface, we... we don't have—'

She grips my shoulders. 'Just say it!'

The awful truth bursts out in one breath. 'Lydia says they dismantle and recycle the units we send them. We don't have any weapons.'

Rebekah's jaw drops. 'But how are we supposed to defend ourselves?' She collapses beside me. I force my tired body to sit. I see her eyes well up—I've just shattered her dream.

'We can't, or,' the thought forms as I speak, 'perhaps we don't have to.'

She turns; a tear runs down her cheek. 'I don't get what that means.'

'Mother doesn't think we need them, so perhaps there's no threat.'

Rebekah runs her hand through her hair. 'But why would she lie about the enemy?'

I watch the tear run down her throat and disappear down the front of her shirt. I take a guess. 'To make us scared? Stop us going outside before it's safe? Who knows what she's got planned, but it doesn't make sense. Or,' I look to the door, 'it's some sort of a trial.'

'Trial?'

'To test our commitment to the cause.' But inside I'm not so sure. I try again to reassure Rebekah. 'To see how determined we are to see in The New Dawn.'

She takes my hand and, with surprising strength, pulls me to my feet. Her chest rises. 'Then let's get out of here, and pass the test!' We turn and take a step towards the exit.

I see a circle in its center. 'It's the same type as the one below.' I squeeze her hand and lead it to the door. 'You do it.' She claps her hands and turns the handle. It clunks and hisses, dropping back towards us. We both take hold and slide it open; hand in hand, we step through into the bright world beyond.

# 34

I raise my hands and screw my eyes shut against the wall of brilliant light. We stumble forward. Rebekah laughs. 'I can't believe it. We're outside!'

I press my palms into my watering eyes. 'I wish we could see it. The sun's so bright.'

She lets go of my hand. 'And warm!' She moves away and calls back. 'I'm going to open my eyes.'

'Wait!' I hold out my hand, wriggling my fingers to find her. 'Let's do it together.'

'Too late.' She gasps. 'Dear Moses! It's so beautiful, it's, it's like nothing I could have...'

'Rebekah?' I drop my hands and blink away the tears. At first I see nothing, just Rebekah's outline against a shimmering green. Slowly, the world reveals its wonders. My mouth drops open. Tall trees, taller than I thought they could possibly grow, surround us on all sides. Giant trunks, like stone pillars from the ancient buildings Mother showed us in school, thrust upwards from the ground, strong enough to support the roof of the world high above. My eyes are drawn up the thick boughs, onto twisted branches whose fingers reach lovingly up to stroke the sky. The sky! It's nothing like the dull, flat skies Mother creates on the dome.

Something moves. I gaze between the leaves. White, wispy shapes float across the deep blue, blown by the gentle breeze ruffling my hair. My fingers itch to touch them, roll them in my fingers and maybe ride one across the treetops.

I look to Rebekah. She's strolled to the edge of the opening; my overall lies in a crumpled heap by a tree. The drab grey looks like a dirty mark, a smudge on a picture I'd drawn using all the colored pencils I could find in the nursery. But it's now Rebekah that attracts my eye. The sunlight behind streams through her thin clothing, revealing more wonders than I think I can take in one go. I mutter, 'Beautiful.'

She turns. 'Sorry, did you say something.'

'I said, can you believe all this?'

She beams. 'I know. Isn't this better than anything you could have *dreamed* of?' She throws out her arms and twirls.

I look up and turn in a circle, taking in as much as I can. 'The sky! It's so blue, so big, it's... it's alive.' My head begins to spin. I steady myself and for the first time, notice the long, green grass covering the forest floor. But it's not all green. Countless flowers of hues I cannot name, hold their heads proudly above the swaying grass to bask in the golden sunbeams.

I bend to stroke their soft petals and collapse onto my back. My fingers tingle as I run them across the tops of the grass. I breathe in, letting the sweet, scented air nourish my starved body. Above, the leaves flutter like the wings of tiny birds, rustling in the breeze to sing just for me. I roll onto my side. 'Rebekah! Come and lie with me, it's softer than my bunk.'

She turns and wades through the grass. Her hand takes mine as she kneels and lies beside me. 'This is more than I could ever have hoped for.' She sounds different, her throat freed from the worries of below.

I close my eyes and let the fresh air flood into my lungs. I sigh. 'The air, it smells... sweet, like my—' I stop, I don't want to think of my past life.

'Like what?'

'Oh, nothing. I've never smelled anything like this before.'

I turn. Rebekah's eyes are closed. I watch her face. She looks more beautiful than ever, as the flowers frame her face in the sunlight. I smile. 'Just one more thing will make this perfect.' She opens her eyes. I almost cry out my answer. 'Birds.' As soon as I speak, a song descends from the sky. Not a harsh song like our anthem, but a soft, lilting sound that reaches inside and awakens memories that I know are not mine alone. I whisper, 'Perfect.'

Dozens of birds fly above the branches, flitting this way and that as if being alive is enough to bring them joy. A new song joins the chorus. I search the sky and high above the others, a single white bird hovers. Its song sounds in some way urgent. I turn to Rebekah to see if she's heard it, but she's looking out through the trees. She notices my attention, turns and strokes the back of my hand. But her smile fades. 'Before today, I didn't think anything so beautiful could exist.'

I push myself up onto my elbow and lean over. The words flow before I can think. 'Oh, I did. And you're still the most beautiful sight I've ever seen.' *Did I really say that?*

Her cheeks redden as her eyes search mine. 'Do, do you really mean that?'

I brush a strand of her hair away from her face. 'Every word.' Her hand moves to my face, but stops. She looks away. I slide my arm under her shoulders and pull her closer. 'What's the matter?'

She turns away. 'I can't go back.'

'What?' We sit. She cups a bunch of blue flowers in her hands.

She looks back to me. 'Let's stay, just the two of us. We can learn how to grow food and look after ourselves.'

Dear Moses, please! I groan. 'There's nothing more I could want. That would be my dream come true.' I sigh. 'But what about the others?'

She raises her hands and examines the roots sticking out between her fingers. Her voice is barely a whisper. 'I can't face it, going back there, not after seeing this, and...'

She lets go of the flowers. 'What if this isn't a test and Mother stops us coming back and sends us to The Trench for disobedience?' She rubs the soil from her palms. 'I couldn't live another second in that hole knowing what's up here.' Her eyes light up. 'We *could* stay. We don't have to go back to tell the others.'

I shake my head, seeing the faces of Abraham and Seth. 'I really want to, but we'd be letting everyone down.'

She turns and grasps my hands. 'No we won't, we've done our duty. Once Mother's notices we're missing, she'll come looking for us, send out the prefects. And when they see it's safe, they'll all come.' She climbs to her feet and wanders to a nearby tree.

I stand. I want to believe she's right. 'But what if she doesn't? She might not want the others to know.'

She spins back. 'But there must be more workers that think like us. They'll start looking, and if we found our way out, so can they.' She holds out her hand. 'So you see, we don't have to go back.' The grass tickles my legs as I stroll to join her. She turns to look into the woods. 'All we have to do is wait here.'

'But what would we eat and drink?' Her mouth drops open. I cannot refuse her. I put my arm around her shoulder. 'No, no. You're right. We'll wait here for them to follow us. We don't have to go back.'

She smiles and rests her head against my neck. 'Thanks.' I hope I've made the right decision. What if the enemy find us first? Ignorant and defenseless.

I let go. 'I've got an idea.' I step up to the trunk and look for a foothold.

Rebekah claps her hands together. 'Oh good. What is it?'

I speak over my shoulder. 'I'm going to climb this tree and look for a river or lake so we—'

'What?'

241

'We need water, I'm parched.'

She shrugs. 'No, I mean, what tree?'

I stop and look back. 'Well this—' Rebekah is peering over my shoulder into the distance. 'This one. Can't you see it?'

'But there's... no tree.' Her body sags. 'Noah? What can you see?'

I don't want to answer. I force my lips to move. 'Trees. We're in a forest, aren't we?'

She shakes her head. When she speaks, she sounds like a child. 'No. I'm on a beach.'

# 35

'I can see sand, the sea and,' Rebekah raises a limp arm and points to her left, 'mountains, over there with snow on their tops.' She collapses and clasps her hands to her face. 'We've been tricked. We're still underground.'

I reach out to touch the tree. My hand tingles, as it sinks a little way into the trunk. My arm drops to my side; I look up to the sky—surely that has to be real. But the clouds and color have been wiped clean, leaving a harsh white screen. The birdsong, rustling leaves and breeze are gone; only Rebekah's sobs for her lost ocean fill the empty space. She lies on her side, curled into a ball, hugging her knees to her chest. I want to go to her but I cannot move, rooted where I stand, willing the trees to stay. But they too begin to change; like a painting I'd spilt water on in the nursery, they fade, their greens and browns running into each other as they drip from the paper into a murky pool before seeping into the floor.

My strength follows. I drop to my knees and sag forward but somehow manage to stay upright. It's just me, Rebekah and the crumpled overalls lying nearby in a harsh, empty room with a dome for a ceiling. I summon all my energy to crawl over to Rebekah. Now I collapse. I wrap my arms around her shaking body, and curl up beside her. Her body stiffens at my touch but I don't let go. I hold her tight, not wanting anything to take her from me.

What do we do now? I can only see one option open to us, but I daren't suggest going back yet. Rebekah sniffs and wriggles from my arms. She sits suddenly as if hit by a blast of cold water. Her red-rimmed eyes find me through her matted hair. She shakes her head and purses her lips. 'I'm not giving up. I'm not. She won't stop me.'

'But—' Her eyes flash.

She looks up. 'If Mother thinks this trick will stop me, she's wrong.'

I roll onto my back and stare at the blank dome. My stomach aches as if the tree roots had been ripped from inside. But Rebekah's right. We cannot let this setback break our spirit. I sit. *Think, Noah, think.* I peer towards the edge. 'Is this the same size as our level?'

Rebekah follows my gaze. 'It's hard to tell with it being empty. But yes, I'd say it's around about the same size.'

I stand and help Rebekah to her feet. 'Remember, when I asked you what you wanted to see when we got outside. You said the sea.'

Her eyes widen. 'And you said, a... what is it? A forest! One with trees.'

I nod and smile. 'This place knows somehow knows it. It showed us our dream, yours *and* mine.' I take her hand. 'Mother doesn't want us to dream on The Workers Level because we'll be distracted, so perhaps this is—'

'Paradise!' Rebekah beams. 'The Chosen must come here to rest after study. Mother did say there'd be time for leisure.' She gasps. 'The others, Rachel, Isaac, they have to be around here somewhere. There must be another door!' She tugs at my arm. 'We have to find them. And you have to tell them what Lydia told you.'

'Wait.' I point to the overalls. 'You should put those back on.' She grimaces. I pick them up. 'It might be cold out there, and we'll need them for when we go—'

'No!' She stops and twists around. '*You* can bring them if you like, but I'm not wearing them.' She looks out towards the wall. 'If this is Paradise, I want one of those bright uniforms.' Her eyes drop to her bare feet. 'And their soft shoes.'

I decide not to argue and tuck them under my arm. 'Okay, but I reckon we've only got five hours at most before morning, and it's going to take at least an hour to get back.'

Rebekah shakes her head. 'I'm not going back.'

'But what if we can't—'

'It makes no difference. I'm *not* going back.'

I step to her side and take her hands. 'Then neither am I.' *Dear Moses. What have I just said?*

She bites her lip. 'Thanks. I'd rather die up here than live another day below.'

I scan the perimeter of the dome. 'Well, that won't be too far away if we can't find water.'

She pulls my arm. 'Then we'd better see what lies behind that door over there.' I turn to where she's pointing. 'See.' She sets off at pace, then breaks into a run calling over her shoulder. 'That's not the one we came through, it's definitely wider.'

'Careful, it might be another—'

She laughs. 'Careful? What for?'

I laugh with her, suddenly free of my worries. She's right, yet again. We've already broken so many rules, Mother couldn't possibly punish us further.

We reach the door panting from the run, and rest our hands against the wall. My voice croaks. 'Let's hope we find Isaac and Rachel, and the rest of The Chosen. Once they know we've wasted all those years in the factory, they're bound to join us.'

Rebekah approaches the door. 'I wonder how many are up here.'

I run my hand across the faint line. 'The more the better. If there's a hundred or more we can build shelters, grow food and,' I take her hand, 'Mother can't make us go back inside ever again.'

Her eyes light up. 'It can't be far to the surface from here. I can feel it. Can you?'

I nod but can't say I do.

But Rebekah seems sure. 'I can smell the fresh air. It's close.' We raise our hands and push.

# 36

'Oh.' Rebekah's hand drops from mine. She pouts. 'I thought it would open.'

'Perhaps it only opens for The Chosen.'

Rebekah turns and slumps against the wall. She folds her arms. 'Then we'll have to wait for them to come to us in the morning.'

*Morning!* My empty stomach churns. By then, Abraham will finally have something to say to Mother in his report. My absence will be noticed. And then what? Will she send the prefects after us? But I've made a promise to Rebekah. I slide down beside her. 'I hope they bring water. My tongue keeps sticking to my mouth.' She looks into my eyes and sees the doubt.

She pats my knee. 'We're doing the right thing. You'll feel better once we've spoken to Isaac and Rachel. Remember, they're The Chosen. Mother will have to listen to them.'

I watch her face as her eyes wander up to the dome; not for the first time, I wish I had her courage. Rebekah turns. She smiles then looks away as she realizes I've been watching her. She speaks to the floor. 'Do you remember coming up from the Education Level?' I see the straight line of prefects dressed in black on my first day.

'Of course. It seemed so big... at first.'

'No, I mean, did you climb a ladder, or was it stairs?' She stops and frowns as her eyes wander across the large, empty space. 'I have no memory of how I actually came up.'

'Well it must have been by the... I think it was...' I scratch my head, 'No. No, I can't.'

Rebekah rubs the back of her neck. 'The last thing I remember was standing with Elizabeth and Judith at the front of the class.' She tips her head back and closes her eyes. 'Mother spoke to us on the screen.' Her eyes move behind their lids and her head nods lightly as she speaks. 'Mother told us it was time to devote our lives to The New Dawn, and it was a great honor to serve the people of The Ark.' Her eyes open and she turns to me. 'But that was it. The next thing, I'm in The Square waiting for the prefects to assign us to a tour party.' She tilts her head. 'Don't you think that's strange?'

I've never given it any thought. I sigh. 'Perhaps the shock of the wide space erased the memory of the way we came up. But as you said, this place can do funny things to our minds.'

'And another thing,' she turns back to me, 'did everyone from your class make it?'

'Make what?'

'Graduation.'

'I think so. Why wouldn't they?'

Rebekah tucks her knees to her chest and studies the floor. 'There was one... Esther, yes, I think that was her name. She was the same age as me, and also had red hair,' she twirls a strand hanging by her face, 'we were the only two in the class.' She sits up. 'But when we turned eleven she disappeared... and no one saw her again.'

'Perhaps—'

'So where is she? What happened to her?'

'Did she do or say anything wrong in class?'

Rebekah shakes her head. 'No. In fact, she was so quiet you didn't know she was there most of the time. She didn't join in and sat at the back. She used to rock,' Rebekah tilts back and forth, 'like this. I remember being a bit scared at first, but then I felt sorry for her. I tried to speak to her a few times but she didn't respond. And then one day she wasn't at class, but no one dared ask Mother where she'd gone.' She stops, looking like a young girl struggling to solve one of Mother's puzzles.

I edge closer. 'From what you say she probably wouldn't have made a good worker anyway, she'll be down *you know where.*'

Rebekah straightens, raising her voice. 'But she never got the chance to prove she could do the work, not even as a server in the canteen. It didn't seem fair. She wasn't allowed to finish school and do something productive.' She looks up to the dome. 'I wonder why it suddenly disappeared.'

'What?'

She looks past me. 'The sea, mountains, and your trees. We could have only been here for few minutes before it all vanished. If this is some sort of *Dream-maker* for The Chosen, it doesn't seem long enough if it's meant to be a reward for their work.' She stands and walks a few paces away, then turns with her finger poised in the air. 'No wait. It all changed as soon as we realized we weren't seeing the same scene, so we knew it couldn't be real.' Rebekah strides back and grabs my hand to pull me up. She beams. 'But what if we want to see the same thing? Would it last longer?' She spins around. 'Let's give it a go!'

'But what about the—?'

'Oh go on. It could be hours before The Chosen arrive.' She strokes the back of my hand. Her eyes have never looked bluer as she holds my gaze. 'It would be a shame to not use it. We might never get the...' Her shoulders drop.

I cannot say no to those eyes having seen her dream evaporate only moments before. I grin. 'What shall we see?'

She jumps up. 'I want to show you what I saw.' She sees my expression. 'No, the *real* sea, not the one we see in Mother's night stories, what it really looks like.'

I nod. 'Okay, but when we finally get outside you have to promise to come to a forest with me.'

Her eyes light up. 'Deal.'

'So what now?'

Rebekah shrugs. 'We just think of the sea, the one from Mother's story will do for you, it's close enough I guess. Then let's hope the *Dream-maker* will—' The dome shimmers. Rebekah squeals and clasps my hand. She looks down to the overalls under my arm. 'I think you can put those down. You won't need them on the beach.'

I let them drop, along with my jaw as Rebekah's wish takes form. But before I see, I hear. The song of the sea rushes to greet me from near and far, awakening a longing in my heart to be somewhere else, away from here to a place I could call my home. Now I see. Wide blue, restless waters tempt me with a promise of undiscovered wonders beyond its horizon. I answer the call and glide across the shallows to the deep, dark waters out to sea. It's alive, not flat like Mother's. Sunbeams bounce from the rippling surface like a million tiny stars glistening in the night sky.

Rebekah claps her hands. 'Watch.' I turn just as a wave topples over and crashes onto the sand, exploding into tiny flecks of foamy, white water. It surges up the beach towards my feet. I look down to see it roll over my toes like a blanket. I laugh. 'It tingles.'

She bends and scoops her hand through the water, sending glittering arcs of color up into the breeze. We wade along the shoreline, but my eyes are drawn back to blue line of the horizon. Rebekah flicks water into my face. 'Hey! Don't look so serious.' I flinch and even feel it run down and soak through my shirt. She laughs and ducks as I try to splash her back.

I throw back my head. 'This is paradise!'

She spins me around. 'Don't forget the mountains.'

Rebekah guides my attention inland. Beyond the hills rising gently from the edge of the beach, sheer-faced, grey monsters with gleaming, white caps thrust ruthlessly up through the Earth. *Mountains*! Just to speak of their name gives me strength.

Rebekah skips ahead, shouting over her shoulder, 'When we get out, we're going to climb one of those.' She stops and gawps at their jagged peaks clawing at the sky. 'Just imagine what the world would look like from up there.'

My stomach turns over at the thought. 'We'll need a long ladder.'

'Nonsense. Explorers only had ropes and hooks, there are no ladders tall enough in the world to climb a mountain.' She holds out her hand. 'Come, let's sit over there.' We stroll from the sea up onto the drier sand. She sits and pats the ground. I happily join her, but the joy has gone from her face. She looks me in the eye, then back to the sea. She whispers, 'Now, will you tell me what happens on the third visit?' The sky shimmers. She stiffens, gripping my hand. 'No! Don't lose it, not yet.'

'I'm sorry, but you reminded me that all this is—'

Rebekah scowls. 'Don't even think...' then softens, 'sorry, I didn't mean to shout.' She looks down, buries her hands into the sand and lifts them to watch the grains spill out between her fingers. She waits for her hands to empty before speaking. 'I wasn't totally honest with you earlier.'

'What? When?'

'On the ladder when I asked about the visits. I know a little.' She takes a deep breath. 'I know that it involves a boy and a girl, and that it has something to do with what Mother wouldn't normally let us do, and... you know, what you tried to do on our first meeting.' My heart thumps louder than the breaking waves. Does she know what I've done with Naomi? Rebekah tugs at my torn sleeve. 'Noah? Am I right?'

'Well, it's... sort of, nearly—'

She pulls me closer, putting her sandy finger to my lips. 'Shush. You don't have to tell me. I want you to,' she lays back on the sand, 'show me.'

I don't need to think. I roll to her, the heat surging through my body. I look down onto her face, her fair skin, searching eyes and red lips, putting anything the *Dreammaker* could show me into the shade. I lean over and press my lips to hers. Her mouth opens, my head explodes. She tastes like my cake—only sweeter. Her tongue pushes forward, seeking out mine. I pull her closer, not wanting even a grain of sand to come between us. This is different than with Naomi. That was duty, but this is sheer pleasure. I don't want to be anywhere else, this is Paradise, this is... wrong.

I sit up. 'No, no, I can't.'

She pushes me away. 'What! Why not? You said—'

'It's not that.' I look into her eyes and almost surrender. 'I really want to, but Abraham said Abigail, the girl he... he lay with, disappeared shortly afterwards.' I see the pain in Abraham's face. 'He's not seen her since.' I look back to Rebekah and take her hand. 'I don't want that to happen to us.'

She sighs and turns to take a last look at the sea. I place my arm around her shoulders and pull her close. 'When we get out of here, we can do whatever we like.'

She blinks away a tear. 'That can't be soon enough.' We watch as the beach fades, dragging us back to the middle of a room that dangles our dreams before our eyes before cruelly snatching them away. Her attention stays fixed on what should be the horizon. My heart aches to see the pain on her face. I know I'd do anything for Rebekah to see the real sea.

She takes a deep breath and turns to me, interlocking her fingers with mine. 'What did you want to be when you were young?'

I see Jared's back as he left the nursery. 'A prefect.'

Despite our loss, Rebekah laughs. 'A prefect! Really?'

'What's funny about that?'

She shakes her head. 'I can't see you as one of them, that's all.'

My shoulder sink. 'I always thought I'd join them. I would do Mother's work and make sure everyone did as they were told. And...' I look to the crumpled overalls nearby, 'I wanted to wear the black uniform and be important.' Rebekah strokes the back of my hand. I see the wooden blocks lying in a collapsed heap on the floor of the nursery. 'But I must have done something wrong because she chose Jared from our class and I got to be a factory worker.'

She lifts my hand and looks into my eyes. 'But a good worker, on the best team. So you see, you *are* important.'

I scoff. 'I've spent most of my life making useless machines for others to pull apart and send the pieces back again.' Her hand goes to the nape of my neck. I turn. 'What about you? Did you want to be a lab worker?'

She shakes her head. 'I always believed we would be the first to surface, so I wanted to travel, see mountains, deserts and of course the sea.'

'I guess that's why Mother gave you a book about the explorers. You know what we say. Mother knows—'

'No. Don't say it.' Rebekah releases my hand. 'It's more like a cruel joke.' I see my birthday cake. 'To show us what it's like on the surface, but then to keep us stuck down below.'

'But we don't know. It could be too dangerous. She might—' Rebekah's mouth drops open. I close mine.

'Even now, you believe Mother knows best? Do you really think she's going to let us return?'

'But why wouldn't she if it's safe? Mother's been down here for longer than anyone. Surely, she wants to return to her home.'

'There's only one way to settle this.' She gets to her feet and glances back to the main entrance. 'We can't wait. We have to go now.'

'But what about Isaac and Rachel?'

Rebekah turns and sets off the way we came in, calling over her shoulder, 'I have a funny feeling in my stomach. We can't risk staying here any longer.'

I bend to pick up my overalls and run to catch up. 'But don't we need The Chosen?'

She shakes her head, keeping up the pace. 'No. The more I've thought about it, the more I think we have to find out for ourselves.' She stops and turns to me. '*Then* we can speak to The Chosen.' Her hand goes to my shoulder. 'But if we wait and the prefects find us, we'll lose our only chance to get out.' Rebekah spins on her heels and points. 'That's it.' She sets off again. 'That's where we came in.'

I see the dark slit in the blank wall. 'But what about the ceiling? How do we go any further?'

She doesn't stop. 'You said there was a vent. We could get through that.'

'Only if we can move it.'

She looks over her shoulder. 'Oh I'll *move* it. If I have to beat my fists bloody, I'll move it.' We reach the door. Rebekah passes straight through without a second glance back. I duly follow and see she's already several rungs up the ladder. She looks down. 'At least we've had a break from that cold wind.'

I hold up my overall. 'You should put this back on. You don't know when you might—'

'No, you wear it. If it gets cold you can always warm me up,' she winks, 'like an explorer.'

I smile, quickly pull on the rags of a worker, and clamber up beside her. I blink and let my eyes adjust to the light; just above our heads I see what I hope to be the final barrier between us and the surface.

'Water!' I cry out in glee as drops of cool water land on my upturned face. I push upwards and suck the glistening droplets from the vent. Right now, it tastes better than anything I've drunk in my life. I let it trickle down my throat before looking down to Rebekah. 'There's not much but it will help.' I watch as her tongue runs across the smooth metal, and listen to her moans of pleasure. I forget my thirst. She stops; her lips move but I miss her words. 'Sorry?'

'It looks wide enough for us to get through.' Her fingers curl around one of the bars and she shakes. It rattles. Her eyes widen. 'It's shifting.' I move my free hand next to hers. 'Push or pull?'

'Perhaps best to push.'

She nods. 'Okay. Together.' We push. It opens with ease. Rebekah's face beams in the light of the ladder. 'You go first. It's your turn.'

I take one step up, just as something far below clangs, signaling the return of the wind. I scramble through the opening, slide to one side and reach down to help Rebekah. She feels light as she slips through and lands beside me. I slam the vent shut against the cold air. 'That should take the sting out of that.'

Rebekah steps back and squints into the murk. 'So what now?' The little light coming up through the vent reveals the only detail.

I step forward and take hold of the ladder. 'More climbing.' As before, the rungs glow, lighting the shaft until it's swallowed by the darkness. I take her hand. 'Together?' We step up and begin the next stage, both silently hoping it will be the last. With each step I long to see the white glow indicating a door, but they remain red. Rung after rung, we pull ourselves up edging slowly closer to the surface. The shaft walls close in, echoing back our grunts and groans. This is worse than below. I don't know how much longer I can climb. Already, my numb fingers and toes cannot feel the ladder, but I look to Rebekah and see the set muscles in her face—I cannot let her down.

She sees my discomfort. 'It can't be too much further. We have to be well above the second dome by now.' I glance up. *What if there are more levels?* We could climb for days and never reach the top. Mother must have delved deep to keep us beyond the reach of the enemy.

I try to smile, but Rebekah senses my concern. She stops. Her eyelids flicker. She opens her mouth but her quivering lips don't allow her to speak. I place my hand on hers. 'What is it?'

Her voice breaks as she speaks. 'Have we failed?'

I shake my head. 'No, we're going to get out. I promise.' But I'm not sure I believe my answer. I see the fight drain from her face. Her eyes roll up; the whites of her eyes shine bright in the glow. She tips back. 'NO!' I lunge and grab at her arm. But my numb fingers can only grasp onto her thin shirt. I yell, 'Rebekah!' She stirs as she slips from my hand. Time slows like the moment we exchanged our first glance on the walkway. Her eyes bulge; her arms flay but her outstretched fingers find nothing to stay the fall. Her mouth gapes. I know she's screaming but it fails to reach my ears. I have one chance left to save her. My hand shoots out. Contact. I clutch her wrist, knowing I cannot hold her for long. But it's enough. Rebekah's free hand snatches at the baggy sleeve of my overalls, nearly wrenching it from my arm. Her kicking feet clatter against the rungs until one finds safety. Her weight releases from my sleeve and I wrap my free arm around her shaking body.

Sounds come crashing back. She gasps, 'Don't let go, don't let go.'

I cling onto her with all my remaining strength. 'I've got you. I'll never let go, never.' I repeat my vow over and over as my mind sees the darkness below snatching her from me.

I feel her body relax. She pants. 'What happened?'

'I don't know. Your eyes went white, then you let go.' Her fingers grip tighter. I pull back to see her face but she looks away.

I strain to hear her low voice. 'You... you won't tell anyone.'

'What? Tell them what?' Her eyes come back to mine. I take a breath. 'Yes. I promise I won't tell anyone.' A single tear brims. I try to comfort her. 'You're safe now, it won't happen again, I won't—'

'It's not the first time, and it won't be the last.' Her head drops.

I place my hand under her chin and lift her face so I can look her in the eye. 'I promised I won't tell, but I don't understand. This is our secret, why would I tell?'

'No. not the ladder, me, passing out. It's my... secret shame. Another girl on our team had it, and she was taken away. No one else must find out, they'll say I'm weak and question my commitment, or think I'm an agent and send me down... there. Only two people on my team know, but they've kept it quiet.' She pulls away and looks over my shoulder. 'I thought it might stop once we left that place. But obviously I was wrong.' She shuffles across the rung. 'Sometimes it lasts longer, and they tell me I shake, and then I start talking, saying things, using words that don't make sense.' I think of mad Enoch. Her eyes look down between her feet. 'I don't want to hold you back. If you want to go on without me, I'll understand.'

'What? Without you? No, no, I can't.' I place my hand on her cheek. 'I can't do this without you. You're the reason I'm here. We're a team.'

This time she holds my gaze and nods. 'But only if you're sure.'

I stroke her skin with my thumb. I smile. 'Yes I'm sure.'

'Thanks. I should have told you but—'

It's my turn to put my finger on her lips. 'It doesn't matter.' I look up. 'Now let's find the way out. Then we'll find the tallest tree in the world, and climb to the very top and then, together we'll touch the sky.' I watch her confidence return as she reaches up.

'Noah.' Her voice sounds suddenly calm. 'Look.' The rung under her hand glows white. She looks up. 'It's the end of the ladder, but I can't see a vent, or a door.'

# 37

'But there has to be.' I twist, desperate to find she's mistaken, but she's right. No door; no vent. I gape at her. 'It can't stop here, what's the point of a ladder that goes nowhere? There has—' I freeze. The shriek sucks the air from my lungs.

Rebekah's nails dig into my arm. 'That's close!'

I gasp. 'It came from up there.'

'What is it?'

'Wait. Listen.' A low throbbing sound fills the air, similar to when I hear my heartbeat in my pillow.

Rebekah lets out a long breath. 'It's okay. That sounds like machines, like the pumps we use in the lab.' She climbs another rung and stretches up to hear. She whispers. 'It could be the filters.'

'Filters?'

'At the surface!' She grips my shoulder. 'The air we breathe is filtered from the surface. Noah!' Her hand reaches up. 'That's not the ceiling, there's a bend.' She clambers up the last rungs and steps onto my shoulder, calling down. 'Sorry, hope that didn't hurt.'

I shake my head. 'What can you see?'

'A short tunnel, then another bend, and...'

'And what?'

'There's a flickering light.' I hear her shuffling along the tunnel.

'Like the sun shining through leaves?' She doesn't answer. I call louder. 'Wait! I'm coming up.' I scramble up the last few rungs in time to see Rebekah's feet disappear around the bend ahead. She screams. I call after her. 'Rebekah!'

'Sorry, didn't mean to scare you. There's a gap, not a vent, and the light, it must be sunlight!' I reach the bend and crawl up to Rebekah's feet. She grabs my shirt. 'See. There's some sort of cover but it's hanging half open.' I shield my eyes against the glare as I drag myself face to face with her. Rebekah hugs me. 'This has to be it!' She reaches out, takes hold of the edges and pulls herself forward so her head pokes through the gap.

'What can you see?' Her body goes limp. 'Rebekah? What's out there?' I crawl to the opening.

She looks back inside and sighs. 'It's another room.' She slips out of the shaft and jumps to the floor. I see the top of her head as she turns. She gasps. 'What the—? Dear Moses!'

'What is it?' She doesn't answer. I slide out and drop to the floor. I straighten my legs and turn. I find myself in a wide space similar to the level below, except this has a flat ceiling like the Education Level. At its center, is the source of the light—six large, flickering screens, placed in a circle, facing out to rows of chairs. I look for Rebekah. She's standing a few feet away, staring at something on the floor next to a short staircase built into the wall. She bends, picks up the object and holds it at arm's length towards me.

Her mouth drops open. 'A boot?'

'Enoch!' My skin prickles. I step forward for a closer look—it's a factory worker's boot. Rebekah's mouth opens and closes but no words come. I take it from her. 'It must be his.'

She frowns. 'But how did it get here? I thought we were the first.' I see Enoch on the morning he had his breakdown, dragged away by the prefects, kicking out with his one remaining boot.

The other slips from my hand as the fact dawns. 'He'd been here.'

Rebekah stares at the object laying its claim to her territory. 'You *know* him? Who is he?'

I look at the boot. 'He was our team leader before Isaac. He—'

'Isaac never mentioned him.' Rebekah grasps the rail of the staircase.

'None of us did. We never spoke about him, well not often.' I see Reuben prancing about with his boot in the air on the evening we had our treat from Mother. 'He was an embarrassment to our team.'

'So where is he?'

I shrug. 'I don't know. The prefects took him.' I join Rebekah on the first step of the staircase and turn away from the glimmering screens.

Her eyes stay focused on the boot. 'So how do you know that belongs to Enoch?' I move to put my arm around her, but she pulls away, climbing to the next step.

'He turned up one morning with a boot missing, screaming and shouting. Then the prefects arrived and took him away. They said he had what's called a breakdown.' I take another step. 'I thought he'd just got back from his morning report to Mother, but he must have been up here.' I look for the top of the stairs, but they pass into shadow just above the level of the ceiling. I speak my thoughts. 'What did he see up here that sent him mad?'

Rebekah slumps onto a step. She whispers to the floor, 'What was he shouting?'

'I can't remember.'

'What?' She straightens. 'Surely you'd remember something like that!'

I shrug. 'He was mad, it didn't make sense.' I force my mind to go back to that morning. 'We were taken to see Mother shortly after. She said we shouldn't be worried about his outburst, and he was under a lot of pressure and had lost his mind when the morning delivery hadn't arrived.'

Rebekah sniffs. 'It doesn't change anything.' She stands and peers up the stairs. 'We go on.'

'But what about Enoch?'

'What about him?'

I shiver. 'He saw something up here that drove him mad. What if the same  ?'

'It won't.' She turns her back and climbs, not waiting to see if I follow.

I watch as she disappears into the shadow. Her footsteps stop. 'Rebekah?' Her feet come back into view as she slowly descends.

Her eyes stay fixed ahead as she speaks quietly. 'A dead end, it goes nowhere.' She passes me as if I'm not there—her drooping body looks ready to fall. Rebekah stops at the bottom. Her body shudders, then stiffens as if waking from a sleep. She turns to me. 'What do you think this place is?'

'It must be where The Chosen come to study.' I point to the wall where we came in. 'There must be stairs from below behind those doors.'

Rebekah wipes her brow. 'It's warm here.'

I undo my overalls. 'Perhaps it's coming from outside. At least that means we're not under ice.' I let the uniform fall to the floor and turn to count the chairs in the closest section.

Rebekah scans the room. 'How many are there?'

I finish my calculation. 'Four hundred and eighty. Is that how many Chosen are up here? That seems like a lot.' Rebekah doesn't answer. I turn to see she's already running towards the screens. I follow. But the ordeal on the ladder slows our legs and we walk the last few meters to the chairs. Rebekah's knees buckle and she collapses onto the first seat. I rush forward. She holds up a hand.

'It's okay. I'm fine.' In between her breaths, she gasps, 'They're soft. Much... more comfortable than... our benches.' She slides along and pats the chair beside her. 'Try one.' I sink a little way into the seat—I see Naomi standing before me on my second visit.

Rebekah nods to the front. 'I wonder what they watch on those.'

'Lectures from...' I shiver, suddenly wary her face could appear and see us, 'Mother.'

Rebekah sits up, breathing slower. 'Doesn't matter, it looks like they're not working properly.' She points up. 'But that's different. No dome, it's flat. Perhaps it's the top.' She stands, squeezes past and, with surprising vigor strides down the aisle towards the screens. I stay silent. I force myself to my tired feet and follow once more. She reaches the front several paces ahead and calls back. 'This looks promising.' I catch up. Now we're closer, I hear the faint hiss coming from the screens. Rebekah points to the surface of a desk beneath the first display. 'See. These are like the controls we have in the lab, only these look like they're drawn with a pencil.' She reaches over. 'Perhaps we could open a door with this—'

'No, don't!' I grab her wrist. She twists and glares. I let go. 'I'm sorry, I didn't mean to hurt you. But, what if one of them switches on the screens? Mother will see us.'

The muscles on her face relax. 'No, I'm sorry.' Her head drops. 'I need to stop and think.' She rests her hand on my forearm. 'Enoch was on his own, but there's two of us. Whatever is up here, we can face it together. That makes us stronger.' I smile, but her attention goes back to the desk and I'm left smiling at the top of her head. She taps the desk. 'That one looks like a door.' Her hand moves, then stops. She turns. 'Shall we try it?' This time she sees my smile as I nod. She takes my hand. 'You press it.'

I let her lead my hand to a small square on the desk. My fingertips brush its smooth surface. We both jump back as the screen bursts into color. Thousands of tiny lights explode, brighter than the screen in The Square. I turn, ready to run. Rebekah grabs my arm. 'Wait! It's not Mother.'

We take a few paces back to see the picture. We stand aghast. The screen shows hundreds of differently-dressed people cramming narrow walkways. Rebekah cries out, 'It's a London!'

'A what?'

'A London.' She ruffles my hair. 'Didn't Mother tell you about them? Where millions of people lived and worked together on the surface.'

I can't stop the smirk spreading across my face. 'You mean a city. London was just one of them.'

She looks away. 'Well it doesn't matter now, does it, they've all gone anyway.' We turn back to the city. Rebekah leans closer. 'Funny. Apart from their clothes, and that they're,' she tilts her head, 'rounder, they look like us. They're sad.' But it's not the masses of people that catch my eye. Buildings line the walkways. Buildings taller than trees, buildings taller than The Factory, buildings that must be high enough to scrape against the thin strip of grey sky.

'How did they make them so big? How did they not collapse?' But Rebekah doesn't answer; she's transfixed by the activity on the ground.

She cries out. 'Look!' She pulls me to her. 'What are those? People are sitting in them… and they move.'

'Cars. Abraham has a book with pictures of them. And if you look there,' I point up to between the buildings, 'they can also fly.'

Rebekah gasps. 'So many people, so little space. It's no better than living down here.' She threads her arm through mine and shudders. 'I wouldn't want to live in a *city*. I'm glad they were destroyed. I hope Mother's telling the truth about that.' She steps back to the desk and turns off the screen. 'Let's try this one.' Without waiting, her finger taps the desk. The lights fade. We're left in the dark.

# 38

'I can't see the desk.' Rebekah sounds fraught. 'I can't turn them back on.'

'There's light coming from somewhere. I can see you.' I twist around. 'Over there, the stairs are lit.' Rebekah's face comes into view as she turns.

'Then that's where we go.' This time she waits. I nod and take her hand, but she pulls me back. 'Shush. What's that?' At first I hear nothing. I hold my breath. A low grinding sound, like the plates sliding together at my workstation, but these must be huge. Rebekah clutches my shoulder. She whispers, 'It's opening,' then yells, 'The Ark is opening!' Above, a black spot in the ceiling grows wider like a giant eye looking down on our deed. *What have we done?* We drop to our knees and tremble in its glare. We've opened The Ark! We've revealed its existence to the world outside—and laid ourselves bare to the enemy.

'It's gone!' Rebekah pulls me to my feet. I look up to see the sections of the ceiling have fully retracted, but I can't see what's above in the dark. 'Look!' Rebekah tugs at my arm. All around, the walls sink silently towards the level the ceiling once occupied. Again, I strain to see what's outside, but the wonders beyond remain hidden from our position just below the surface.

I cry out, 'The stairs. We can get out.' We run. I feel lighter, energized by the thought we'll be free in seconds. Beside me, Rebekah almost skips, shrieking with joy. We run. Hand in hand towards the unknown, desperate to feel the air on our faces, not caring what dangers await outside. But we must be fast. Mother must know we've found the way out.

We reach the stairs. I glance up—it's dark. Rebekah shouts. 'It must still be night.' We fly up the steps taking four at a time. She calls out, 'I can see stars!' We stumble out onto a narrow, circular walkway. Rebekah's hand drops from mine as our heads tip back to take in the view. She whispers, 'It's beautiful. It's...' We stand and gape at the star-speckled expanse; so many stars, brilliant, bright stars in the black sky.

I look to Rebekah and see their reflection in her eyes. I struggle to find my voice. 'I didn't know they moved like that. I've only ever seen pictures.'

Rebekah beams. 'It's so... big. I didn't know the sky could be so... big.'

I wrap my arm around her waist. 'Five more steps and we're out of this place.' We take the first. I stop—two figures shrouded in shadow stand opposite. I release Rebekah as the figure outside does the same. I frown. 'It's glass.'

Rebekah looks around. 'How do we get out? Can you see a door?' I check both directions. The walkway extends around the edge of the room below. But now I see two higher walkways connected by stairways, and higher still, a new ceiling like a large, dark moon stuck onto the night sky.

'Noah?' I turn. Her joy has gone. 'Something's not right.' Her eyes dart from the sky to the floor and back again.

'What?'

'I don't like it.' Her pale face turns to me. 'This can't be the surface.'

I look back to the stars. 'It has to be. There's—' We duck. A dark object scythes past the window.

Rebekah cries out, 'Have they found us?' She drops to the floor, covering her head. I cannot move. We've betrayed Mother. We've opened The Ark and alerted the enemy. My head feels light as I watch the stars swirl. I flinch as another object swoops by, and fall to my hands and knees. But I have to know what's outside. I crawl to the edge and see more of the world beyond. My heart stops.

'What is it?' Rebekah's voice comes from another time and world behind. I pull up and press my hands and face into the cold glass.

'Dear Moses!'

'Noah?'

'It's not the stars, it's us, we're moving.' My breath obscures the awful truth. My forehead slides down the glass. 'We're on some sort of a... ship.' Now I turn, I strive with my slack jaw to speak. 'We're not on Earth.'

'Ship?' Rebekah edges beside me. Her breath joins mine on the window, but I have no urge to wipe it away—I'm not sure I want to know what's outside.

She presses her hands against the window and sobs. 'Where's the sea? The trees? The...?' The glass squeaks as Rebekah's fingers slip and let go of her dream.

I have to help her. *Do something.* I rise up onto my toes and wipe my view clear as the grey object swoops past again. I whisper to myself. 'A spoke?' I push my head further into the window and look down. Far below, the object connects to a thick tube. A rim. 'It's a wheel, like on Barnabas's trolley.' The spoke sweeps to our left. 'It's spinning. We're in a spoke of a wheel. There are two, it's spinning like us, or... maybe it's still and we're moving.' I turn to her. 'I can't really tell, but if I could—'

'Where are the mountains?' Rebekah slams her fist into the glass, screaming for our lost freedom. 'This isn't happening! This can't be true. This isn't supposed to be here. This can't be...' She twists away. Her legs give way. She slides to the floor and rolls into a ball.

I should go to her, but I can't tear my eyes from the vast space beyond. I strain my neck and force my eyes to the extremes of their sockets to see more of the wheel. Two spokes! I reason out aloud. 'There's more than one spoke. There has to be, it wouldn't come around that quick if there was only one.' I wait for the next. It also has a large window like ours. I see the glass but its grey walls behind are closed—it looks like the ring on Mother's finger. It arcs out of view leaving a whirling sky of stars. The next spoke rises. This one's different, the window is broken. The ring of dark glass opposite has a large part missing; its silver jagged edges clear to see against the black, gaping hole behind. It passes. Another rises to my right—no broken window. I await the next—it's the same. The broken spoke appears next. 'There are three!' Pleased with my discovery, I turn to Rebekah. Her head is in her hands.

She mumbles, 'I don't care. It's a trick.'

I shake my head. 'No. I don't think so.'

'It is! It has to be one of Mother's tricks.' I look down. Rebekah lifts her head. 'She doesn't want us to leave so she puts this thing over the way out.' She clambers to her feet and scans the surface. 'This is like the *Dream-maker* in Paradise, except she decides what we see.' She turns to me. 'This is her doing, but she's not going to trick me.' She rubs both hands across the window. 'We can break it.'

'Rebekah.' I place my hand on her back. 'It's not Mother. I think this is for—'

She drops her shoulder and coils back. 'No! You're wrong!'

'But—?'

She kicks out. 'We have to break out.' Her fingers clutch at the glass, trying to get a grip. 'The sea is on the other side, you'll see.' She gives up trying to find a hold and hammers with both fists, but her silent blows fail to make a dent.

'Rebekah.' The fight evaporates. She steps back, her efforts inflicting nothing more than smears on the smooth surface. Her head drops onto the window, her outstretched arms push upwards as if taking the weight of the whole structure. I edge to her side and wrap my arm around her waist. Her lifeless body sags against me.

She whimpers, 'What do we do now?' It pains me to hear her weak voice. *I have to be strong.* But I'm as lost as Rebekah.

'I don't know.' I watch the relentless spinning of the giant wheel. 'Let me think.' I count. Every eight seconds, a spoke sweeps past our view. Lower down the spoke it looks different, lighter. A shadow? I spin about and peer through the opposite window several hundred meters away. I wait. There it is. A flicker. A bright ball streaks across the window. *The Sun?* I scan the skies. My heart leaps. 'Look!' I point to a small, but distinctively blue-green disk as it follows the sun in the same arc. I laugh. 'It's Earth! We're not beneath it, we're above it!' I clutch Rebekah's hands. 'The Ark is a ship, sailing over the Earth.' I feel Rebekah's body come back to life.

'So why didn't she tell us?'

It's all starting to make sense. 'To protect us. She must have thought we'd feel safer believing we were on Earth and not floating around in space.' I can trust Mother again. A tear forms in my eye, smearing the next pass of the sun. I take Rebekah's hand. 'Let's see what's around the other side.'

'Wait.' She pulls me back. 'Why did she tell Moses and the other workers they were *going up*?' I stop.

'I... don't know. Perhaps it was a false reading, perhaps the air quality wasn't as good as she first thought, or perhaps it was something to do with the enemy? Perhaps—'

'So where are the enemy? Are they up here or,' she nods to the disk, 'or already back there?'

'It doesn't matter. Mother knows best. She'll take care of everything.' Rebekah sighs; her eyes stay fixed on Earth as it sweeps faithfully past once more. I hold out my hand. 'Coming?' Her eyes drift back to me. 'I think we just have time to see what's on the other side before...' I close my mouth and smile. I don't want to think about what we do next. Her arm slowly rises and she lets it hang, waiting for me to lead. I wrap my fingers in hers and take the first few steps. 'This is good, at least now we—'

'Don't.' I feel her hand tighten.

'Don't what?'

'Don't make this any worse than it is.' She turns her head away. I stay silent, keeping my thoughts in my head as we walk.

I'm right. As we work our way around the walkway, the rim of our own wheel comes into view, stretching from the bottom to the top of our window like a colossal grey snake. At the very top of our window, I can just make out the straight line of the adjacent spoke. My stomach turns over at the next discovery. An immense cylinder, stretching out as far as I can see, rises from where the spokes meet in the middle. But unlike us, it's still—we're spinning around its axis. I check if Rebekah has noticed, but her attention is on her feet.

I stop and push my face to the glass. From this side of the room, we can see more of the Earth as it glides through our viewpoint. I risk sharing my thoughts with Rebekah. I turn back. 'It's so blue. Like the sky when Mother...' I change the subject. 'That must mean the clouds have gone. We can tell Mother it's safe to return.'

'That's not Earth.' Her flat tone forces me to stop.

'But how do you—?'

'If that's Earth, then that,' she points over my shoulder, 'shouldn't be there.' I turn to see what's bothering her. My legs buckle. I drop to my knees, I look back to Rebekah's face, bathed in the crimson light now flooding through the window. She heaves a sigh. 'I may not know the name for a city, but I do know Earth has only one sun.'

As much as I don't want to see it, I cannot stop my head turning to watch the giant, red ball join her little sister, shattering our last hopes by her presence.

# 39

Dark grey lines streak down the glass, fanning out a short distance across the floor before its crusting edges stop just short of my knees. *'It's a lie. We're never going to leave. Never! Never!'* I look to Rebekah. 'Those were his words, Enoch's. I remember now. And Mother made us think he'd gone mad.' I rub my thumb across his dried blood. 'Enoch saw this. He just kept repeating the words, *'We're never going to leave. Never! Never!'* Looks like he tried to break the window.' I see his forlorn figure as the prefects dragged him away, cradling what must have been his wounded hands. I sigh. 'He wasn't mad, he was angry. And we made fun of him.' I sit on the floor, turning my back on the giant orb as she slips out of sight.

Rebekah slides down next to me. I have no words. Mother has kept the truth from us, but I cannot find any reason that would justify her intentions. Rebekah entwines her fingers in mine and we watch the spokes sweep past the far window like the hands of a backwards clock. Rebekah speaks, she's calmer now. 'What's your book about?'

'What? Why now?'

She strokes my hand. 'I told you about mine, but what about yours? Is Mother in it?'

I shake my head. 'No, well not directly. It's a story about a group of boys who've run away from her, but they crash on an island and can't escape across the sea. At first it was an adventure to be on their own, but they soon start to fight each other and it all goes wrong.'

'Interesting.'

'How do you mean?'

Rebekah sits up and looks me in the eye. 'Our books are all about Mother in some way. She's either the hero, like in mine and some of the others on my team, or they're about what goes wrong when she's not there.'

'I haven't thought about it like that, no wait, Seth's wasn't a story. He had a book about tractors.'

Rebekah laughs. 'I bet Mother claimed she made them. But can't you see? Even our gifts she so *carefully selected for us* are about controlling our thoughts.' She peers across the opposite wheel. 'Do you think there are others like us? We'd number in the thousands if all the spokes are the same.' She turns to me. 'I wonder if Mother controls them all.' Her hand tightens on mine. 'If we could contact them...'

I look up. 'But how do we get out from here? There's no way up to that ceiling, and the ladder we came up doesn't go any further.'

'There's another way.' Rebekah leans over to the window and points down. 'That way, through the rim of the wheel.'

'But that would mean...'

Her shoulders lift and drop. 'I know it means going back. But we don't have any other choice.'

'Oh.' I'd already accepted we'd have to return. 'No, I meant going lower, down through The Trench and the—'

'Oh come on. Noah. I think we can safely say The Mine doesn't exist, knowing what we know now.' She tilts her head towards me. 'That has to be one of Mother's scare stories, and maybe even The Trench.'

I shudder. 'But the water and,' my nose wrinkles, 'waste have to go somewhere.'

She smiles and shakes her head. 'If we're going to fight back, things are going to get unpleasant.'

My eyes stay on the wheel. 'How do we start? Will anyone believe us? We all thought Enoch was mad, it will be easy for Mother to turn the rest against us.'

'We take our time, we have a year to—'

'A year? Where do you get that?'

'Once Mother can't deliver on her promise, what happens then? What do you think happened to Moses and the others when they couldn't leave?'

I shake my head. 'I don't know.'

'Neither do I, but I don't want to find out. No. We take it slowly and carefully, find others we can trust. We can bring Isaac, Rachel and more of The Chosen up here to prove our story. Then we start with our teams. Once we have a dozen or more it will get easier to convince others.'

I nod. 'I can trust Abraham, Reuben and perhaps Lydia. But not Barnabas, I'm sure he's in with the prefects.'

'I know two others I can trust.' She looks down. 'They've kept my weakness a secret, but we'll have to be cautious. All it takes is one word in the wrong ear and we're finished.'

'But what do we do when we have control?'

Rebekah nods to the window. 'Get Mother to take us to that planet. It looks a lot like Earth in the pictures, so perhaps it has water, mountains and,' she strokes my arm, 'your precious trees.'

My heart lifts, but it's too early to dream. I take her hand. 'And the enemy? What about them?'

'If they exist.' I watch her eyes trace the arc of the blue disk. She notices and smiles. 'Probably just another one of her stories.' She climbs to her feet. 'No point putting this off any longer. Let's go.'

My body feels suddenly tired. I force myself to stand. I look back to the expanse outside—it will be difficult returning to the Workers Level after this.

We try to walk fast, but our legs are reluctant to return. Rebekah takes one last look at what will hopefully be our new home. 'We can't have much time before morning. We'll have to contact The Chosen another night.'

'Then we'd better get a move on.' I take her hand and break into a run despite our heavy legs. We cover the distance to the stairs and descend below the level of the window. I turn to find the vent but Rebekah yanks at my arm. 'Wait!' I skid to a halt. 'The walls are closing.' *Has Mother found us?* I move to run, but Rebekah holds me fast. 'The screens! There's something on the screens.'

I pull back. 'We don't have time!'

She stands firm. 'But it looks important. It won't take long.'

I release her arm. 'Okay, but make it quick.'

The pictures become clearer as we jog down the aisle. 'They're ships!' We stop. Rebekah's eyesight must be better than mine. She reads the words below as the pictures of ships glide across the screen in front. 'Aurora, Bear, Challenger,' she points to the last ship, 'that one must be us.' She turns to me. 'See, it's the only one that has two wheels.' I can see the last name beneath. It reads, '*Discovery*'.

Rebekah gasps. 'I know these names! Well, two of them. They're in my book.' She squeals. 'They're ships of the early explorers.' She grasps my arm. 'That means there are others.'

I squint at the screen. 'So where are they?' I look up, just as the rising walls shut out the blue planet's homely light—I dearly hope we can one day accept her invitation.

My tired eyes seek Rebekah's. For a moment, I see the same promise of hope looking back.

She raises a smile. 'They're out there, somewhere. I can feel them.' I take her hand. We turn our backs on the screen and look for the exit. We don't have to look for long to see my crumpled overalls marking the spot where we came in.

# 40

When will morning come? My mouth is so dry, my tongue sticks to the roof of my mouth in my pounding head. I can't sleep—the light streaming through the slit is too strong for my eyelids to shut out.

We had descended in silence as we both struggled to come to terms with our discovery. Any concerns we had of missing the morning call were put to rest as we found the lights were still full on as we came through the dome. Our spirits sank further as we climbed back into our small world and made our way down the outer walkways, back to Rebekah's dormitory. Our parting was the hardest part. We clung to each other, neither wanting to let go first, fearful we might never see each other again if our plan fails.

I press my hands into my eye sockets and long for morning. But how can I face my team and go about my duties knowing what I now know? I have seen what lies outside—it cannot be unseen. I roll onto my side. I have to keep going, for Rebekah and for our future. I want to climb my tree and touch the sky. I won't let Mother snatch my dream away. Today is a new day. Today is the first day of our rebellion.

This is unbearable. Surely, it must be morning soon. I have to drink. I have to eat. Voices outside! 'She's not going to be happy. Grey sky tomorrow.'

Another calls. 'Lights out in ten. Eight hours till morning.' I stifle a moan. *Eight hours! How long are the nights?* No wonder we wake up stiff. I think of Rebekah. She won't know how much longer we have to wait. I miss her already.

I reach under my pillow and pull out my book. It's been weeks since I last read it. I flick to the page with the tree. Will I ever climb one? I drag my eyeballs along the first sentence. *'The boy with fair hair lowered himself down the last few feet of rock and began to pick his way towards the lagoon.'* When I first read the story, I'd felt frightened for the boys, knowing that running away from Mother could only end in disaster. But now I'm envious; they, at least had a chance to start a new life. I shut the book and read the faded words on the spine, *'Lord of the Flies.'* Would it end the same for us if we rebelled against Mother? But I'm too tired to think, or even care about the consequences now. I place it back under my pillow. I have no choice. I reach for the headset on my sheet and attach it in the hope of some respite from this ordeal. It works.

The light flickers, then scorches my eyeballs like hot blades being thrust into my skull. The others stir. I clench my jaw and clutch hold of the blanket.

Abraham announces the new day. 'It's five o'clock on Thursday, the thirteenth day of May. Everyone up. I want to see breakfast ready when I return.' I jump. The thirteenth! What happened to the twelve?

To be continued...

## BOOK 2: CLOUD CUCKOO

25638184R00167

Printed in Poland
by Amazon Fulfillment
Poland Sp. z o.o., Wrocław